Junior Year Bites

Annie Lisenby

Sir Ferdinand
Publishing

DEDICATION

I dedicate this book to all the people I shared the stage with as an improv actor. You all taught me how to be free with comedy and embrace silliness and comedy chaos.

TRIGGER WARNINGS

To my lovely readers, this book includes some elements that might make readers uncomfortable. This includes mild vampire violence and a scene with violence toward squirrels.

PROLOGUE

Usually, prom doesn't end in a bloody massacre. But that's just how my junior year has gone. One stupid mistake followed by a shitshow and topped off with a dumpster fire of a vampire attack on me and my friends. And it really sucks because the guy I'm head over heels for was literally just about to kiss me. At least, I think he was. And I'm determined to find out...after we win this battle.

Red drips all around the high school gym. Some girl in a hot pink, 80s-ironic dress is splayed across a few rows of bleachers, her dress splattered crimson. I could blame this all on Damn It Doug, and I should because it was his fault that I became what I am. But this wasn't *all* his fault. I know that.

Seeing my stake make contact with Jeff's shoulder, I cringe because I'm in serious trouble. I panic looking for my team, my ragtag band of misfit friends and vampires. I really need them now because I just pissed off the meanest, most vengeful, immensely epic asshole of a vampire I've ever met. And he doesn't play around.

1

COLA CROTCH

EIGHT MONTHS EARLIER

Win the district art contest. Get a scholarship to art school. And be bold. Because there's no way Toby Chan will kiss me if I keep hiding in the shadows. Junior year is going to rock!

I've been practicing this pep talk all summer long. Now, as Zel texts me to hurry up for literally the eighteenth time, I take one last look in the mirror. I hope it all comes true.

"Bye, Mom! Bye, Dad!" I yell at the laboratory door that used to be a beautiful enclosed porch in our house. I don't wait for a reply because I highly doubt they know what day it is, let alone care that I'm going to a party at the Bluffs with Zel. Like most parents in Inman, they know nothing about the Bluffs, nor do they know that all the biggest and best bashes are held there. And lately, Mom and Dad have been hunkered down in their lab much more than usual. I swear I heard a party in there yesterday, a mixture of unfamiliar voices and footsteps. But I haven't actually seen them to ask about it. So, off I go.

I slip my phone into my dress pocket and scratch Pablo, our gigantic orange-striped tomcat, under the chin before running outside.

Zel sits, tapping her fingers on her steering wheel in an overly dramatic fashion. She pushes her thick espresso-colored ponytail over her shoulder as she leans across the cracked vinyl seat.

"The AC's broken again," she announces before starting the engine. I slide into the passenger seat and regret wearing my gray t-shirt dress. It's impossible to hide the pit stains that will surely blossom. I should have dressed like Zel.

Her full name is Rapunzel, but she's refused to acknowledge it as long as I've known her. That was when I moved in next door to her in sixth grade. Her aversion to princesses and her mom's obsession with them has grown exponentially over the years. As we celebrate the last day of summer vacation, I bite back a flicker of jealousy at her wardrobe choice. Short jean shorts and a Captain America tank top. It accentuates her boobs that warp the red, white, and blue shield printed across them.

"Kaysee, did you see Tagg's new TikTok?"

"No," I reply. Social media is the worst. I hate it. I still use it, but I hate it.

"Why am I not surprised?" Zel tosses her phone in my lap. "Look who's behind Tagg, by the cooler."

I tap in Zel's passcode and the screen comes to life. On it is a short video from the Bluffs with Tagg and his other football goons flexing their muscles for the camera and making faces that are supposed to look tough but really it looks like they're taking a group dump. "#BullsRULZ #FridayNightLights #IHSfoot-ball4evr" reads the caption. Behind them, a streak of sapphire blue winds through the various greens of different tree leaves as the river by the Bluffs ambles north.

Sliding my fingers over the screen and enlarging the group of people standing behind the possibly defecating meatheads, my heart flutters. There he is, his dark hair drooping into his eyes giving off a sexy nerd vibe. Toby Chan. My heart jumps with joy as my eyes digest every pixel of him.

Zel slaps my shoulder. "Told you he'd be back. Now give me my phone."

I plug in the aux cord, hit play on Zel's playlist, and drop her phone into the cup holder. Rolling down my window as far as it'll go the hot, end-of-summer wind blows my hair in a way that should make me feel free. Really it makes me wonder why I spent so much time curling it and making it look cute when I knew I'd be riding in Zel's beat-up car with no AC. At least she has a car. And a driver's license. I hold my hair back with one hand to keep it from being blown in a wild tornado as I turn up the volume.

This is when I feel free. When we sing at the tops of our lungs to the newest stupid love song, all done ironically of course. The wind whips around us distorting our voices as houses in various earth-tone shades zip by. And soon Zel's car is bouncing across the makeshift road toward the Bluffs.

"I hate this car!" Zel screams as we hit a big rock and bounce so hard we almost smack our heads on the ceiling. "I swear I'll save up enough money this year and buy a new one." Zel works at the last remnant of a small town in our corner of suburbia, Burgers & Burritos. Her parents own the restaurant and run it with her grandma, whom everyone lovingly calls Abuelita. She makes milkshakes and takes orders for minimum wage at one of the most popular restaurants in town. Everyone in her family works at Burgers & Burritos in some way. Even though they closed the dining area during the last virus scare, she's had to take on more shifts this summer because her brother left for college.

"It looks like everyone's here," I say as Zel maneuvers her car into a tight place between two giant trucks. The Bluffs and the flat flood plain at their base are speckled with people in bright-colored clothes holding drinks in brightly colored cans.

"Well, duh," Zel unbuckles and slips out of the car. "Yeah, everyone's here. After the school shut down in April and prom was canceled, this is the biggest social event in months." Zel flips her ponytail dramatically and poses. One summer of drama camp two years ago, and she thinks she's the next Zendaya. "Plus, everyone wants to mingle and find out who's in daylight school and who's in twilight school."

"Daylight and twilight," I scoff. "What uninspired names. Couldn't they just make it simple like day school and afternoon school?"

Zel shrugs. "Someone told me they chose the names because the superintendent is a huge fan of the Twilight books and thought it would help her connect with the student population."

"Vampires?" I full-on laugh at this as I adjust my dress. "Might as well write about teenage angst in Atlantis. No one believes in all that mythical, gothic nonsense anyway."

Following Zel, I trudge through the rutted mud toward the party at the base of the large rocky bluff. Around us, other socially deprived teens are throwing a football or running past and yelling greetings to Zel. People don't really notice me. This year I want to change that. I don't want to be just Zel's friend, the girl in the shadows. Standing taller I pull my tangled hair into a quick messy bun using the hair tie always on my wrist. This year is going to be different. It's going to be great.

This party on the other hand is terrible. It's just jocks peacocking for all the girls who wore clothes so tight and small that they look like trampy sausages.

"Drinks," Zel commands, taking my arm and steering me toward "Dwayne Johnson." I wish it was the real guy, all muscled and drop-dead handsome. Instead, it's just a flat rock where everyone sets the coolers.

Zel shoves a cold can in my hand. I don't even look at it. My eyes are drawn to Toby. He's leaning against a tree, his foot casually resting against the trunk. When he laughs, his smile calls to me, just like it did in seventh grade when I helped him with an art project. I lift the can to my lips before I realize I haven't opened it. I laugh to hide my mistake, but no one's watching.

Next to me, Zel giggles with Tabitha, another junior girl who's always a total jerk to me. It's easy to leave them behind. I wish Zel would give up on trying to be popular. She's obsessed. When her brother, Heisman, was around he was popular because he passed out free burritos from the restaurant to all his friends, and he had a *lot* of friends. He only stopped because Abuelita caught him and chased him through the restaurant waving a wooden spoon and cursing him in Spanish. With him gone, Zel has made it her mission to achieve the same level of popularity.

Yeah, it stings to have her flat-out ignore me like I'm a ghost. But it's not the first time she's done it, and it probably won't be the last. I shake my head, my messy bun flopping, and shake off Zel's drama because I'm not here for her. I have other plans.

I stumble on a stick, nearly dropping the unopened Coke can as I zero in on Toby Chan, hot nerd of my dreams. "Helpless" from *Hamilton* starts playing on repeat in my mind.

Toby is talking it up with a few other guys from the robotics team. They all wear the typical teen boy outfit of shorts and an ironic t-shirt. Toby is classier, wearing his signature polo shirt in my favorite color, forest green.

The robotics guys all laugh, holding beers. They look awkward as hell. So does Zel. She carries around a giant can of White Claw, but never drinks it. She knows her mom would kill her. These guys grip the cans as though dropping them would set off an explosion.

I sidle up next to one of the nerds, joining the circle. Nodding my head, I smile and try to catch Toby's eye. I have no idea what they're talking about, but when the short pimply guy says, "Conductor? I don't even know her!" I join in laughing. It always feels awkward weaseling my way into conversations.

"Ow, damn it!" I yelp and swat at the mosquito that just started feasting on my arm. Toby and the robotics team stop and stare. Trying to smile cutely, I flip my messy bun making it messier. "Mosquitos. Hungry little blood suckers, they love biting me." I don't mean that to come off dripping with sexual angst. But that's what happens I'm guessing because the robotics guys all turn red and shuffle away. It's just Toby and me, swatting at more mosquitos. Now, who's awkward as hell?

"Hey, you wanna take a walk? I think there's less bugs by the rocks, away from the river," I suggest trying desperately to hide my, well, my desperation.

"Did you know that it's only the female mosquitos that bite?" Toby asks as he steps away from the tree. The Jones River rolls peacefully behind us as we cruise toward an outcropping of rocks. When there's heavy rain and the river rises, the whole area is underwater. My rainbow-flecked Vans stick in the mud as I follow.

"That's really cool," I say sounding like an idiot. A drift of his scent reaches my nose, and holy frijoles, he smells amazing. The clean soap and some exotic spice I can't place infect my brain and add a new level to my intoxication.

"Yeah," Toby says with a glance and a sip of Red Bull.

"Hey, you don't drink either?" I say holding up my Coke. "My parents are food scientists and tell me about all the chemicals in here. All I know is that they taste amazing." I smile and bat my eyelashes trying to draw his attention to my green eyes, my best physical quality.

"My mom won't let me drink. She says it'll kill my brain cells and I need them all to get into an Ivy League school like she did." There is a bitter ring in his tone. And I love it! He's not a mama's boy like everyone says. Toby Chan has a rebel flair that is emphasized by the way he flips his charcoal-colored hair out of his eyes. "Kaysee, let's sit up there. You can tell me about what you did while school was out."

Clumsily, I climb up the rock after Toby, grateful I wore leggings under my dress. No one needs to see my pink unicorn panties. Because with this crowd, someone would snap a picture and post it on Snapchat or TikTok. There would be a buttload of hate-filled comments so terrible that I'd have to move and change my name. As I attempt to sit next to Toby, I slip and land hard, smacking my

Coke on the rock. "Good thing it wasn't opened," I laugh trying to hide my perpetual embarrassment.

Toby smirks, which highlights how beautifully his thick, black eyelashes frame his mocha-colored eyes. I can't tell if he's fascinated with me or amused like I am when I watch cute kitten videos. Oh, please let it be the cute kitten thing. I return the smile and bite my lip. And then there's this awkward pause.

He doesn't say anything. I don't say anything. I don't know what to say. Panic rises. Then I remember something Zel said from her acting class. How when you're nervous onstage you should do something with your hands. So, I finally pop the top of my Coke.

High fructose corn syrup-laden cola deliciousness explodes over us! The sound of the bursting carbonation and our yelps makes everyone stop and turn. Toby jumps up and wipes at his shorts where most of the soda has splashed. He's taken a direct hit to the crotch. And everyone is in first grade again, laughing and pointing at Toby yelling that he peed his pants.

"I'm so sorry!" I jump up, shaking beads of soda out of my hair. With the hem of my dress, I frantically dab at Toby's pants. I want to do anything to make this better. To fix it. Oh my god! I am ruining everything!

"Whoa, Kaysee!" Toby stumbles back. Laughter grows below, and a few cameras flash like lighting over us. His cheeks red and his hands over his crotch, Toby stares at me wide-eyed.

"This was all an accident. I didn't realize. I must've shaken the soda when I tripped."

"Look," Toby holds up a hand, fending me off the way Chris Pratt did a pack of dinosaurs. "I'm just gonna—I'm gonna go. Somewhere. Not here."

As he scampers down the rock racing for his robot team buddies, I gape. It's only the first day of the new me, the one who doesn't hide but puts herself out there, and I've totally botched it.

"Smooth move, Wax Lips." Jason, the most annoying football jerk I know, slides down next to me from one of the higher rocks. Pebbles and dirt follow in his wake. He doesn't notice, but I step away trying to keep the tiny rocks from falling in my shoes.

"Go away," I say bending over to pick up the soda can. Dirt and a leaf stick to the side. I dump the rest of the soda over the edge of the rock.

"No really, quite entertaining." Jason chuckles. He folds his arms over his broad, well-formed chest. It's covered in a crimson and gold Inman Bulls shirt. Like the other jocks, the Inman colors nor the layers of muscles he's perfected can disguise his dark soul. "I especially like the part where you tried to clean him up. You don't seem like the kind of girl to go straight for a guy's junk."

I turn on Jason hoping that he sees the hatred in my eyes. It's been building for years. "Go. Away."

"Oh, come on, Kaysee. You have to admit it was pretty funny." He's taunting me with his dark eyes. I stare him down, hands on my hips. What I really want to do is run and jump in the river and ride it to some place far from here. But I'm not that person anymore. I am Kaysee who doesn't run away and Kaysee who doesn't hide in the shadows. I am bold.

"Piss off, Jason." I climb down the rock in search of Zel. As I pass clusters of people they point and laugh. One guy offers me a high five like I'd planned on soaking the boy of my dreams in Coke before unintentionally molesting him with my dress.

"Zel, can we go?" She's standing with a group of popular girls. They all look the same except in different shades of clothes and makeup. Basically, they each look like a makeup tutorial video, totally fake. And it annoys the shit out of me, the extreme level of their fakeness that Zel can never seem to see. I sigh waiting for her eyes to take in the splatters of Coke covering my dress.

"I'm not ready yet," she says flashing a grin before turning back to the girls who sneer at me.

I huff and roll my eyes as I trudge back to Zel's car. I really wish she wasn't being such a Zel right now. Her car's unlocked, so I slip in, grateful we left all the windows down. Sounds of laughter and yelling as everyone gets drunker fill the air. I grab Zel's earbuds, pop them in, and pull up Olivia Rodrigo's album on my phone. With the sun setting across the field and beyond the river, the light changes and breaks into fiery orange. There's a tall tree that's silhouetted perfectly against the streaking clouds. The beauty of it begs to be captured. Peeling my sweaty, sticky self out of Zel's car, I follow the sunset.

Hiking across the field, Olivia Rodrigo's angsty voice bounces against my ear drums. The mixture of shadow and light makes me wish I had my real camera, but my phone will have to do. The light's too perfect not to capture. The party at the Bluffs rages behind me as I pick my way through the mud that smells like rotting leaves, so gross it makes my stomach flip. Getting closer, I see a beam of sunlight coming perfectly through a break in the leaves. When I crouch down and angle my phone just right, I capture it.

I wish life was as easy as taking pictures. Just position yourself in the right way and everything is beautiful. But it's not. Life is full of changes and disappointments, ones you can't crop out. And sometimes just when you're in the right place for the perfect picture, a soda can explodes and destroys everything.

I snap a few more shots highlighting the tree in the foreground, then focus on the streaks of sherbet-colored clouds drifting past. When the light has disappeared from the field, I turn back toward the party and the tiki torches and camping lanterns scattered across the bluffs.

"Oh, shit!" I yell and jump as something pulls on my arm. I rip out the earbuds. Olivia's vocals are replaced by a laugh I know all too well. "Jason, I said to leave me alone."

"Quit being so jumpy. I just wanted to check on you." His silhouetted shoulders shrug.

"Why do you care?" I push past him, trying not to lose a shoe in the sticky mud as I head back to Zel's car.

"Kaysee, really," Jason is at my side in a few long strides. He moves with a slight limp left over from when his knee got destroyed in a football game last year. "I know you like Toby."

"You don't know anything," I spit, scratching at the blossoming cluster of mosquito bites on my arm.

"You are the world's worst liar. You were staring at him in biology all last year. I'm just saying that you shouldn't be chasing that guy. Find someone who likes you for who you are." I'm instantly mortified and keep walking grateful that he can't see the flush rising to my cheeks.

"Thanks, for the Ted Talk! Now, leave me alone. Go back and party with your jock buddies."

"Those guys are idiots," Jason says with a hint of cynicism.

I stop. "Look. Whatever's happening between you and your steroid-fueled bromance crew, I don't care. Stay out of my life and leave me alone."

"Whatever, Wax Lips," Jason throws the old insult at me. It doesn't make sense. It never did. Something about the lip balm I wore in sixth grade. He started calling me "Wax Lips" and laughing every time. It was just the beginning of his reign of terror teasing me every chance he got.

But I'm not in the mood to waste my time on him. After managing to get back to Zel's car without losing a shoe or falling in the mud, I recline the seat back and start scrolling through TikTok. Zel finally shows up just in time to get home for her 10:30 curfew. As she drives, she blathers on about all the popular girls and what they did this summer and a bunch of stuff I couldn't care less about. We became friends out of convenience. She lives next door. She was with me through those awkward and horrible years of middle school and hasn't left. Don't get me wrong, she's great and lots of fun when she's not focused on her social status. But tonight, that's all she can talk about. Thank god the drive home is short.

I can't sleep. My mind won't stop replaying my encounter with Toby. I refuse to go online because I'm sure there'll be at least a dozen pictures or videos of us that have long lists of stupid comments.

I thought tonight was going to be the night. That I was going to finally kiss him. It's been so long since school closed. These health shutdowns are always a pain. I didn't mind having to do school from home. It was quiet, but this one lasted too long. Now, we're finally going back to school in the morning in full masking mode. I'm sure that everyone will follow the rules just as well as they do the ones about not drinking at football games and not making out in the performing arts center.

Downstairs I hear someone, probably my mom and dad. They usually stay up late working on experiments. Having to work from home isn't a problem for them. They have the lab. They work crazy hours anyway.

Deciding I need a glass of water, I head downstairs for the kitchen. The house is pretty peaceful, but the noises in the kitchen don't exactly sound like my parents. When I hear a cabinet door slam, the ultimate sin in our house, I know something's not right. Standing in the middle of the stairs I have two choices. Just check it out, maybe it's Pablo. Or run for my phone in my room and call the police, which could possibly lead to another embarrassing moment when it's really just the cat.

As I ponder my choices, Pablo runs past me, up the stairs, and into my room. That's not a good sign. I slink down the stairs, moving stealthily across the carpet, and leap for the coat rack. After years of living in St. Louis, we still keep a baseball bat near the front door. I tighten my fingers around it as I peer around the corner.

Oh my god! There's someone in the kitchen, and it's definitely not my mom or dad. Standing in front of the open fridge, the light silhouetting him, is a skinny guy scanning the contents. He looks like one of the freshman boys with long, gangly arms and legs.

The skinny guy turns and sees me. I watch in fear as the realization reaches his eyes. I lift the bat higher, right at the level of his skull. His eyes widen in panic as he sneers, sharp teeth glinting in the light from the fridge. He runs at me so fast I don't have time to do anything but scream. I can't even swing the bat before he's on top of me and my shoulder's burning like I've been bitten by a shark.

"Doug! No!" Mom screams as the lights snap on assaulting the darkness and my eyes.

That's when I get a close look at the skinny boy. But he's not a boy. He's something very different. His gray eyes gleam with inhumanity. And sharp teeth drip blood down his chin as he hisses over me.

2

DAMN IT DOUG

Arms and legs tangle with mine all fighting to yank Doug off me. I feel like I'm at the bottom of a dogpile in a football game pushing at random body parts to free myself. And, oh, holy hell! My shoulder burns like it's on fire!

"Get off! Get off!" I scream at the strangers who've poured into my kitchen.

A foreign voice with a British accent adds to my screams. "Damn it, Doug! Let go!"

"Doug, let go!" My dad bellows, his glasses knocked askew as he wrangles the oddly strong Doug. Doug responds by snapping at me like a rabid dog. His hands are clamped around my arms so tight my pulse crashes against them.

Mom's voice blends with the others begging Doug to let me go. I dodge to the side just in time to avoid Doug clamping down on my neck. "Get this guy off of me!"

"Get back," someone pushes through whipping a thin scarf from her neck and wrapping it around Doug's mouth like a gag. With the speed of a cheetah and the gracefulness of a prima ballerina, she yanks Doug to the side with her scarf. A quick kick and a spin and she's pinned Doug to the floor. "You must be Kaysee. I'm so excited to finally meet you," she says with a thick accent and a smile. Doug bucks under her, and she punches him in the nose making him still.

I cough as I sit up and survey the scene in my kitchen. Blood pools on the floor. Deep punctures in my shoulder ooze, soaking my shirt. Dad stands back looking between the badass girl and me like he's watching a tennis match. Mom cries as she races to me with a towel. Casually leaning against the counter, the British accent guy studies me, his eyes creased in concentration.

"Kaysee, are you okay?" Mom presses the towel against my shoulder.

"Ow," I recoil. "Mom. What's going on?"

"Nugget, we need to get you cleaned up. Here, hold the towel on your shoulder and I'll get some peroxide." Mom shuffles away. "Michael!" Mom snaps her fingers at Dad and nods at me still on the floor.

"She doesn't need peroxide," the British guy says shaking his head. He has perfectly tousled chestnut wavy hair that defies gravity.

"Yes, she does," Mom commands. Her eyes are squinted like she's trying to make her words true, even though she knows they're not. "It's just a minor bite. We'll clean it, and it'll be okay."

"Emily." The British guy draws out Mom's name in an apology.

Mom drops her head and whispers, "Damn it, Doug."

Dad kneels at my side, the hem of his white lab coat dipping into my blood puddle. Something about the blood is immensely fascinating. I watch it soak through the white fabric and inch up toward one of his large pockets as my head begins pounding and my shoulder throbs.

I drop my head and groan. "Can someone turn off the lights?" Dad places his hand over mine and presses the towel against my shoulder. "Dad, stop. That hurts."

"I'm sorry, nugget," he says into my hair. I lean against him, nestling my head against his chest like I did when I was a kid. We used to watch movies cuddled up together on the couch and I would always fall asleep listening to his heart and the deep rumble of his laugh.

"Kaysee, love," the British guy crouches in front of me. "My name's Oscar. This is Baihe," he nods to the badass girl with eyes deep brown like Toby's. She still pins Doug to the floor. Her name is strange, sounding like he's saying, *Buy, huh?* "And you've met Doug. I'm sorry this happened. But we can help you." His voice, melodic with the accent, is soothing. I look into his deep blue eyes and trust him immediately.

"Are you a doctor?"

"Not in this life, love. But maybe in the next one," he smirks.

"Oscar, what do we do?" my mom pleads, standing defeated over the sink.

"We wait for nature to take its course," Oscar says, resting his hand on my foot.

"It's going to hurt," Baihe adds with a dour look. Her intricately braided raven-colored hair falls over her shoulder. And everyone in the room is frowning. Except for Doug. He's still unconscious.

"What is happening? Someone needs to explain this now!" I scream, my voice reverberating off the insides of my skull. If dousing Toby in Coke isn't in my plan for starting junior year, being attacked by a crazy guy in my kitchen absolutely isn't either. Everyone glances around the room, waiting for someone else to start talking.

Finally, Mom turns to me and forces a smile across her face. She looks torn, putting on a happy face while trying to hold back pools of tears in her sorrowful eyes.

"Well, Kaysee, you see," Mom clears her throat. "Oscar and Baihe can explain a lot of it to you in time, but I can address the scientific aspect of the changes you are experiencing."

"Mom, if you're talking about puberty, you're about four years too late," I say squinting against the light. It bores into the back of my brain like a laser.

"Well, that's not it exactly," Mom stalls. "But it is a change. And you'll see some new things happening with your body, very different kinds of things." She waves her hands like she's casting a magic spell. "Proteins have already started metabolizing in your body. Your cellular structure will never be the same again."

"What is she talking about?" I look up at Dad.

A single tear escapes his eye as he shakes his head. "Damn it, Doug."

A flash of light splashes through the windows followed by flashing red and blue lights.

"Oh, no! Oh, no! It's the police," terror fills Mom's entire body. Her eyes widen as she grabs more towels and throws them to Dad. "Clean it up quick!"

Dad wipes the white tile floor sopping up my blood. It smears, the crimson strokes looking like a Valentine's Day card I painted for him in first grade. "Help her up," he orders Oscar. Next to me, Baihe drags Doug into the lab, smacking his head against the door jamb with a thud. His eyes flutter open, conscious again.

"Wait, what's going on? What's the change?" I ask, looking for an answer clearer than my mom's mumbling about proteins. "Someone needs to *really* tell me what is going on now or I'm going to totally lose it! I mean, seriously, I'm bleeding everywhere and Mom's not making any sense at all! And who are these people?"

"This might be hard to take in," Oscar helps me to my feet. "But to put it simply—"

"You're a vampire now," Doug smirks droopy-eyed as Baihe drags him into the lab and slams the door.

My gaze whips back to my mom, and her weak smile confirms it. I'm a vampire. What the hell? Vampires aren't real. I can't be a vampire. They're just in books and movies, not in Inman, Missouri.

I whip my head around, "Dad, this is a sick joke." And from the way he freezes with his mouth gaping like he's pondering a chemistry formula he can't solve, I can tell something is really wrong. But there's no way in hell I'm a vampire. Because vampires aren't real!

"Police!" yells an officer pounding and rattling our front door in its hinges.

Mom holds her finger to her lips and whispers, "Please, Kaysee, keep quiet. This is really important." She straightens her lab coat and her ponytail before reaching for the knob.

"Don't say anything," Oscar whispers in my ear. "Please. You'd be saving our lives." The levity in his voice makes the room spin. But what he says doesn't make any sense. How could I save his life? Aren't I the one that needs saving right now?

Leaning against Oscar, I let him guide me from the kitchen into the living room. I groan when he drops me on the couch.

"We had a noise complaint. Neighbors said people were scream-ing," the police officer barks from the front porch. I lean forward trying to see the officer, but Oscar tosses a blanket to me and gestures to my shoulder. I pull it up to cover the wound that is now fizzing like that time Zel and I put Pop Rocks in a soda on her back porch and watched it bubble and ooze.

Mom laughs nervously, "Oh, that! We were just happy. Happy screaming." Her laugh pitches higher with her lie. Maybe she needs to go to drama camp because there is no way anyone in their right mind would believe her. Geez, Mom.

Out of sight of the officer, Dad tosses the last of the towels into the garbage and steps behind Mom. While Dad is a brilliant scientist, he'd also be an excellent used car salesman. Thrusting out his hand to the officer, his voice booms, "I'm Dr. Michael Fehr. It's nice to meet you, officer. Sorry for the disturbance." He pumps the officer's hand a few times and drops his arm over Mom's shoulder leaning into her like they're out on a date.

"I'm sure you understand that I need to come in and look around." The officer pushes past Mom and Dad and steps into the living room looking at me and Oscar on Mom's prized heather grey couch. My sticky blood soaks into the fabric making me wonder how pissed Mom will be that the couch is ruined. But honestly,

I hurt too much to care. If she's going to let me get bit by some vampire guy, she gets to deal with a bloody couch.

"See, officer, nothing out of the ordinary here," Dad says with a nod and a smile.

"It's kind of late for so much commotion," the officer says taking in the room with skepticism. His eyes linger too long on the muted grey walls and family photos trailing up the staircase.

"Well, you know teenagers," Dad punches the cop on the shoulder. He glares at Dad and straightens his shirt.

"What's that on your shirt?" the officer moves closer to me.

"Um," I stall, pulling the blanket higher and looking at Dad for an answer. He cringes. "Paint?"

"Paint?" The cop raises an eyebrow and takes out his notepad.

"Yes!" I say too enthusiastically. The cop snaps his eyes to me, and my head starts pounding again. "I was painting and Mom and Dad surprised me." I wave my arm imitating the act of stroking my paintbrush across a canvas.

"What about him?" The cop points his pen at Oscar who leans in and drops his arm over me. The force of his hand on my vampire-bitten shoulder makes me cry out. I try to turn my gasp into a cough.

Oscar jumps in. "I'm Oscar," he answers with a smile, relaxing confidently into the plush couch.

"You live here, Oscar?"

Behind the police officer, Dad nods his head vehemently, his glasses vibrating down his nose.

"Apparently I do now," Oscar replies, his words dripping sweetly.

A commotion from the lab steals everyone's attention. Baihe's muffled voice meets the sound of crashing glass.

"What the?" the cop asks.

Doug bursts through the lab doors, Baihe holding his arm. "Let me go!"

"I'm gonna have to call this in," the cop reaches for his radio.

"No!" everyone screams in unison.

We all freeze, looking at the cop before Dad jumps in. "Really, officer, it's all okay. Just a misunderstanding."

"Misunderstanding, huh? That girl's covered in paint that looks like blood. This guy doesn't know where he lives. And these two are obviously up to no good."

"I can explain it all," Mom says, her voice level and calm. "This is our daughter, Kaysee. We surprised her tonight with," she gestures in turn, "Oscar, Baihe, and Doug. Our new, uh, you see, our new foreign exchange students. Kaysee was painting when we told her, and she, you know, spilled her paint. So, um, there's nothing vile going on here." Mom is less than convincing, making me hold my breath to see how the cop responds.

"Foreign exchange students?" The officer squints as he process-es. "I can tell you're not from around here," he points at Oscar.

"From across the pond in jolly old England. God save the queen and Downton Abbey," Oscar says. I elbow him in the ribs to make him stop verbally vomiting Britishisms.

"What about you?" The officer turns to Baihe and Doug.

"China!" Baihe says still holding Doug's arm. "*Wo hen gaoxing renshi ni*!" she adds with a meek smile. Of course, no one under-stands a word she says.

"Uh huh," the cop replies. "And you? You sound American enough."

The energy in the room plummets. We've all added to this elaborate lie. I still don't fully understand why, but I know that if what Oscar said was true, their lives somehow depend on it. They depend on Doug. The guy who bit me with his strangely sharp teeth. Jerk. Wait. Maybe, vampire jerk?

"I know right?" Doug smiles and pulls Baihe to his chest. "My girlfriend here loves my American accent." He pulls Baihe in for a kiss. She stiffens and does something to his back that I can't see, but it makes Doug stand bolt-upright as though he's been electrocuted.

"Oh, Doug!" Dad laughs. "He has such a strange sense of humor. He's Canadian." Dad shrugs almost apologetically.

"That explains it," nods the cop with a sneer. "So, they startin' school in the morning?"

"Of course," Mom answers with way too much enthusiasm. "We'll be dropping them off first thing." Heads bob around the room in agreement, even Doug's. Although, it looks like Baihe is controlling him like a puppet. He groans in protest.

The officer flips his notebook closed and sticks his pen in his pocket. Turning to leave he says, "Better get everyone to bed. It's late. And no more surprises tonight, okay?"

When the door closes behind him, everyone sighs in relief. I collapse forward fighting against the burning in my stomach. My whole body throbs.

"That was close," Mom says looking terrified. "Everything could have been lost."

Dad takes her into his arms and holds her close. A lick of searing pain shoots from my shoulder down to my toes. Moving the towel away from my shoulder, all I can see are two small marks that look more like pimples than puncture wounds. I wipe the towel over the wound in disbelief. So much has happened in such a short amount of time. My head is screaming and I'm reeling from the shock.

"Nicely played, Drs. Fehr," Oscar tips an imaginary hat to them.

"Get off!" Doug yells, twisting from Baihe's grip. "Geez." He pulls off his t-shirt stained with my blood to reveal his scrawny, hairless chest. All bones and pale skin.

As a wave of nausea rolls over me, I lift my hand. "Can we stop for a second here? And someone tell me what the HELL IS GOING ON!"

A chorus of voices assaults me. The only one not participating is Doug who's returned to the refrigerator. I try to comprehend everything they're throwing at me. While the words make sense, their meaning doesn't. They're wrong. This can't be happening.

Dad sits next to me on the couch. He strokes my hand and tells me everything will be okay. Mom joins him, their voices blending. Oscar is saying something about long histories. Keeping an eye on Doug, Baihe adds to Oscar's story.

The more they speak, the hotter I get and the more my stomach churns. The room is spinning. The light too bright. I focus my eyes on the stack of old science journal magazines abandoned on the coffee table, but they fade in and out. Without warning, my stomach lurches and I puke. Everywhere. I didn't know my body could hold that much. It is absolutely the most disgusting thing I've ever done. Luckily, I pass out right after that and fall into a blissful silence where I'm 100% sure that this has all been a dream.

3

But I'm a Vegetarian

Holy shit. It wasn't a dream.

Waking up the next morning, Pablo is curled next to my legs. His soft fur against my bare skin feels so normal, not like anything from last night. I've pushed off all the blankets, which is really weird because I'm always freezing cold. But not now. Now, I'm blazing hot. A slit of sunlight shines on my face. Ugh, everything is just too bright. I roll over as another wave of nausea attacks me like a steamroller.

It doesn't help that my mind won't stop flashing through everything that happened last night, from the exploding soda all the way to my parents explaining that I'm a vampire and tucking me into bed.

Grabbing my phone, I stare at a dead screen. Dead like me, is that what I am now? When I plug it in, it starts chirping with messages, all from Zel. Scrolling through the long chain of texts I cringe at her mentions of Snapchat and TikTok posts. Dropping my phone on my nightstand, I look at the time. Oh, no. I'm late for school on the first day. I already missed Zel's ride and school started two hours ago. No! Two hours!

Jumping from my bed I don't get far before I'm sticking my face in the plastic bucket Mom left within reach on the floor. I dry heave for a few minutes before my body gives up. My lips are chapped from dehydration. I'm dizzy. My head buzzes. I'm still struggling with the idea that vampires are real and not ready to admit that I got turned into a freaking vampire last night!

There's a soft knock on my door followed by Mom's whisper. "Kaysee? You okay?"

"No," I groan and drop to the floor resting my head against my bed. "I'm late for school and I feel awful."

Mom cracks the door open and sticks her head through. "I can help with both of those," she smirks. Mom doesn't smirk often, she's usually your typical analytical, boring scientist with her head in a book or her hands on some test tubes. When she smirks, it's for good reason. The last time I can remember her smirking was a few years ago when she brought home Pablo. Whatever she's got cooking must be good.

"Come on," she steps into the room and reaches for my hands. "You can at least make it downstairs. I have something special for you."

Standing, I have to lean against her. My body aches in places I didn't know I had. In the hallway, I squint at the bright sunlight. "I've already missed a bunch of school. Zel is not happy." My phone trills with a message emphasizing my point.

"Don't worry about that. I called the school and changed your schedule from daylight schedule to twilight schedule. You don't have to start until 2:00." Mom smiles.

"No! You can't," I complain, groaning with each step down the staircase. "Zel and I made a plan. We scheduled our classes together."

"Oh," Mom says, her brow furrowing. "Well, I'm sorry, but this is how it has to be now. Daytime classes aren't really going to work for you."

A chorus of good mornings greets me as we round into the kitchen. Mom deposits me in a chair at the dining table, and Dad swoops in to kiss my forehead. He hasn't done that in years. I rub my hands over my temples trying to dull the ache caused by a lifetime of change happening in a few hours.

"*Zaoshang hao*!" Baihe says way too loudly as she sits next to me. "That's 'good morning' in Mandarin. Your dad said that you like, totally want to learn to speak it."

I wrack my brain trying to remember any conversation I ever had with my dad about speaking Chinese. Maybe it's because of those crazy kung fu movies grandpa loves to watch with me. I don't know. I give up and quit trying to make sense of anything. I feel like I've awoken in an alternate universe.

"Um, okay," I say weakly.

"You should drink this," Oscar sits on my other side and slides a glass to me. My stomach rolls again.

"Is that?" I can't muster the word to describe the thick, red liquid. It's horrifying. "I can't drink—"

"It's not blood, love," Oscar sits back and sips from a teacup.

"We made it. In the lab," Dad says proudly, sitting across from me with a plate full of eggs and bacon. "Try a sip."

I dip my nose toward the mystery liquid and take a whiff. "Is there any meat in it?"

Oscar laughs. I glare at him. "I'm a vegetarian," I explain.

"Oh," Oscar says, making no attempt to hide his amusement. "That creates quite a conundrum." He giggles.

"Ignore him," Baihe says. "He's an elitist. Thinks he's so smart because he's the oldest."

Mom sits next to Dad. "It's mostly cherry juice, some beet juice, tofu, and some chemical enhancers and stabilizers." She shrugs and dips her spoon into her oatmeal, the same thing I usually eat at breakfast. But the sight of it makes my lips curl today.

Lifting the glass to my lips, I tip it slightly letting the liquid coat my tongue. It's thick and sweet like syrup, but kind of salty too, and takes a few swallows to push down. I wait for my stomach to react, to start retching again, but it doesn't. Everyone around the table watches me with anticipation.

I shrug, "It's not so bad." Something in the juice is instantly addictive. I keep sipping until all that's left is crimson red coating the inside of the glass.

"Vampire transition: step one complete," Oscar raises his teacup to me with a wink. "Feeding."

"Wait. What? Was there blood in that?" I turn to my dad. "Dad?" He keeps his face buried in his eggs. "Mom? What was in that?"

I want to be really angry with them for tricking me, but I'm suddenly feeling better. Like a lot better. My headache has faded, and my body has stopped tingling like I'm being pricked by a thousand needles.

"Okay, Kaysee, there was a *little* blood in it. Not much, just a few CCs. You need it right now for your metabolism," Mom shrugs away the last three years I've committed to being a vegetarian like it means nothing. To her it probably does, but when I committed to no meat, I meant it for many reasons. She just doesn't understand, she never has.

As my righteous indignation at their trickery grows, so does a shocking realization. "Whose blood was it?"

"A donor," Dad says taking the last bite of his breakfast. His casual attitude as he sits back to clean his glasses throws me off kilter. "The juice is a project we've been working on, synthetic blood for those who need it."

"Like vampires?" I ask not even trying to mask my disgust.

"Yes, like vampires. There's quite a big market for it actually. That's why Oscar, Baihe, and Doug are here, to help taste and test the product," Dad says.

I lick my lips, my body already craving another glass of their concoction. "But vampires aren't real. I'm definitely not one, and I didn't just drink someone's blood. And, oh god, this is just a nightmare, a stress dream before school starts. I'm going to wake up in the morning as my boring self." I bury my face in my hands

"Oh, Kaysee, you're not boring," Mom says concerned.

"But vampires *are* real," Oscar says. "And you are one now. So sorry, love."

"Yes. That was an accident. It was not intentional," my mom emphasizes by smacking the table. We all jump. "Doug was out of line."

"Maybe Doug shouldn't have been here at all," I feel my anger rising. Normally, I'm not like this. I stay calm, but realization is hitting me like a hurricane. "Maybe you shouldn't have brought vampires into the house who would bite me. What about you? Are you two vampires too? What else are you hiding from me?"

Oscar's hand on my arm stops me. I don't even know when I stood up, but I'm pounding on the table as my blood pounds in my veins. I have never been so angry in my life.

"We didn't have a choice," Mom says staring into her oatmeal bowl. "When work shut down because of the pandemic, we got laid off." She meets my gaze, wiping at tears before they can trail down her face. "It was taking so long to open the labs again that they let us go. We had to branch out on our own or just live off of our savings, which wouldn't have lasted long. We could have lost the house, our cars, everything. So, we used our savings to invest in the blood alternative research. Once we can market it, we'll be okay again and never have to go back to the labs. There's a high demand for it."

"Very high," Oscar adds. "You see, Kaysee, being a vampire isn't a walk in the park. There are some really great parts to it, but there's also the need to feed on humans that ends up putting a damper on everything else. Your parents are doing something great. You shouldn't have gotten mixed up in it. It's really a shame, love. But we can help."

"We want to help," Baihe takes my arm. "I could totally use a vamp sister." Her smile is infectious. Something about Baihe is innocent, as long as you overlook the whole eating humans to survive part.

"We're all in this together," Dad says.

"I didn't sign up for anything." Yawning, Doug steps into the kitchen doorway. A thick crease line travels down his cheek from his pillow, and his blonde hair juts out at weird angles.

"Oh, good, Damn It Doug's awake," Oscar says into his teacup with a thick layer of sarcasm.

"Shut up, grouch," Doug kicks the leg of Oscar's chair as he passes by. "What's for breakfast?"

"Doug, I think you have something to say to Kaysee," Mom says in her firm mom voice.

"Yeah," Doug speaks into the pantry cabinet, his words flat and lacking emotion. "Sorry I bit you and turned you into a vampire. My bad."

"Doug," Mom sings his name the way she does mine when I'm in the worst trouble. It's mildly entertaining to watch someone else on the receiving end of her annoyance.

Sighing, Doug turns to me, a box of Pop-Tarts in his hand. "Kaysee, I'm really sorry I turned you into a vampire. But you shouldn't have come at me with a wooden bat. I was just defending myself."

"Damn it, Doug. An apology isn't an apology if you blame the other person," Mom says.

"Right-o, it's not her fault you were creeping around the house and that you can't tell the difference between a baseball bat and a wooden stake," Oscar adds.

"Fine!" Doug drops the Pop-Tart box on the counter. "I'm sorry," he says mockingly. "I shouldn't have bitten you. I'm sorry it happened. I'm so, so terribly sorry. I won't do it again."

With a yowl, Pablo traipses into the kitchen and jumps up onto the table. "Aw, *mao mi. Hen ke ai*!" Baihe coos, passing Pablo a piece of bacon, which he inhales.

"Pablo, get down," Mom says in unison with me. I grab the water spray bottle and squirt him in the face. Pablo hisses. It takes two more squirts to get him off the table. Seeing Doug near the stove, Pablo starts rubbing against Doug's legs meowing, begging for more scraps.

"Feed the kitty," Baihe says, smitten with Pablo.

"No! He's too fat. The vet put him on a diet," I explain turning to Pablo with the spray bottle. "Pablo, go!"

"Yeah, cat, scram!" Doug nudges Pablo with his foot, which Pablo doesn't appreciate. He bats at Doug and hisses. Doug hisses back. The two fall into a hissing battle, with growing intensity. I spray Pablo, but engaged in war with Doug, he doesn't move. Instead, he latches on to Doug's ankle with his claws.

"Pablo, stop!" I yell unleashing more water at the cat. Doug continues hissing, and my anger builds again. This time at the madness around me. Remembering the exploding soda from last night, (was that just last night? Geez.) I aim the spray bottle at Doug's nose. He squeals in response. "Doug, stop!"

"Doug, quit pestering the cat!" Dad yells, sidestepping a stray squirt of water. My aim is passing between Doug and the cat like I'm playing one of those water blast carnival games trying to win a crappy stuffed animal. They won't stop hissing at each other.

"Kaysee, stop for a second," Baihe orders. She slinks toward the cat and cradles him under her arm. He swipes his claws across her hand. "*Mao mi! Bu hao*!" But her anger vanishes a second later when she rubs Pablo under the chin and is treated to one of his crazy loud purrs. Mom relives Baihe of Pablo and pushes him out the back door into the yard.

"Just when I thought the day couldn't get any weirder," I say dropping the water bottle back on the table.

"You okay, Baihe?" Mom asks.

"Oh, totally," she replies wiping her hand with a napkin. She plucks a Pop-Tart out of Doug's hand and plops back down in her chair with a playful smile.

"Okay, I think I've had enough of Vampire 101 and learning that my parents are now cooking fake blood like meth in the lab. Thank you for the mystery cherry, beet, blood juice," I say to Mom. She smiles, proud of her achievement. "But I seriously need a shower."

Everyone is quiet as I leave the kitchen. Climbing the stairs, I ignore Pablo crying at the back door, begging to be let in for more bacon.

As I reach the landing, I hear my dad say, "That went better than expected."

Good god, my parents are insane.

4

WEIRD STUFF IS HAPPENING

It's amazing how human I feel after getting out of the shower. It's also amazing to think that I'm not really human anymore. Or am I? All the questions about my new body keep piling up. Staring at my reflection in the mirror, I look for anything about me that's changed. Nothing really. Wasn't becoming a vampire supposed to make me hot, or at the least cute? I guess not. I have the same limp, boring brown hair. Same green eyes. I smile. And there it is.

My scream echoes across the house...again. I run my tongue over my teeth, my canine teeth in particular. They're sharper and longer. Not much, but it's absolutely noticeable. It's the first evidence I've seen that I really am a vampire. And if that's so, then vampires are real. And, holy hell, this year is such a flaming disaster that I can hardly take it.

After I catch my breath and continue inspecting myself, I notice something else that's off. Yesterday, I'd spent ten minutes covering three pimples on my forehead with thick concealer. They're completely gone now. Maybe there are a few things about being a vampire that aren't so bad. I really hope so.

Then I look at my body. I'm the antithesis of Zel. She's all curves in the way women want to be curvy. Me? I'm like a stick. Too tall. Too thin. And too flat. All the movies say that vampires don't age. That's ludicrous to think about. But what about my body? Will it never change? Am I going to live for eternity with no boobs?

I pull my towel tight around me and slip out of the bathroom. Padding along the thickly carpeted hallway to my room I shut the door. My clothes are hanging in the closet, ones I'd picked out last week with Zel. She insisted that the forest green t-shirt with the lace trim was perfect with a tight jean skirt she talked me into buying at the mall last year. I haven't worn it once, even though she said it made my legs look awesome. It's too short for me and rides up uncomfortably higher when I sit down. Zel has been trying to dress me like her doll for years. Like usual, I toss the jean skirt aside and exchange it for the flower-printed flowy skirt I found at the thrift store this summer. It's soft cotton that blows in a breeze and hugs my legs.

I head back to the bathroom to get my hairbrush and try not to look at my mouth in the mirror. I still run my tongue over my newly sharp teeth, each time hoping that I'll wake up from this weird dream. My hair is long with split ends. Really, it hasn't been cut since before Christmas family pictures last year. It looks so drab and sad that I just pull it into a braid to keep it out of my face.

The handle turns on the bathroom door. "Mom, I'm in here!" I yell.

"Let me in, I gotta go," Doug panics from the hallway.

"Damn it, Doug," I say under my breath, slapping on some deodorant before opening the door.

He rushes in and shoves me out, slamming the door behind me and announcing, "It'll be a while."

"Gross!" I yell over my shoulder as I return to the solace of my bedroom. I don't know how Zel does it. All those sisters sharing one bathroom.

As if she knew I was thinking of her, my phone vibrates on my desk with a new message. I grab the phone and flop on my bed next to Pablo who'd been let back in and has nested in my blankets, his head contentedly perched on my pillow. I rub his back as I read through Zel's message. She is completely pissed, and rightly so.

Sorry. Parents. I tap on the screen and drop my phone next to me. She is going to lay into me when I see her next. We spent most of the summer making plans to be in classes together this fall. Even back when everyone was getting sick and talking about who was "in your bubble" Zel proclaimed that I was in her bubble and that I wasn't allowed to hang out with anyone else. It's not like there were many other people to hang out with. I have a few other friends like Maddy and Maeve from art class, but they live across town. Since my parents refuse to let me get my driver's license, there's no way I'd get to see them anyway.

The thought of my parents not letting me get my license, and why, makes me snort. It's so absolutely ridiculous that they refuse to let me learn to drive because teenagers are so often hurt in car accidents. I run my tongue over my newly elongated and sharpened teeth and laugh. Me becoming a vampire wasn't anywhere on their radar. Maybe they need to acknowledge that there's really no way to protect me.

"Open up, Doug!" Baihe yells in the hallway, her voice accented by pounding. I can't make out what Doug says in reply, but whatever it is, makes Baihe pound harder and break into a string of Mandarin so harsh her words alone might break down the door.

I run my fingers over Pablo's furry head. He leans into my hand and lifts his chin with a purr. "Well, Pablo, I guess this is life now. Not exactly how I saw this year going. I guess everything continues to get weirder and weirder."

Grabbing my phone again, I scroll through the messages from Zel that started at 5:45 a.m. In the three and a half hours since she sent that first message, she's flooded my inbox with 38 more that grow in panicked intensity. The first ones start off teasingly, making fun of me for not being a morning person, like my parents. The only reason I'd agreed to daylight classes was because Zel had to work at the restaurant in the afternoons. The 6:00 a.m. to noon schedule worked well for her and her family. Now, I'm stuck in the 2:00 p.m. to 8:00 p.m. schedule. I shift to avoid a stream of daylight streaking across my arm. It wasn't bad at first, but soon my arm started to burn, and now there's a red line where the sun had been. Fantastic, daylight is now my enemy.

As I get to the end of Zel's messages, I send another quick one to her. She'll be in chemistry now, a class she didn't want to take without me. Science has never been her forte, so she was counting on me to help her through the class.

Sorry again. My parents changed my schedule. Weird stuff is happening. I'll explain later. I hit send and lay back trying to fathom how in the holy hell I'm going to explain this to Zel.

"You can't tell anyone you're a vampire," Dad says ten minutes later. He's sitting in my desk chair running his hands through his rumpled hair. "Your mom is going to take the four of you to the school in a bit to get your schedules set. Oscar's working on a cover story. But you can't tell anyone the truth. Don't even mention the word vampire. After all those vampire TV shows and how crazy this year has been, we don't want to cause a panic." Dad takes a long sip from his coffee mug.

"What about the sun?" I ask petting Pablo, who is curled up on my lap. I sit on my bed, the drapes drawn to keep out the light.

"Your mom is making a plan for everything with Oscar. Oh, Kaysee," Dad sighs and shakes his head. "You have to understand that your mom and I never thought anything like this could happen."

"Dad," I sit up, the back of my shirt damp from my hair. "You brought bloodthirsty murderers into our house and didn't tell me. How could you have thought that was a bright idea?"

"We didn't think you should know because you'd get upset," he protests.

"Upset?" I stand quickly. Pablo yowls as he's expelled from my lap. "Here you go again. You and Mom are always so focused on your experiments and your lives that it's like you've forgotten I even exist."

Dad stands to meet me and holds his hands out. I brush off his touch. "Kaysee, please."

Emotions rage through me, coursing through my veins. I've never felt like this before, so utterly and completely pissed off. My mind is racing through fantasies of throwing my desk chair through my bedroom window and watching it shatter into pieces on the patio outside. I take a deep breath trying to control myself. But every breath feeds my rage.

"Please leave," I whisper through gritted teeth. I'm clenching so hard to keep in more harmful words that a headache is blossoming. My fists are balled into the folds of my skirt tight enough that the bones pop in my right hand.

"Kaysee, come on—"

"Leave," I shout, blood rushing to my face.

My dad is hurt. It shows all over his face.

He backs away followed by Pablo and softly closes my bedroom door behind him.

And that's when I totally lose my shit. I scream so loud that it tears at my throat and I swear the walls shake. I grab the pillows off my bed and slam them over and over against my mattress. I keep screaming and attacking my bed until the energy fueling me switches from anger to pain. Lots of pain.

Yes, my head hurts, but this pain is deeper. My soul, my innermost being, hurts. Not just because I'm now a freaking vampire, a mythical unbelievable beast, but because my parents botched it again. They've missed art shows, school performances, field trips. They've never messed up a science experiment though. Not once.

They've shown me again and again what is most important, and it's never been me.

Something inside me breaks as all the hurt from the years of my parents ignoring me flashes through my heart. I fall to my knees and flop forward on my bed. Then I cry. Now, this isn't the kind of sweet crying you see in movies and in those teen dramas where a single tear slips slowly down the girl's cheek as piano music plays in the background. Hell no. This is a snot-filled explosion of all kinds of liquids from my face. I sob. I wail. I cry until my comforter is soaked. It's disgusting. But it also feels good to let it out.

Eventually, my heart slows and I can sit back on the floor as I suck air through my ripped throat. After a few minutes of calm, there's a knock at my door.

"I'm fine, Dad," I say. My voice sounds weird, tired.

"It's not Dad," Oscar says through the door, his lilting accent softened like he's approaching a rabid animal. "May I come in?"

He doesn't wait for an answer and pops his head in the door. "I brought tea," he says stepping into my room and around the pillows I'd thrown on the floor. "It always helps calm my nerves."

I take the teacup he offers, one I bought a few years ago when our art class went on a field trip to the Crystal Bridges Museum. "Thanks, but I don't trust anything you offer me to drink," I say not withholding my ire.

"Touché," Oscar says with a suave smile. His lapis blue eyes look gleeful. "But I can assure you this is purely tea, not proper tea, but some American brand that is passable."

"No blood then?" I ask.

"No, blood. I promise on my honor as a gentleman." Oscar raises his hand with a flourish.

I take a tentative sip, and it tastes like normal tea. The comforting warmth coats my throat. Oscar sits in my desk chair patiently watching me drink. There is an intensity in his eyes, something about them that makes me curious. But the more he stares at me silently, the more I feel like he's examining me like a zoo animal.

"What?" I ask, eyeing him cautiously.

"That was quite a spectacular display of emotion," Oscar replies and gestures at me. I feel instantly self-conscious which starts to quickly morph into anger. Heat grows in my stomach, rising through me. "Take a sip of tea," Oscar orders.

Surprisingly, I find my hand moving as if it had a mind of its own. The mug finds my lips and tips, allowing in a slow stream of warmth that brings down my fury. When my hand drops again, questions bubble inside but I can't find the words to start asking them.

"It was a mind trick," Oscar says. "A little thing really, just a little persuasion that can work in our favor."

"A vampire thing?" I ask, taking another sip of tea but this time of my own free will. I had to do it just as a test to make sure I had control of myself.

"Yes, a vampire thing. And your outburst was another vampire thing." Oscar leans forward, resting his elbows on his knees. It shows off his sky-blue collared shirt and how well it matches his dark jeans. He's impeccably dressed. "You have a lot to learn. I'm here to help. There are things about being a vampire that can be overwhelming, difficult to conquer. That's why so many of us turn into bloodthirsty vampire stereotypes." The rhythm of his voice is soothing. I don't know if it's just the British accent, but my body, my muscles, relax as he talks.

"What about you? Aren't you a bloodthirsty vampire?"

Oscar scoffs, his smile accenting a perfect row of pearly white and deadly sharp teeth. "Good god, no. I'm too refined and self-controlled."

"So, this can be controlled? How?" I ask, resting the mug on my knee.

"Have you ever seen *Out of Control*?"

Oscar moves to sit next to me on the floor. He straightens his shirt as he stretches his legs out. I look at him wide-eyed, confused, and shake my head. "No? Really? That's too bad. It's quite good television. See, there are these people who have let their choices and behaviors control their lives for so long that their families send them off to the wilderness with others of their kind. The worst part of it is that often their friends or family had been enabling them, providing them with whenever they ask. These people usually have reasons for their poor choices, trauma from their childhood and such. They choose to deal with their issues by overeating, drinking too much, alienating everyone with their constant anger, and so on."

I sigh and rest my hand on Oscar's arm. "Oscar, what in the world does this have to do with being a vampire?"

"I was getting to that part. Oh, you Americans are so impatient," he says with a smile. "You've been through something traumatic. You have a choice now," he says holding out his hands like the scales of justice. "You can self-destruct, you know eat the proverbial four boxes of Twinkies or scream until your voice box explodes and then become a stereotypical bloodthirsty vampire who takes out all her aggressions on a helpless bed. Or you can choose to overcome and learn how to deal with being a vampire, the non-bloodthirsty kind. The good thing is that you have me, your parents, Baihe, even Doug to help." He finishes by bumping his shoulder against mine and sloshing my tea, splashing a little on my skirt.

Oscar stands and moves to lean against the door jamb. In the softer light, he is magnificent. Amazingly attractive in a way that makes my breath catch. Soft, wild curls accentuate his gorgeous eyes and devilishly charming smile. "Meet me downstairs in ten minutes. I've got something for you."

"Is it Twinkies?" I ask with a smirk, my lips lifting so that I know they are exposing my new vampire teeth.

"Maybe. Maybe not," Oscar quirks an eyebrow. "Probably not though because Doug has been tearing through your pantry all morning." He sighs and winks. "See you in ten."

For the first time since I became a vampire, I feel a sense of normalcy. But it feels so strange. Not like the normalcy of yesterday going to the Bluffs with Zel. This makes me feel that life as a vampire might actually be possible. As I stand and set my mug on my desk, I take a deep breath. *Maybe things won't be so bad after all*, I think as I cross my bedroom to grab my sketchbook from my backpack. I want to take a moment to sketch Oscar and see if I can capture the fantastic floppiness of his hair. As I reach for my bag, a stray thread of sunlight streaks across my arm leaving a line of blazing pain and a pink streak from my wrist to my elbow.

Well, shit.

5
VAMP LIKE A CHAMP

"What does it mean to be a vampire?" Oscar asks, looking over the lenses of a pair of Dad's discarded reading glasses. He paces across the living room carpet, the coffee table separating us. Motioning to an assortment of items on the table, he continues. "Yes, you'll need your kit, but it doesn't matter if you use these items to preserve yourself if you don't know what you're preserving."

"Get to the point!" Doug yells from the kitchen, a lump of food bulging in his cheek as he works his way through a bag of Takis.

"Shut up, Damn It Doug!" Oscar turns to shoot Doug a glare over his shoulder before he continues pacing. I can't stop a smile from creeping over my face. "As I was saying, there is a long history and tradition of vampirism through the millennia, one that I encourage you to embrace."

From the kitchen, Doug blows a big raspberry, flecks of half-chewed chips flying across the counter. This is just when Baihe walks past him. In one fluid movement, she snatches a chopstick from her hair, raps his knuckles with a thwack, and returns the chopstick back to her updo. "Shut up, Damn It Doug!"

This time I can't hold it back. A laugh escapes. Doug responds by slamming the chips on the counter with a huff. He faces Baihe and preens like a peacock, puffing his chest and trying to match her height.

"Enough!" Oscar rubs his hands through his hair and somehow makes it look even better with the frustrated gesture. "Doug, have you printed the documents?"

"Yeah," Doug snorts, not backing down from Baihe.

"Then, please gather them for Dr. Fehr. We're due to leave for the school soon," Oscar says with a smile.

"Fine!" Doug grabs the crumpled chip bag and heads upstairs.

"I still say we should have left him in San Francisco." Baihe crosses to sit next to me on the couch. She's wearing tight stretchy jeans that highlight her long, slender legs. Paired with that are stylish blood-red clogs and a baggy black tank top hanging loose over her hips. It's bejeweled with a red rooster. On me, this outfit would look absolutely ridiculous, but on Baihe, it looks fabulous. Glancing between her and Oscar, I wonder if being fashionably fabulous is a requirement for vampires. *If so, I've got a lot more to learn*, I think as I look at my legs covered with the thrift store skirt.

"You know that was impossible," Oscar chides Baihe and her suggestion before turning to me to explain. "Damn It Doug is a bumbling fool, one who has put us in many precarious situations. But we keep him around because neither Baihe nor I are able to produce legal documents as Doug can."

"This is very *ke ai*!" Baihe interrupts, pointing at the face mask on the coffee table.

"Zel's Abuelita made it for me," I explain reaching for the mask. It's homemade, covered in swirling stitches of green and blue. Plus, it fits perfectly and doesn't pull too hard on my ears. "We were both supposed to wear ours together to school today."

"If there is any bright side to pandemic fiascos, it's that vampires can now easily disguise their teeth with masks," Oscar smiles. "But that is not your only problem. There is also the issue of the sun."

"I noticed," I snark, rubbing the pink streak on my arm.

"You see," Oscar stands and paces like a college professor in one of those movies where the professor inspires all the students by jumping on desks and tossing textbooks out the window. "That is part of the downside of vampirism, sensitivity to the sun."

Mom walks into the kitchen with a stack of papers in her hands. She tilts her head in our direction not trying to disguise her eavesdropping. As Oscar continues, she slowly makes her way to the living room.

"But really, it's only a sensitivity," Oscar continues. "Thick sunscreen and sunglasses are sufficient to overcome it."

"It's because of the newly developing cells," Mom adds. "There are some fascinating scientific papers on it." She pushes her glasses up her nose. She's dressed like a soccer mom today: purple capri pants, a grey t-shirt, and sneakers. There's no lab coat in sight. She even left her hair down. Her brown locks spilling over her shoulders make her look younger, make her look like me. The thought pisses me off because I'm still really mad at her. I fidget with the end of my braid. "It's what also causes the perceived immortality, heightened healing abilities, and the emotional firestorms." Mom's gaze drops.

"Exactly. Your experience this morning was just one of those firestorms," Oscar explains with a nod.

"So, it *is* like puberty," I say with an eye roll.

"Not really. Puberty is due to hormonal changes and growth of the body," Mom says. "Vampirism is a change on the cellular level. It's like a virus that sweeps through your body and manipulates every cell in its path."

"Okay, so I've managed to avoid getting sick all summer, but now I've got a vampire virus?" I say standing up. This is all just too much. As soon as Mom starts speaking in technical jargon a firestorm starts brewing in my brain. She never gets it, only focuses on the science. She doesn't see me or how freaking freaked out I am. "How am I supposed to go to school if no one can see my teeth and I can't be in the sun, and oh, yeah, I have to feast on human blood?"

♥

"Here they are," Mom says as she pushes a thick envelope to Mrs. Cole. She started as principal last year, coming in with fresh eyes and big ideas. The pandemic dumpster fire of my sophomore year dulled her brown eyes and sprouted straggly grey hairs that escape her unruly bun.

"Susie at the front desk said she already made copies, and Mrs. Whitehead has everything in order," Mrs. Cole says disinterestedly glancing at the envelope. Lifting her mask to take a long sip from her travel mug, she looks over Inman High School's newest exchange students. "I hope you enjoy your year here as an Inman

Bull. If you need anything, please reach out to Mrs. Whitehead, your counselor."

Oscar meets her eyes, smiling kindly. Baihe sits ramrod straight in her chair as she glances at the pictures of Mrs. Cole's family on her desk. In the corner, Damn It Doug is living up to his name by crunching loudly through a bag of Cheetos. He keeps sticking his fingers under his paper mask, streaking the mask in orange dust. Mom gives him a quick scowl over her shoulder.

"We look forward to a brilliant year and many new friendships," Oscar says, drawing everyone's attention back with his formal but friendly attitude. He stands and extends his hand to Mrs. Cole. She jumps back, tucking her hands under her arms. Oscar whips his hand back and awkwardly bows. "My apologies. I still forget that it's a faux pas to shake hands nowadays."

Living through a pandemic has changed people a lot, but the part that is most strange to me is not being able to touch people.

Of course, right now, the person I'd most like to touch is Doug, touch him with a punch on his arm. He's loudly smacking as he licks flavored chip dust off his fingers. Baihe must be thinking the same thing because as she stands, she scoots her chair back. The screech of the chair leg scraping across the cheap tile floor is loud enough to cover the sound of Doug grunting when the back of the chair careens with his groin. I'm really starting to like Baihe.

We follow Mom through the school office, our new schedules in hand as we step into the commons. A few people are filing in to start twilight session. Across the commons, a cluster of masked and gloved janitors wipe cafeteria tables and door handles like they're cleaning up a crime scene. Posters have been plastered over the cinderblock walls informing students to protect against the virus, against STDs, against bullying. Their mixture of colors brings some life to the sterilized space. Too bad there weren't any posters telling me how to protect against vampire bites. That would have actually been helpful. I wonder if anyone can see the change in me, the molecular changes that make me a vampire.

I adjust the elastic strap of my mask and turn to Mom, who is hovering. "Mom, we're good here. I can show everyone where to go."

"She's right, Dr. Fehr," Baihe adds. "We've done this *lots* of times before," she says conspiratorially.

Mom sighs, looking around to see if anyone is watching us. "There is one last thing." She reaches into her big black purse and pulls out small bottles with weird labels on them. They kind of look like sports drinks, but not quite. "Here," she hands one to each of us. "It's the new formula. Kaysee, I don't know how long you can go without...refreshing yourself."

I turn the bottle in my hand to see the label. "Cherry beet juice," I grimace and push it back to her. "I'm sure I'll be fine, Mom. Besides, you already got me once. I'm not falling for it again. No meat means no," I look around and whisper, "blood."

"Kaysee, please. Like I said, there's so much changing in your body right now that you need more proteins than you'll get from the peanut butter sandwich you threw in your bag."

"I have crunchy chickpeas too," I say feeling stupid. After what happened this morning with my epic vampire tantrum, I'm suddenly afraid of what might happen if I go unhinged vamp at school. Mom tips her head, looking over her glasses, and gives me a perfectly executed Mom shame glare.

"Okay," I say taking the bottle.

"Don't worry, Dr. Fehr, we'll keep our eyes on young Kaysee here," Oscar says. "I trust that she will have a normal first day of school where no one will notice anything different about her."

Mom hesitates. I think she's considering kissing me on the cheek like she did before school every day up until fifth grade. Instead, she shifts her bag on her shoulder, nods, and heads for the door. I watch her, kind of wishing she had kissed me. It would have been nice to have something normal today. She pisses me off, but I can't help still wanting her there to tell me everything will be okay. And that pisses me off more. Mom only looks over her shoulder to smile before being swallowed by the bright red double doors.

"You're going to be fine," Baihe links her arm through mine.

Oscar links my other arm, a wall of vampires ready to tackle eleventh grade. "Come, Doug," Oscar says snapping his fingers like he's calling a dog.

Baihe laughs, a tinkling laugh that makes me smile under my mask. "We got you, Kaysee. Before you know it, you'll be able to vamp like a champ."

As we walk in step together, Doug trailing behind us, I know she means well. But Baihe has to be full of shit. There's no way I'll be able to pull this off, not when I've only been a vampire for half a day. My heart thumps harder with every step down the hallway toward health class where Oscar and Doug have first hour.

After the boys have been deposited to Coach Anderson's care, I spin Baihe around and guide her down the hallway toward the math classroom. I find my arm tightening under hers as I clench my fingers over her wrist. When we get to her geometry class I can't let go. My eyes widen and my breath disappears.

Noticing my freak out, Baihe turns to me. "Kaysee," she says in a soft voice. "You need to relax and breathe. I'm afraid we're about to witness another vampire gone wild incident if you don't calm down."

"I don't know how," I whisper, fear welling inside me and mixing with frustration and anger. It's all the emotions all at once, and they're making my chest tighten and my eyes lose focus on the world around me.

Baihe pulls me aside and pinches my arm so hard I can feel a bruise forming immediately. "Ouch," I yell.

"Refocus. That's the key. Find something else to focus on. Right now, that's pain," she explains with a knowing glance. "You're welcome."

"I can't do this," I protest. Baihe lifts her hand again aiming for the same place on my arm. I jump back to avoid her attack. "Hey!" I complain. "Stop!"

"Refocus. Remember that, Kaysee," she says. "Don't worry. You are already vamping like a champ."

6

NO CHEMISTRY IN CHEMISTRY

All through government and English classes, I kept fidgeting with my mask. I couldn't seem to keep my hands still. When popular girl Tabitha cleared her throat and crossed her eyes at me, I dropped my hands to my lap and played with a loose string on my skirt. I stared at my lap as Mrs. Martin finished class by reviewing the lengthy reading list for the semester.

I made it through those first two classes by trying Baihe's advice to refocus. When my feelings started boiling inside, I tried to find things to distract me. Nothing in the classroom was very interesting, just your typical walls of classic literature and a smattering of inspirational posters. My classmates didn't help either. They were all in first-day-of-school good behavior mode, taking notes or sneaking peeks at their phones.

Indigo, a girl from my art classes, the one who always wins first place at contests, was my only source of distraction. She's small-framed, like a rabbit, and just as flighty as one. Her dirty blonde hair sticks out in odd directions. Over the years I've known her, she's always nervously had a finger in her mouth gnawing at a nail or cuticle like a bunny with a carrot. But, wearing a mask makes this nervous tick impossible. I counted each time she lifted her hand to her mouth only to drop it back down dejectedly. After 29 failed attempts, my heart couldn't take watching her any longer.

When the bell rang to end the period, I grabbed my backpack and slipped out the door as fast as I could. The hallways felt strange as I headed to chemistry. I missed the crush of bodies filling the halls, the high fives for reasons I never knew, the girls hugging and taking selfies, and the one person who was always racing through the hordes of students pushing people out of the way as they went. The halls today are depressing. Everyone seems afraid to touch each other. Eyes skitter around trying to guess who's under the masks. And most people keep their hands tucked in their jean pockets like toddlers in a China shop.

Only one person isn't afraid to push their way through. "Watch it! Watch it! I gotta go!" comes Doug's voice cracking with puberty as he presses his way down the hallway. He has his mask on, but it's tucked under his chin and he holds his backpack over his head as he shoves his way toward the bathroom. I guess all that guy can do is eat, crap, and accidentally turn people into vampires.

I stop in the doorway of the chemistry lab watching Doug turn the corner. A few girls in tight shirts and short skirts jump out of his way as he lunges for the boys' bathroom door.

"Excuse me," a smooth voice with the tiniest hint of an accent tickles my ears. I turn to find Toby Chan waiting outside the chem lab. He's wearing his typical collared shirt and khaki shorts with Adidas sneakers. His hair drops perfectly over his almond-shaped eyes that look at me questioningly, or seductively I hope. It's hard to tell since half his face is covered with a plain black mask.

My heart skips a beat as I step to the side and blurt out a quick, "Sorry." Bumping into the door, it bounces against the wall and back against my head with a smack as Toby passes me. I rub my head, grimacing and watching him walk to a lab table. My heart floats from my body like a balloon released into the sky. The scent of lab chemicals, bitter and sweet, swirls around me as I watch him drop his backpack at an empty station.

"You okay, Wax Lips?" Jason Hancock hovers over my shoulder. My eyes narrow as they turn on him. He nods at me, his thick, wavy, dark cinnamon-colored hair flopping with the motion. Around his red Inman High School mask, I can tell he's smirking.

I roll my eyes at him and join the flow of students into the chem lab. I have to fold my arms over my chest to keep from flipping him off. He's such a jackass.

"Toby!" Jason bellows from behind me as though they're long-lost friends. Toby glances over, apparently as confused as I am. Jason brushes past me, pointing his finger at Toby. "Lab partners!" he declares.

I watch in horror as Jason plops down on one of the flimsy lab stools and drapes his arm over Toby's shoulder like they're best buds. Is he trying to ruin my life? My moment of elation at seeing Toby at twilight school has flipped to complete abhorrence of Jason. And as the emotions swirl, I fight to refocus. But, on what? Damn, this really sucks.

"Kaysee, come join us," Jason says wiggling his eyebrows and nodding. And I freeze. Like I always have. Junior year was supposed to be different, not just a repeat of all the boring years of school so far. I was supposed to be stepping out of the shadows, bolder.

"Screw it," I say under my breath and smile in a way that it's visible in my eyes since my mouth is hidden behind Abuelita's homemade face mask.

"Everyone, have a seat," Mr. Garcia bellows as he steps back into the room. His glasses are fogged from his mask. He looks like a cartoon, no eyes and a broad, balding forehead shining in the fluorescent lights. He's even wearing a tie with little beakers on them. "Lab partners will be in groups of three or four."

As soon as I hear that, I let my new boldness take over and jump for a stool across the lab table from Toby.

"Laney said she wanted to be my partner," Toby says, confusion written across his face.

"Laney Preston?" Jason asks, dropping his arm to rest his hands on the waxy black tabletop.

"Yeah," Toby nods.

"My man," Jason laughs. "You don't want her to be your lab partner. I know. I dated her for a few weeks last year, and that girl has no gift for science. I don't know how she passed bio."

"Really?" Toby looks across the table at me. I smile again and flutter my eyelashes for emphasis. I don't really know how girls do this. I'm obviously not great at the art of seduction. But I remember a little of what Oscar said and decide to stretch my new vampire muscles.

"You definitely don't want her," I say emphatically, lowering my voice because I think that's what Oscar did.

Jason quirks his head at me, a little too amused at the scene playing out before him. I'm waiting for him to botch the whole thing.

"Yeah, you definitely don't want her," Jason repeats, imitating my eye flutter but more dramatically. "Besides, Kaysee here, her parents are chemists. She's probably learned a thing or two." He pauses and leans forward, nodding at me with the *you know what I mean* look. "A thing or two about chemistry."

Oh, dear god. There he goes again. If the tables weren't solid underneath, filled with cabinets, I would kick his shins. Instead, I slap him on the shoulder, my hand landing harder than I'd intended and making a loud pop.

"Mr. Hancock, have we got a problem?" Mr. Garcia asks squinting from the front of the classroom. He has his glasses in his hands, wiping them clean with the edge of his sleeve.

"No, sir, Mr. Garcia," Jason snaps upright. "Just talking about how much we love chemistry. All kinds of chemistry." He winks with emphasis, which sets off a wave of giggles around the classroom.

Red creeps up my neck and over my cheeks. At least this isn't as bad as exploding soda across Toby's crotch. Of course, everyone in the classroom knows about that. Stupid social media. I duck my head and slip my phone out of my bag, pressing the awake button and checking for more messages. Zel finally stopped flooding me with texts. I really want to talk to her and explain, but what am I supposed to say?

I drop my phone back in my bag and sneak a peek at Toby. His head's dropped, scanning the first pages of the chemistry textbook that Mr. Garcia asked us all to open. I risk a glance at Jason, who meets my eyes and nods with satisfaction. Well, if his goal was to make my first day in chemistry with Toby Chan the second most awkward encounter I've had with him, then he should be satisfied.

Scowling at Jason, I open my chem book and prop it up like a fence, separating me from Jason. He doesn't need to see how much he's flustered me. I pinch my arm really hard to keep him from finding out.

"Being a vampire sucks!" I scream-whisper across the table. I scratch at my cheek, grateful to have my mask off. I was able to grab one of the outside tables in the shade, and even though it's still hot and steamy, I'm grateful because not many others have chosen to sit near us. I can speak a little more freely with Oscar and Baihe.

Baihe shrugs, "It has its moments." She takes a bite of her cafeteria cheeseburger as Oscar slips into the bench next to her. He settles his tray on the table and drops his backpack on the ground.

"Dear Kaysee, I'm afraid that you've been thrown into this world a bit abruptly," Oscar says as he squirts individual packets of ketchup into a mound next to his fries. "Doug had a rough go of it too, but that was a very different time. And he didn't have a good coach like you do." He smiles and shoves fries in his mouth before gingerly dabbing at his lips with a napkin.

"So, this is coaching?" I ask. "Baihe telling me to refocus and you telling me that it could be worse?" I drop my elbows on the table and plop my head in my hands, frustration vibrating through my body.

"Baby steps, love," Oscar rests his hand on my shoulder. The scent of fry grease on his fingers makes my stomach heave, gurgle, and growl all at once. It sounds like my insides have just eaten themselves. I reach for my backpack and pull out my PB&J. This has been my standard lunch since I gave up meat. Sometimes I mix it up with almond butter or honey, but good old peanut butter and strawberry jelly has always been my favorite.

I pop open my plastic sandwich container and sink my teeth into the soft bread and chewy mix of salty and sweet. The peanuts dance with the strawberries. I'm halfway through eating my sandwich with the fervor of a bear coming out of hibernation when my stomach lurches again. This time it's worse. I can feel the muscles in my stomach rejecting my sandwich. I bend over in pain, a groan escaping.

"She needs the juice," Baihe whispers. I glance up to see the concern on her face. Her eyes dart to the clusters of students at the other tables. Then she starts laughing and leans across the table to slap me on the shoulder. "Oh, Kaysee, you are so funny!"

My stomach lurches again. I feel like I have a dying star inside my guts. It's collapsing inward, devouring everything in the galaxy to disappear into a black hole. Oscar uncaps a bottle of Mom's vamp juice and pushes it to me. A little splashes on the table leaving drips that look like evidence from a crime scene.

I take a sniff, willing myself to drink it. I know what's in it, beet and cherry juice, but also at least a small amount of human blood. The thought of it sends a wave of nausea cascading over me that my stomach fights against. I can feel the longing, the need. It's in every cell of my body screaming out to drink. I look up at Oscar pleading with my eyes for another way, another answer. He frowns and lifts the juice to my lips.

When the juice hits my tongue, my body explodes in celebration. I guzzle it like a football player in a Gatorade ad. A thin line of red drips down the side of my mouth, but I don't care one bit. It feels so good to have the vampire drink hit my stomach and start coursing through my body that I force out any thoughts of human blood.

When I set the empty bottle on the table and use the back of my hand to wipe the sticky trail of vamp juice off my chin, Oscar and Baihe are smiling at me like we all share an inside joke. My body tingles as it digests my parents' concoction. It makes me feel more alive, like the colors around me are brighter in the late afternoon sun. The taste of it lingers in my mouth, hints of cherry and maybe lime. I start laughing. It's a deep laugh, the embarrassing kind that you usually only have when it's the middle of the night at a slumber party and your belly is full of cookie dough and Dr. Pepper. Oscar and Baihe join in, their eyes sparkling at their young disciple. At this moment, I feel hopeful. Maybe I can overcome this vampire curse after all. Maybe?

"You guys eating magic brownies?" Jason Hancock asks from behind me. I recognize his deep voice and mocking tone.

I turn on Jason, pissed that he's showing up again, but also kind of ready for a fight. I don't know if it's my pledge to be bold or the happy vamp juice, but something about me feels different. "Why are you always around?" I sneer.

Jason tilts his head back and holds up his hands defensively. "Geez, Wax Lips, I just wanted to make sure you're okay. I'm not a total asshole. It looked like you were going to be sick, then you were laughing like a serial killer with a new knife."

"I don't think we've met," Oscar stands and steps to Jason. He runs his hand through his thick curls, tousling them in a way that make him look like he'd just stepped off a movie set. Oscar follows the tousling with a seductive tight-lipped smile. "I'm Oscar Marlowe, newly arrived from across the pond."

"Okay, hey," Jason nods and takes an almost imperceptible step backward.

"And this is Li Baihe, or as you Americans would say it, Baihe Li. From China," Oscar gestures to Baihe who has come to stand by his side. She is also smiling, but her chin is dipped and her lips don't show her teeth. And I instantly realize that I'm grinning showing off the glory of my new teeth. I grab my mask and slip the straps over my ears.

"They're exchange students staying with me," I add trying to sound natural. Oscar'd said that it was extremely important that we don't reveal ourselves, so I continue the lie that began with the cop. "There's another one. Doug. He's from Canada."

"The skinny kid you walked in with?" Jason asks.

"That would be our Doug. He's always good for a laugh," Oscar says, inching closer to Jason.

"Maybe that's what you'd call it, but I saw him hitting on any girl that passed by him today. You might want to tell him to tone it down." Jason shifts his backpack. The straps are tight across his thick chest. I can't help but notice the muscles bulging from under his shirt, especially the pectoralis major. Details from anatomy in bio class last year flood back as I imagine each layer of muscle and the blood pumping through his body to keep them working, taut, in perfect shape.

"So, yeah, that's Oscar. This is Baihe. Doug's the weird kid from Canada. And I'm perfectly fine, thanks for asking." The words cascade from my mouth like a flood, barely decipherable. But after the thoughts that were just running through my brain, I know I need to get Jason out of here ASAP because all I can think of right now is how much I *need* to bite him. Heat flashes through my body, the kind that burns both painfully and delightfully filling me with warmth like an electric blanket on a snowy day.

"You're acting really strange, even for you," Jason steps closer, reaching for my forehead. "Are you sure you don't have a fever?"

I slap his hand away, shocked by the contact of our skin sending pleasurable sparks up my arm. "I'm fine," I say too loudly. People at the tables around us turn and stare. I take a deep breath, struggling to find something to refocus on. Glancing across our table I see my phone peeking out of my backpack. "Look, I gotta call Zel. She's pissed I changed to twilight school." I lunge for my phone and start gathering my things.

"Okay?" Jason says, more of a question than a statement. "I guess I'll see you later then."

"It was so nice to meet you," Oscar says with another charming smile.

"See you later. *Zai jian*," Baihe adds steering Oscar back to our table.

My fingers tremble as I unlock my phone searching for another message from Zel. There's nothing but a few email notifications. She's ghosting me, which means that she's really going to let me have it when I see her.

I take more deep breaths as I gather my things, trying to keep refocusing and shutting out the pictures I envisioned of my mouth on Jason's muscled neck. My lips sucking his pulsing artery.

Oh, dear god, this has never happened before! I'm totally losing control. It must be a vampire thing. Slinging my backpack on my shoulders with a groan I repeat, "Being a vampire sucks."

I grab the empty bottle of vamp juice noticing that there's still a tiny bit left in the bottom. I tip it back and drink the last few drops hoping that the magic from this bottle will calm me for the rest of the day.

7

ROMEO AND JULIET'S DEMISE

After lunch, I float through my last classes not really paying attention. My head starts to throb by the time I get to my last class, art. It was the class I was most looking forward to this year. I love Mrs. Carroll. She's the perfect mix of art knowledge and artistic exploration. Basically, she'll let me do almost anything as long as I have a valid justification for it.

The only downfall to art class is that Indigo is there too. She sticks to a corner of the room nearly hidden behind her easel. Occasionally, she lifts her hands to her mouth. It's not as much as before, either because she's adapted to wearing the mask or, like me, she just feels more relaxed being surrounded by easels and all the colors of paint. I know I shouldn't hold a grudge against her. But when she moved here during freshman year, I was suddenly taking second place in all the art contests. And every first place she got set me further back from my goal of getting to art school. What art school wants to accept a student who is always in second place?

By the time Mom drives up through the circle drive in front of the school, my face itches from my mask, and my stomach is hinting that it's going to go supernova again soon. I squeeze into the back seat of our old Ford Focus after Baihe calls shotgun with a smile. I don't even care that I end up in the middle wedged between Oscar and Doug. Sure, Doug smells like wild onions that have been rotting in the sun, but having him this close, I'm ready to elbow him if he does anything stupid again.

"Well, that was an experience," Oscar says with a sigh as he pulls the door shut.

"Seatbelts," Mom calls out automatically and joins the slow flow of traffic away from the school.

While the others buckle up obediently, I huff. "Why does it even matter? Aren't we immortal?"

"Yes and no," Mom shrugs. "It's hard to explain."

From the front seat, Baihe turns to Oscar. "Do *Romeo and Juliet*!" she says gleefully.

Oscar chortles and settles back. "I'm assuming you've read *Romeo and Juliet* or are at least familiar with the story?" he asks handing me the strap of my seatbelt. I roll my eyes as I click the buckle.

"Of course, it's required for freshman English," I answer. I breathe in a whiff of fresh air as Doug rolls down his window and rests his arm so it's hanging outside the car.

"Very good. I'm glad American schools aren't slacking on the essential classics," Oscar says. "Do you remember what brought about Romeo and Juliet's demise?"

"Being stupid," Doug laughs.

Oscar ignores him and continues. "Particularly, do you remember how Juliet ended up in the tomb?"

Flashes of the movie we watched in class after reading the play flicker through my memory. "It was the medicine from that monk," I say.

"Exactly. Bravo! The American education system is not a complete failure," Oscar grins. "The medicine from the apothecary slowed Juliet's heart to where it nearly stopped."

"That's like us!" Baihe says.

"It's the virus, honey," Mom adds. "It slows down your system so much that it appears that you're dead. If I were to check your pulse right now, it'd be so low that any doctor would call a code blue."

My hand drifts to my chest to feel the rhythm of my heart. It's beating at a rate where I can count to three between each beat. "So, vampires aren't truly undead. But I can still die in a car wreck?" My head has started to pound and my stomach to flop relentlessly. I'm so tired of vampire lessons and vampire juice and vampire anything!

"That's the other side of the coin," Oscar says with a smirk.

Baihe twists in the front seat again. "The virus also helps us heal. Isn't that crazy?" She digs around in the compartment between her and Mom and comes up with a plastic knife lost from a takeout bag. "Watch this," she says conspiratorially and rakes the knife across the base of her thumb. A thick red stripe follows in its wake and blossoms wider, dripping into the discarded McDonald's napkin Baihe presses against her hand.

"Baihe!" Mom yells, swerving the car. A minivan next to us honks. "What are you doing?"

"Just a little demonstration," she dabs as the cut. "See it now," she passes her hand toward me, a new trail of blood dripping from the cut. The sight of the blood makes my stomach roil again. "Now, count to ten."

Next to me, Doug starts counting but running the numbers together so fast that they sound like one singular word. "Onetwothreefourfivesixseveneightnineten!"

"Doug," she says throwing the bloodied, wadded-up napkin at him. He bats it away and it flies out the window as we turn off the main road into our neighborhood. "Look," she holds her hand out to me again. The cut is still there, but it's much thinner and shorter, less red. "Magic vampire healing," her eyes twinkle with mirth. "It's one of the better perks."

"I get it. Vampires can't die," I say rubbing my temples and turning my eyes away from the passing car lights.

"Not exactly," Oscar says, his tone heavy. I tip my head to him expecting more of an explanation. I mean, he's basically a walking Wikipedia of Vampirism. Surprisingly, he purses his lips together and looks out the window.

"There's Zel," Mom's two words heighten the fear in my already flummoxed body. As Mom pulls into our driveway, I catch sight of Zel leaning against the bumper of her car. The glow of the street light highlights her crossed arms and that she's chewing on her lower lip. On a normal day, I'd know that allowing her to let loose and verbally process her anger and then offering to bake her my special vegan cookies would soothe her. But today is far from normal in any way, shape, or form. Mom stops the car and shifts it into park. Baihe, Doug, and Oscar open their doors and climb out. I linger a moment too long, not wanting to meet Zel's wrath.

"Hey, baby," Doug says, nodding his head suggestively at Zel. She stares daggers at him, her deep brown eyes narrow so sharply I can feel the power of her disgust as clearly as I can feel the drip of sweat trailing down my back.

"Zel, you haven't met our new foreign exchange students," Mom says brightly. As she introduces my new vampire crew to my best friend, I drag myself out of the car and sling my backpack over my shoulder.

Zel listens to Mom and gives the occasional "uh huh" response as she twists the end of her ponytail draped over her shoulder. Eventually, Mom runs out of steam and steers my new roommates into the house.

"Nice to meet you," Baihe says with a smile and a wave that lingers unnaturally long. Zel doesn't see it, but I do. Baihe's hand is completely healed.

"So?" Zel says accusingly.

"Zel, I'm sorry. My parents—"

"Stop," she puts up her hand dramatically. "We made a plan. All summer, we planned to go to daylight school." She emphasizes *daylight* with air quotes. "We were doing it because it'd work better for me at the restaurant and because all the football players would be taking daylight school too so they could go to games and stuff."

"I know. I'm sorry—"

The hand stops me again. And I know this is my cue to wait. Usually, I would just sit back and let her unleash on me. But, right now, my stomach is twisting in a new way that prevents me from thinking straight. And something stranger is happening. As Zel talks, I can't ignore the pulse of the artery in her neck. It's like she put it on display by pulling her hair back into a high ponytail. Flicking her head to make a point shows it off in a way that I can actually feel her pulse radiating through my body, calling me to her. Words lose meaning as I stare at that throbbing artery.

"Kaysee!" My attention snaps back. "Quit ignoring me. It's not fair. Just like it's not fair that you changed *everything* without even sending me a text."

Thump, thump, thump.

Her pulse is slowing, taunting me.

Thump, thump, thump. My stomach aches, crying out for, oh no, crying out for blood. I lick my lips as my mind focuses on what Zel's blood would taste like. How it would slip smoothly down my throat.

She won't stop talking, and my heart is thumping like a tympani drum. "Oh, god!" I yell. Zell stops mid-sentence and stares at me slack-jawed. "You wanna talk about unfair? Look, I didn't want this! My mom and dad—they changed my schedule because my body is—it's changing. Like, crazy stuff is happening. And I can't go to daylight school because of the sun."

"The hell?" Zel gives me full attitude. "Kaysee, you sound insane. Are you high?"

"No! It's just—it doesn't make sense!" I yell, my stomach flopping again. I look over my shoulder to see Oscar and Baihe watching me through the living room window. I'm trying to remember everything they said, but it all comes out a mess, like all the bits of vampire training I had were tossed into a blender and pulverized beyond recognition. "Look, I gotta go," I say backing away.

"Kaysee," Zel whines, concern invading the anger written across her face. "What's going on?" She steps to me, and being closer to her beating heart makes me jump with the need, the need to feed.

"I can't explain it. It's Twinkies and *Out of Control* and *Romeo and Juliet*'s demise. It's, I'm a—"

"Kaysee," Mom sings from the front porch. "Snack time." I run my tongue over my sharpened teeth again and take a breath. Mom's voice is tight, putting on a show like she did with the cop.

"I gotta go. I'll text you later," I stammer over my shoulder as I bolt through my front door. I drop my backpack, hearing my laptop crash against the tile floor in the entryway. In the kitchen, Dad hands me a vamp juice. Before it reaches my mouth, I tip back the bottle and guzzle as fast as I can. Sticky syrup spills over my chin and cheeks. But I don't care. When I'm done, Dad passes me another bottle. I drink this one less like a Neanderthal, slow enough to taste the flavors of cherry and the salty aftertaste. My body celebrates with every swallow. And I force myself to ignore the fact that I'm drinking someone's blood.

After my blood bender, I go upstairs and flop on my bed next to Pablo. Sensing my anguish, he nuzzles up next to me and rubs his cheeks against my arm with a purr. Stray bits of his soft fur float into the air as I pet him and close my eyes.

When I wake up later, I reach for my phone but realize I left it in my backpack and it's probably still sitting in the front entryway. The old alarm clock I've had since I was a kid glows 10:04 from my desk. When I shift, Pablo hops off the bed and saunters out of my bedroom. He probably wants to go outside to do some night hunting, so I follow him down the stairs.

Opening the back door, a thick breeze sweeps over me. It fills me with a deep longing to be outside, so I follow Pablo, not bothering to turn on the back patio light. Outside, the stars twinkle brightly through the thin Suburban haze and light pollution. Pablo takes off for the bushes in the back corner of our yard. I know there's a place where a wood plank in the fence is rotted. He can squeeze under and explore the neighborhood.

I meander over to the old wooden swing hanging from the sweet gum tree and sit on it, my body enjoying the normalcy of my butt on that hard piece of lumber. The first year we moved to Inman, Zel and I would spend hours playing in my backyard.

Our favorite game was to sit in the swing and have the other person twist it until the ropes were tight and couldn't bear any more pressure. Then we'd let go, sending the other into a wild spin. We'd see how long we could take it before one of us was on the verge of puking.

She was so great then, so much fun. But once high school started, she changed, wanted something more that I couldn't give her. The fun Zel from middle school still comes out sometimes. But she's hidden a little deeper every year. *I miss middle school Zel,* I think as I begin spinning and watching the ropes twist over my head.

"You always gave up first," Zel's voice breaks through the night. I stop the swing and find her standing at the fence staring at me warily.

"What are you doing?" I ask.

"Taking out the trash," Zel replies closing the gate behind her. She walks in silence toward me and leans against the trunk of the sweet gum tree. I don't know what to say, so I maintain the silence, listening to the sounds of suburbia: crickets, a barking dog, the loud rumble of a big truck passing down our street.

"Look, I'm sorry," Zel starts. "I overreacted. I know that."

"It's okay," I say not ready to fully forgive her but also relieved that after drinking all the vamp juice I'm able to talk to Zel without daydreaming about devouring her blood.

"I'm changing my schedule in the morning. Daylight school was pretty lame anyway. Mr. Harris spent most of first period trying to keep everyone awake." And there she is. The old Zel shining through all the drama and angry verbal processing. She's just Zel, just hanging out and talking like a normal person not like someone whose one goal is to social climb through the high school ranks.

She laughs as she continues. "It was pretty funny to see how riled up he got. At first, Mr. Harris was only dropping books on the table, but by the end of class, he'd thrown two erasers at Tagg."

Being that Mr. Harris is the most mild-mannered English teacher at school, I join Zel laughing at the image she paints. Tagg, a poster child for what happens when football helmets don't work, was slumped over his desk, a squishy eraser bouncing off his head.

It feels so good to laugh with Zel. For a moment I forget the whole vampire thing. That is until her story swivels to Hailey Atwood taking off her mask in speech & debate to protest her rights being taken away by government liberals and I laugh so hard I snort. But my heart drops because I realize how visible my new teeth are. I just hope that in the dark they don't show. There's no way Zel could handle my new lifestyle yet. Hell, I can barely handle it myself.

"Thanks, Zel," I say tapping her knee with my toe.

She crosses her arms over her chest, her face hardening. "Kaysee, are you okay? You said it was some medical thing that made you change classes. Is it, like, are you okay?"

I stand from the swing and lift my arms to display my normal boring body. The only visible differences are my teeth and clearer skin, which I will never complain about. "I'm fine. Really. It's just this skin thing. I can't be in the sun much," I say hoping it sounds believable. Of all the new traits I'm living with, this seems like the most plausible excuse and the one that keeps Zel from thinking I have something horrible like cancer or something.

"Really? Like, you're okay? You promise?" Zel asks, scanning me.

"I promise," I answer with a tight-lipped smile.

"Good," she stands straighter and pulls me into a hug. "Come here, pod partner." My arms find their way around Zel's shoulders and I relax into the hug. With all the pandemic stuff going on, I've hardly touched anyone except my family, and they aren't touchy-feely people anyway. Zel and I had decided from the very beginning that we'd be in the same pod so we'd have a person to escape to when our parents were driving us nuts or when Zel's little sisters wouldn't leave her alone.

Zel pulls back from the hug, and from the ambient light cascading from her backyard, I can see a mischievous crinkle in her eyes. "I fixed everything anyway. Your mom gave me your schedule, so I lined up our classes."

"What about the restaurant?" I ask surprised that her parents, who'd been insistent that she help with the dinner shift, would be willing to let her change.

"I'll just switch to breakfast and lunch. Jasmine started working dinner shift last week, and she's a mess. I couldn't get anything done without her asking me for the thousandth time how many ketchup packets to put in a to-go bag. She's totally hopeless," Zel sighs then smirks. "I'll let Abuelita straighten her out."

8

My Condition

After surviving the first day back to school as a vampire, the next day should be smooth as silk, right? That's what I'm thinking as I slather on sunscreen and adorn my dark sunglasses. With my lunch, Mom has included two bottles of vamp juice. I cringe drinking one at breakfast, but less than yesterday. I absolutely and totally hate the fact that I'm drinking even a few drops of human blood, but there is no way to describe how it makes me feel. The headache disappears, and my body feels stronger, less like a wet noodle.

Of course, my parents aren't helping this whole, "vampires are real and now you're one" situation. They hover over me with every sip of their concoction, their scientific minds clocking my every reaction. I don't care if they succeed with the vamp juice honestly. I'm still really pissed that all this happened. And all the raging emotions coursing through me make me want to rip off Oscar's face every time he tells me it'll be okay. He says it a lot.

School is okay. My mask hides my new teeth, and the fluorescent lights in the school don't hurt my eyes like the sun does. I glide through my first few classes on autopilot. But as time nears for chemistry, my heartbeat quickens. When my English teacher starts wrapping up, I steal a sip of vamp juice. I want to be on my best game for chemistry.

The juice does its job. I sail into chemistry class and catch sight of Toby Chan sitting at our lab table all alone. As in, no Jason! I'm so excited I have to hold myself back from skipping across the room. I don't want to put on display for the whole world exactly how desperate I am. Which is, like, super desperate.

I adjust my mask as I sit on the rickety stool. Toby is laser-focused on his phone, tapping away. Mr. Garcia greets students at the front of the class waiting for the bell to ring. I set out my notebook and pen keeping my eyes on Toby waiting for him to look up from his phone so I can bite—I mean initiate conversation.

The classroom fills around us, other students taking their seats and either chatting or staring at their phones. Toby still won't look up, and I'm being bold here, so I lean across the table. "Anything interesting?" I ask trying to sound seductive.

Toby lifts his head to meet my eyes. He squints at me like he's surprised to see me at his lab table. "Oh, yeah," he stammers. "It's a game some of the guys told me about. I was trying it out to see if it's lame or not."

I lean back to sit on my stool. "So, what's the verdict?" I ask.

Toby scoffs, and by the tightening of his eyes, I can tell that there's a smile hidden under his mask. It's the same smile he gave me when I showed him how to use a dry brush in art class years ago.

He's always got everything together so much, that I loved being able to help him paint. "Totally lame," he says.

"Are you talking about the assignment in French?" Zel says dropping her rainbow sequined backpack on the lab table. "Because that one is trés lame." She rolls her eyes as she sits and shakes her loose hair off her shoulders.

"Zel, what are you doing here?" I ask, bewildered by her interruption.

"Mr. Garcia said to sit here. All the other groups are full." She pulls a notebook and pen out of her backpack.

"But, Jason…" I start.

"What? Jason Hancock?" Zel asks, emphasizing his last name with raised eyebrows.

"Yeah, he's our lab partner," Toby chimes in.

Zel laughs. "He's not here now. Mr. Garcia said this is where I should sit." Zel tilts her head toward me. "And, now you can help me get through this class." Her words are light, but the message is there. Zel can't pass this class without me. I think I only do okay because my parents have exposed me to their experiments since before I could walk. They had my highchair set up in the corner of their lab next to a pack & play. I'd crawl around and play with my toys while they experimented with various concoctions.

"Besides," Zel continues with a smirk. "He's a total *boron*."

Toby's eyes dart to Zel. "Was that a chemistry joke?" he asks with a quirked eyebrow.

"Yes. Yes, it was." Another hair flip. "See? I'm a billion times more fun than Jason Hancock."

Toby chuckles and drops his gaze back to his phone. Zel turns to me and pulls her mask down to show off a huge, goofy grin.

Smears of bright red lipstick color the inside of her mask. I bite my lip telling myself that this is okay. It's fine. Totally fine. Zel won't screw everything up with Toby. She knows I like him. She's just being fun Zel, not sexy, playful Zel flirting with the boy I want to be sexy and playful with.

"Zel," Mr. Garcia warns from where he leans against the whiteboard. "Masks up at all times."

I nudge her foot with mine as Mr. Garcia shuts the door and starts class. Toby has to turn in his seat to see the notes Mr. Garcia writes on the board, so I spend most of the class flickering my gaze between the whiteboard and the back of Toby's head. And what a lovely back of a head he has. I'm daydreaming about running my fingers through his hair when Zel leans over and taps her pencil on my notebook. My mask hides my flush, which is good. But by the side-eye glance Zel gives me, I know I've been caught.

Yeah, I think, *Zel would never ruin this for me.*

"Bay hi?" Zel asks with her eyebrows raised.

"It's like saying," Baihe explains using her hands to accentuate her words, "the word buy like to buy an awesome dress. And the word huh, like huh? It costs how much?"

"Okay, I'll work on that one," Zel takes a bite of her apple. We're sitting together for lunch at one of the outdoor picnic tables. A humid breeze snakes through our group as Oscar and Baihe introduce themselves to Zel. Doug dropped by earlier, but he zipped away real quick. He never seems to stay in one place too long. We have English class together, and he's always bouncing his foot or bopping his head as though holding still would cause him great pain.

"You're here all year?" Zel asks, turning her eyes to Oscar. And I don't blame her. He is smoking hot in an animalistic, Hollywood hottie kind of way. He's pretty to look at and has a magnetism that makes everyone turn his way when he enters a room.

Oscar takes the bait, shining in her attention, he leans forward across the weather-worn and warped wood planks of the table. "All year," he smiles and leans back to take a bite of his banana.

"And your mom's okay with this?" Zel turns to me. "I mean. It's your mom. She hates even having Pablo, so I never thought she'd be someone who would take in three foreign exchange students. Right?"

I had a feeling this would come up. The charade is hard to maintain around Zel. She knows me and my parents too well. Every time someone opens their mouth, I think she's going to guess. I mean, she might not go straight for the whole "everyone's a vampire" theory, but she'd know that something was not right. Anxiety steals my words. I glance at the time on my phone as I try to make a coherent lie appear out of thin air.

"It's like culture and stuff," I say, my hands twitching.

"But I thought with all the virus stuff no one could travel, so how did they even get here?" Zel hits me with a glance that makes my whole body tremble.

"Um," I stammer. My head swims. The light is suddenly too bright. As I blink, I realize that I'm not nervous about talking to Zel about this. I'm having a low-blood vampire crisis. I'd put off taking out my bottle of vamp juice, but if I don't eat now, I know

I won't be able to pull my gaze away from the inside of Zel's arm. I can sense her pulse. It vibrates through my body that quivers in sync with the exposed part of her arm below her Captain Marvel t-shirt line. Thump. Thump. Thump.

"We got stuck," Oscar says too loudly, at least too loudly for me. I can feel his eyes on me and hear Baihe squeak a little, like a duck quack. "We were here last year and couldn't go home. All the quarantines and such, so the Fehrs took us in." Oscar weaves the elaborate lie. Zel turns to him leaning forward, resting her chin in her hand, and buying everything he says.

I'm inching closer to Zel, the desire to feed overtaking me when Baihe presses a bottle into my hand. I unscrew the vamp juice as fast as I can and tip it back. The juice quells my overwhelming desire to feed on Zel and fills me with gratitude until I hear Zel asking, "What's that?"

I tip the bottle down only long enough to reply, "Nothing." Then I chug the last gulps as fast as I can, choking a little. My cough sends tiny red splatters across the picnic table.

"Let me see that," Zel pulls the bottle from my hand and inspects the hasty label Mom and Dad plastered on. From a distance, it looks like any sports drink. But up close, you can see that it's totally homemade. "What is this stuff?"

"Mom and Dad made it," I say reaching for the bottle.

Zel pulls away, holding the bottle to her nose and sniffing. "Smells weird," she grimaces.

"It's the chemicals," I blurt. "They're super healthy but the formula isn't set yet. It's still a little bitter."

"Bitter?" Zel scoffs. "You just drank this as fast as Thor would have downed beer when he was all drunk and fat. It must be good."

Zel lifts the bottle to her lips.

"No!" I scream lunging for Zel. We tangle and end up splayed across the table. The bottle goes flying and lands in the grass. I scramble over Zel. She protests with a grunt as I accidentally jab my elbow into her chest.

"Kaysee, ouch! Not the boobs. Geez! Get off!" she complains. I scramble away to snatch the bottle and forcefully toss it into a garbage can.

"You can't drink that. It's *my* juice." The people around us have stopped packing up their lunches to watch me acting like a crazy person. Laughter is mixed with WTF expressions. "It's for my—my condition."

"Your condition?" Standing, Zel brushes off her shirt and pushes her hair back.

"Remember?" Everyone is staring at me. I wanted to be bold this year, to be noticed, but not this way. I nod knowingly at Zel.

She gets the message, but her acting classes leave her overdoing her response. "Ohhhh," she says with a dramatic nod. "Your condition." The air quotes she uses makes it look like she is 1000% talking about an STD. I am horrified.

Snickers ripple around, and my face flushes hot. I'm so glad I already drank all the juice because if this had happened before I drank it, I swear to all things holy that I would rip off every laughing face. One by one.

"Oh, grow up!" I yell. "It's a real medical thing. Get your minds out of the gutter."

I stomp back to the table and toss the remains of my lunch into my backpack. Slinging my mask over my face I stomp into the school with my ears burning. The laughter grows behind me and is only silenced by the door slamming shut behind me.

9

I Can't Keep Trying to Eat My Friends!

"You have to do something! I can't keep trying to eat my friends!" I whisper to Baihe the next day as I climb out, slam the door to Mom's car, and let out a sigh. My stomach rolls. Damn it! My stupid vampire body is becoming insatiable. I'm still struggling to believe that vampires are real, but my stupid body keeps reminding me. Argh!

I really don't want to drink more blood. I promise. I don't. That's my mind talking. My stomach, on the other hand, has a different thought on the subject. It's like I'm two different people. One person is just plain Kaysee, too quiet, likes art, is a vegetarian 100%. The other is an angry bitch with only one goal and purpose: drink blood.

Baihe stops on the sidewalk. Angry grumbles are shot at us as we block people filtering toward the school doors. "You get used to it," Baihe shrugs. "Just like anything else. You know, Kaysee, when I was a girl in China, like back in the 1950s, my father had a bad business dealing and we became very poor. We went from eating pork nightly to eating only rice. We were always hungry. But with time, we got used to it."

"Baihe," I say, my mind picturing a dusty Chinese village and a skinny Baihe begging for food. "That's terrible."

She links her arm in mine, and pulls me forward. "Yes. It was," she says simply. "But I got used to it. You'll get used to the blood cravings too. You're lucky your parents are making all the vamp drinks. It really makes a difference. You can't imagine what I went through trying to get blood at first."

"Keep moving," a teacher's voice booms over the flow of bodies. Warm bodies. Delicious bodies.

Shut up, bloodthirsty, bitch! I think so strongly that I'm surprised no one hears me.

Our conversation dies as we enter the school and go our separate ways. But she makes me think. I don't really know anything about our new "foreign exchange students." I watch Doug follow a trio of girls in short skirts down the hallway that I know doesn't lead to his first class. Oscar is laughing with a tall, skinny guy I think I had PE with last year. I've seen them, talked to them, but I don't know anything about our "foreign exchange students." Who are these vampires that are now so deeply intertwined with my life?

By the time I reach Chemistry class, I've entertained multiple scenarios for Oscar, Baihe, and Doug's backstories. My classes were boring, so the stories in my mind are quite intricate filled with broken hearts and unrequited love, except for Doug. I'm guessing he just went down the wrong dark alley one night.

I'm dropping the heavy chemistry book on the lab table when Jason slides in to the stool next to me. "Miss me?" he says, raising his eyebrows. Mischief brews in his deep brown eyes.

"Not at all," I reply hoping to sound nonchalant. "I didn't even notice."

"Unlikely," he winks.

"You're back," Toby sets his backpack on the lab table.

"He missed me," Jason says with a triumphant pound on the table.

"Whoa, keep it together, Hancock," Zel says coming to stand behind him. "And you're in my seat." She looks comical standing behind him, only five feet tall. Sitting down, Jason is still taller than her.

"You're not at our table," Jason refuses to move from the stool.

"Yeah, she is," I say excited at the prospect of him moving farther away. He has a special skill of bringing out the worst in me, and I really don't want to go all emotional vamp crazy on his ass. The thick, musky scent of his deodorant even pisses me off today. Stupid vampire emotions. Of course, a quick glance at his muscled neck gives me another thought that makes my stomach roll.

"She is at our table," Toby confirms dropping his gaze to his phone.

"If you weren't skipping school on the second day, you'd know this. Now, move," Zel pokes his shoulder.

Jason picks up his backpack and bristles. "Mr. Garcia, Zel isn't socially distancing," Jason yells across the classroom.

"Sit down, Mr. Hancock," Mr. Garcia dismisses him with a wave of his hand.

"Han-COCK!" shouts a guy in the back of the room. A tittering of giggles follows the taunt, a taunt that's followed him as long as I've known Jason.

Jason glances over his shoulder to see if Mr. Garcia is looking before he throws a pen at the guy and sits down. As Mr. Garcia starts scribbling a formula on the board, Jason leans across the table, looking pointedly at Zel. "I wasn't skipping," he shifts his gaze to me. "I had to go to physical therapy for my knee."

He shifts in his chair, turning his back to us. Zel shrugs and opens her chem book as I doodle pictures of robots around the margins of a page in my notebook. Mr. Garcia's lesson is very basic, so I only occasionally jot down a note or two that's framed by two robots holding hands in front of a sunset. Every glance I sneak at Toby, and there are quite a few, I only get the back of his head.

It makes me wonder if I could figure out Oscar's mind tricks and if they work subconsciously. Deciding to give it a try, I start repeating in my mind, *Toby, look at me.*

It doesn't work. He doesn't even flinch. I'm switching to the new mantra, *Toby, you want to look at Kaysee. You want to kiss her* when the bell rings.

As everyone stands and moves for the door, I catch Jason peeking at my notebook. Instantly, I slam it shut. He doesn't need to see my rendition of me and Toby as robots in love. He laughs, slings his backpack over his shoulder, and steps in line behind the guy he threw the pen at. They begin one of those teen guy rituals of slapping each other's shoulders. I've never understood how guys enjoyed hitting each other. It's so violent. As a vegetarian, I've also committed to pacifism. I stop short.

"Damn it," I whisper under my breath. If I have to eat people, I can't be a pacifist or a vegetarian. My stomach flops with hunger, vampire hunger, making me swear with more creativity than usual as I walk to the commons for lunch.

After chugging two bottles of vamp juice at lunch, I cruise through the rest of the day until my last class, art. My art buddies Maddie and Maeve chat with me while Indigo stays in the corner still trying not to bite her fingernails. At the end of class, Mrs. Carroll takes us outside to do some sketches as the light shifts to sunset.

As soon as I step outside, I am on fire. Any exposed skin feels like it's burning, baking, blistering. The sun is just high enough in the sky that its rays are like lasers on my body.

"I'm going over by that tree," I say abandoning Maeve and Maddie to talk about some new Netflix true crime show. As I walk, I pull on my sleeves, but they're too short. My arms are turning red. I feel a lash of heat spread across the back of my neck and pull my ponytail holder out, letting my hair shield my neck. Still, I can't move fast enough to the shade of a small tree with low-hanging branches. I'm sprinting as my arms bake in the sun and not paying attention to the fact that another person is also hiding at the base of the tree.

"Hi, Kaysee," a voice squeaks. I whip to my right and find Indigo, her mask off and her fingers pressed to her mouth. She looks at me sheepishly like she's afraid of me.

"Indigo, hi," I sputter. "I didn't see you here."

"Yeah," she bites at a cuticle. "I thought the shadows would be nice here." She points up under a cluster of branches. Stepping in her direction, I look through the twisted tree limbs and fluttering leaves. They catch the light, and with their movement in the breeze, the underside of the leaves change to a lighter green color. Dark brown, forest green, mint green, the cobalt blue sky. The blend of colors is beautiful.

Beside me, Indigo has stopped chewing on her fingers and is sketching in quick, sharp strokes across her sketchpad. They're light on the paper, capturing the shadows, with a few heavier marks to recreate a bending tree branch. If she didn't frustrate me so much, I'd like her work. It is good. Like, really good. No wonder she keeps beating me in contests.

Slipping my mask off and stuffing it in my pocket, I pull out my phone and snap a few photos of the light playing on the tree and let the world and the work envelop me. This is one of my favorite things about art, I can get lost in it. The world disappears, all the sucky things, and I can release my creativity from deep inside my soul. Conversations from other kids in class drift on the breeze as I hold my phone waiting for one cluster of leaves to flutter again so I can capture a perfect flash of minty green. My moment of artistic bliss is broken by Indigo.

"Mrs. Carroll is calling us back," she says as though it's not the first time. I slip my phone into my pocket and Indigo flips her sketchpad closed. She drops her pencil. Both of us reach for it and we bump into each other. I lose my balance and thrust my foot back to catch myself, reaching out for a branch. But I miss, and the rough edges of it scrapes across my sunburned arm. I gasp and jump back grabbing my arm.

"I'm sorry," Indigo says. "Are you okay?"

The sting from the scrape sizzles across my skin. The burn is better than it was before (thank you vampire healing superpower) but it still hurts like a mother. I press my hand over my arm as I gasp.

"I'm fine," I spurt attempting to form a smile.

Indigo's gaze moves from my arm to my mouth and freezes. A wrinkle forms between her eyebrows as she studies my mouth. No, not my mouth. My teeth.

No. No. No! No! No! No!

Faster than I thought possible, I sling the loops of my mask over my ears. How could I have been so stupid? "I'm fine. Really," I say wishing I'd taken the drama classes like Zel.

"Okay?" Indigo questions, tucking her pencil in the spiral loops of her sketchpad.

I start walking back to the classroom across the crunchy grass always found in Missouri in late August. She follows adding, "I just thought your arm looked bad."

"Oh, yeah. No, it just surprised me." I lift my arm, a beam of sunlight hitting it and reigniting flames across my skin. Indigo can't see the forced smile I'm wearing under my mask as I quicken my pace.

She continues next to me and we step back inside to the coolness of shade.

I'd never really talked to Indigo much before, never really had a reason. As my mom would say, she's an odd duck. But the arts seem to attract these kinds. *I guess that would include me,* I think as I make my way down the hallway feeling every heartbeat around me. Suddenly ravenous, I can't ignore the rhythm of pulses that echo against my sunburned skin. I pick up my pace and dive for the bottle of vamp juice that Mom offers me in the car. I'm so hungry. I want to eat every living thing I see.

10

Six, Eight, Four

Six. That's the number of vamp drinks I *must* drink each day to function.

Eight. That's the number of vamp drinks I should drink each day but am currently trying to avoid because even though I've been a vampire for a month now, I still can't get over the whole drinking human blood thing. Disgusting.

Four. That's the number of vamp drinks I drank last Thursday. AKA, the day Oscar had to hold me back from eating my geometry teacher, Mr. Jones. I haven't been able to look him in the eye since I lunged for his arm when he found me after school to return a quiz I'd dropped.

Luckily, Oscar and Baihe were there. Oscar used his persuasion to make Mr. Jones believe that I suffered from low blood sugar. He said this is a pretty common excuse vampires use because people rarely question it. And it really works because what I needed in that moment was to eat and it did involve blood. Baihe had pulled me into a tight hug, pinning my arms down and pinching me in the ribs so hard I still have a faint bruise that even super vampire healing hadn't erased yet.

It was so embarrassing. No one really saw and Mr. Jones doesn't remember a thing, but I remember. While I faltered then, in the one month of my new vamp life, I've progressed a lot. Vamp drinks are always in tow. SPF 100 sunscreen is my new best friend. My emotional rages have gotten less intense too. And I've finally come to terms with the fact that vampires are actually real and that I am one of those real vampires.

Now, as for my love life, that has gone nowhere. No. Where.

It's like Toby can't see me. Geez, I'm a vampire, not a ghost. I've tried to get his attention, but he always has his eyes on his notebook or on his phone. What is he doing? Is he addicted to TikTok? Is he researching colleges? Is there a girl he's chatting with? I keep hoping not, but it doesn't look good for me. My whole plan to conquer junior year is disappearing faster than Doug can eat a whole bag of chips, which by the way, is 89 seconds. Baihe and I timed him once. If he weren't such a jerk, I'd be impressed.

At least today is Saturday. No school. No Toby ignoring me. No Jason pestering me.

I'm glad that Zel is in chemistry with us because she's gotten pretty good at getting Jason off my back. The only bad part is that now it's like a game to him. Jason makes snide remarks to me, and Zel zings him in return. I think they're both enjoying the game way too much. And it's all at my cost, which isn't much fun for me.

But, it's Saturday. *Take a deep breath*, I think sitting outside on the swing after a rainstorm. Missouri has magnificent rainstorms. The one this morning came rolling through with heavy claps of thunder and flashing cracks of lightning. Now, the sun is nicely hidden behind a bank of clouds. As I sit on the swing drops of rain drip from the tree branches above me. It's bliss.

I can almost ignore Doug sniffing around the corner of the yard. Thankfully, our privacy fence keeps his antics from view of the neighbors. I watch wondering what in the world he's doing crouched over a bush in the corner. His back is damp from the dripping trees. His red t-shirt sticks to the ridges of his ribs and spine. Pablo was sniffing around the same area earlier but ran off when Doug showed up.

"Hello, lovey," Oscar says walking outside with a mug of tea. He closes the door behind him and crosses to me. In the past month, Oscar has become one of my favorite people, or favorite vampires. He's always encouraging, and he's always good to look at. Today, he's paired dark jeans with a form-fitting wintergreen button-down. His hair is a mass of thick, wild curls defying gravity in a way that makes him look uber sexy yet also approachable. My baggy jeans and a black t-shirt can't hold a candle to his flaming hotness.

"That for me?" I point to his mug. He makes the best cup of tea. When I asked him about it, he just winked and said that he'd had more than a century to perfect his technique.

"No, but this is," he pulls my phone from his back pocket and passes it to me. "The thing keeps making noises. Maybe it's a Zel emergency," sarcasm drips from his words. Sipping his tea he watches Doug still cowering by the bush.

Unlocking my phone, I find eight text messages. Seven are from Zel complaining about working with her sisters at Burgers & Burritos again. If Abuelita doesn't intervene, I'm afraid there'll be a story about them on *Dateline* sometime soon. The last message is from an unknown number. I'm tapping to open the message when Oscar says, "What on earth is Doug doing?"

Shrugging, I respond, "I have no clue. I thought this was something he just did. You know? Sniffing around in weird places." Oscar blinks at me before his eyes trail back to Doug. Sensing the tension in Oscar's gaze, I stand from the swing and step toward the corner of the yard for a closer look.

On his knees, bent over with something in his hands, Doug's head moves strangely. He goes side-to-side then flicks his head back like Pablo when he's playing with a cat toy.

"This is a Doug thing, right?" I ask with trepidation, my palms starting to sweat. Living with Oscar has been easy. Baihe? A total breeze. But, Doug. Living with Doug has been weird, strange, just plain bizarre. It's not only that he's always eating and chasing girls at school. But he also spends hours locked in the basement storage room where Mom and Dad set up a bed for him. He says he likes it because the Wi-Fi is stronger there, so I always tell myself that he's playing video games online and not doing other weird online things.

"Something's off," Oscar says and sets his mug on the patio table. "Doug!" he calls across the yard. Doug's head flicks in our direction revealing something streaked on the side of his face. Probably, with as rainy as it's been, he's gotten mud smeared across his cheek from digging around.

"Doug?" Oscar repeats, his voice like a dad scolding a kid. "You're not doing it again, are you?" Oscar takes two steps closer to Doug.

Curiosity overtaking my sensibility, I mimic Oscar and step forward. "Oscar, what's going on?" I ask.

He ignores me, which makes me worry. He never ignores people.

"Oscar?" I plead, worry creeping in faster.

"Doug?" Now, Oscar's pacing toward Doug, his mouth drawn tight. "We talked about this. You can't do it!"

And that's when Doug turns and I can see his face fully. It's not mud. Oh, my goodness. It's so disgusting. It's revolting!

Blood and sinew drip from Doug's chin. His hands are spattered with red, and a lump of bloody, pulpy, fur lies limply in his hands. I freeze, thinking that the fur is Pablo's. I wouldn't put it past Doug to eat my cat. But, seeing a pile of small furry animals at his feet, I realize he's not eating my cat.

Doug's eating squirrels! There must be eight or ten of them all piled on the ground in front of him. Their eyes are glossy, their mouths hanging open.

"Doug!" Oscar yells. "I told you, you can't do this again! Damn it, man!" He tries to pull the squirrels away from Doug, but Doug turns on him. Baring his sharp vampire teeth, Doug hisses at Oscar. A thin trail of squirrel blood squirts from his mouth.

"What the hell?" I exclaim aghast.

"Kaysee," Oscar says keeping his eyes on Doug. "Go get Baihe." His voice carries a controlled calm, the kind that makes a chill creep down my spine.

"Leave her out of this, Oscar!" Doug yells as he tosses the squirrels' remains over the privacy fence. "I needed to feed. On something real, not chemicals."

"Doug, mate. You can't. We discussed this. It's not what we do." Oscar keeps his voice low, his hands held up ready for a fight.

"It's not what *you* do," Doug spits. Bending, he grabs a cluster of squirrels that hang like rags in his hands. "This is what *I* do. I can't live off those drinks. Come on, Oscar. Don't you miss the taste of warm blood when you can still feel the heart beating?"

"Of course, I miss it." Oscar hisses. "But this is not us. We agreed when we came here. And you remember why we came here. I know you do."

Doug shoots me a side glance. Blood is caked around his chin and even though his eyes are squinted, they shine with the intensity of a ravenous tiger. If he were a larger person, I'd be so scared I'd probably pass out just from that glare.

"I remember," Doug says through gritted teeth. His grip on the squirrels tightens as he faces Oscar again.

"Then, this can't happen again. Ever." Oscar says, his hand slashing through the air with finality. "Now, clean this up."

With a vengeance, Doug tosses the handful of dead squirrels over the fence and scoops up the remaining cluster of lifeless animals. They're flung through the air to join their dead comrades, landing with a crunch in a pile of leaves in the Davis' yard. Hopefully, they fell to the bottom. And luckily, Mr. Davis works so much that he rarely works in the yard. I've heard Mrs. Davis yelling at him in their driveway to clean things up while threatening to run off to her mother's house. They're new neighbors. Mom said they only got married a few years ago.

Oscar passes by me to retrieve his tea mug and takes a sip as if nothing happened. I'm wondering what he was talking about with Doug. Where was the last place? And why did they have to leave it?

Just as I'm opening my mouth to ask these questions, Oscar says, "Drat. Gone cold. I'll scurry inside and heat this up a bit." With a wave of his mug, he steps back inside.

Doug, his shoulders drooping in a pout, walks past me so close a breeze blow off him. Under his breath, he whispers something that I don't catch. It sounds mostly like a string of swear words. I'm okay that he doesn't stop for a heart-to-heart chat because seeing him with blood crusted around his mouth and staining his shirt makes me feel sick.

A chime sounds from my phone. *It's probably Zel*, I'm thinking as I pick it up. Strangely, it's not. It's another text from the unknown number. I open the thread to read the two messages.

U home?

I need chem notes

I look again at the number but don't recognize it. This is strange because I don't really give out my number. But strange seems to be the theme of the day.

Who is this? I send while trying to figure out who in chemistry would ask for my notes. Maybe it's Toby? My heart skips a beat at the thought.

Oscar's voice drifts from inside. He sounds angry like he's scolding someone. I can't hear Doug responding, but I'm certain he's the brunt of Oscar's anger.

I unlock my screen when my phone chimes again.

jason

HANCOCK

I'm walking 2 ur house now

get them NOTES!!!!

My pulse thrums, speeding up and making my skin itch. Who does he think he is? That he can just come by anytime he wants and take my notes. I huff and go inside where Oscar's voice is louder and clearer. He's yelling at Doug, something about Cleveland. The lack of response from Doug is sending Oscar's pitch higher until I hear something crash.

I grab my notebook from my backpack lying by the front door. *I really should put that away*, I think as I walk outside. Something about being a vampire has made me messier than I used to be. Maybe it's the impending cycle of time that's bound to stretch on for centuries ahead of me. Or maybe it's just that school is crazy and I've been sleeping a lot more.

Out in the front yard beneath the big oak tree, Baihe is slowly moving through a series of tai chi moves. She looks magnificent. Totally in control yet also deadly. With her hair pulled back into a long raven-colored braid and her eyes squinted in concentration she is a badass warrior. She told me that tai chi is like kung-fu in slow motion. Watching her shift forward and gracefully press with the palms of her hands, I'm imagining her shoving someone. I've seen her use her kung-fu moves on Doug a few times, and she was impressive.

"Kaysee!" I look down the sidewalk to see Jason with his hands cupped around his mouth yelling my name from halfway down the block. He smiles when I meet his gaze and trots to meet me in my driveway. I'm glad Zel's at work. If she saw this, she'd explode with questions and suggestions to insult Jason.

"Those the notes?" stopping in front of me, he points at my notebook.

"With all the other people in class, why are you bothering me to get the notes?" I cross my arms and press the notebook against my chest. If he wants me to help him, he's going to have to work for it.

"Playing hard to get? Nice. Okay," Jason runs his hand through his hair then rests his fingers on his chin and pierces me with a glance. "You're pretty. Now can I have the notes?" he asks, his eyebrows dancing with mirth.

"You're a jackass. So, no," I say turning back to my house.

Jason runs a few steps to get around me and blocks my path. And I swear I hear Baihe giggle.

"Whoa, hold on."

Jason stops so close to me that he has to dip his chin to meet my eyes. It feels weird. It's uncomfortable being so close that I can feel the heat emanating off him. With a smile that I'm sure has charmed a lot of other girls, he continues. "Please. Really. I missed those few days for physical therapy, and we have that big test coming up."

He shrugs and sighs, and I think this is the first time I'm seeing the real Jason. Not Jason the jerk who's always cracking jokes and goofing off in class. But this is the real guy, vulnerable and needing my help. His eyes are pleading as he licks his lips.

"Okay," I give in. He's giving off such a lost puppy look, that it overrides my better judgment.

"Sweet!" he yells pumping his fist. From my pocket, my phone chimes with another text message. I slip it out to discover it's from Zel again. Something about how Ariel spilled a giant jug of salsa on Zel's new shoes. I slip my phone back in my jeans pocket. I can respond later. For now, I just want to get rid of Jason.

"Is that Zel?" Jason asks as he opens my notebook and scans the first few pages.

"Yeah," I say. "Drama at work with her sisters."

Jason chuckles, his mouth moving into a surprisingly handsome shape. I haven't seen him smile much and find myself intrigued by how it pleasantly changes his appearance.

"I texted her first. She blew up my phone saying 'no' about twenty-five times." Jason says.

"Did you try Toby?" As soon as his name escapes my lips, I know I've set myself up for ridicule. I haven't talked to Jason about Toby since the night at the Bluffs. Well, he's talked to me about Toby, but I keep ignoring him... and trying not to imagine sucking all the blood from his body until he looks like a raisin. When it comes to drinking blood, I've craved eating all my friends at some point now. But Jason's the only person I've seriously considered.

To my surprise, Jason simply says, "Yeah. He's out of town with his grandma."

And that's it. I stare at him slack-jawed waiting for the teasing, the jokes, for him to call me Wax Lips for the billionth time. But all he does is turn the page in my notebook.

Another chime from my phone breaks my stupor. It's Zel again. I'm beginning to wonder if she's actually doing any work. With the way she's been blowing up my phone, I'd guess not.

"Tell her that she owes you a burrito if she texts you again. One of the big ones, with extra beef."

"Ew!" I reply with a scowl. "I'm a vegetarian."

"Then one with extra beans and guacamole," Jason shrugs with a glance at my phone which is chiming again in my hand. I shoot him a glare.

"You know that's why everyone loved Heisman, right? That guy gave out free burritos to everyone," Jason adds.

"I don't care about Heisman. The restaurant burritos don't compare to Abuelita's home cooking. For the new year, she made green chile tamales that would melt in your mouth." I'm interrupted by another chime which makes me groan.

"Give me that," Jason grabs my phone and starts tapping in a message.

"No, give it back!" I yell reaching around him as he turns his back on me. He lifts the phone high over my head, laughing as he taps away. With every dodge, I become more infuriated. Rage fuels my vamp emotions. The feeling of prickles racing across my cheeks warns me that I'm turning bright red. The prickles pour over my whole body when Jason whips around on me and I careen into him, chest-to-chest. There is so much contact between our two bodies that the old Kaysee is mortified. But the new vampire Kaysee is enticed by the contact. And I hate myself for even thinking that having my boobs pressed against Jason is a good idea in any way, shape, or form.

"Social distance please!" Jason laughs as he steps back.

"Give. Me. My. Phone. Now." The muscles around my eyes are cramping, they're so tight from staring daggers at him.

"You want it? Come get it," Jason says turning and sprinting down the sidewalk past Zel's house.

"Jason!" I scream in hot pursuit. "Get back here!"

He laughs over his shoulder, lifting his arm over his head and taunting me with my phone as it chimes again.

Pumping my legs faster, my body vibrates with the rhythm of blood thumping through my veins and arteries. Strangely, it feels amazing. Watching Jason turn the corner only ten yards ahead of me I know two things. First, oh god it feels good to run! I've never been a runner before other than when necessary for P.E. But, today, my body is crying out to me to keep going. Keep moving.

The second thing is that I'm surprisingly not focused on drinking Jason's blood. Which is weird. Just a few moments ago, vamp rage was making my stomach flip and cry out for blood. Maybe this is what Baihe was talking about. Distraction. So far, the only thing that had distracted me from the horrible blood cravings was pinching the inside of my arm. I've had a line of bruises for weeks.

Running, the only blood I can think of is my own pumping through my body and filling me with a new intoxicating energy. So, I push harder, lengthening my stride and forcing my legs to move faster. The old Kaysee would have given up twenty feet past Zel's house, but this Kaysee is racing, relishing the feel of my muscles straining and the wind in my face as I splash across the puddled sidewalk. Not even Jason's laughter can take away this freaking incredible feeling.

As we cross the next street, I reach out and grab a handful of his shirt and yank. He stumbles, knocked off balance. Trying to right himself, he twists and lands in the muddy grass, sliding to a stop next to a planter full of purple and yellow flowers in someone's front yard. At least he's quit laughing.

I'm surprisingly not out of breath. In fact, my heart feels like it's pumping with a rhythm that says, "Kaysee, keep running."

Sprawled with mud streaks across his gym pants, Jason is gasping for air on the wet grass. A smile plays on his lips when he reaches out for a hand up.

I shake my head. "I want my phone," I spit.

He lifts his other arm producing my phone that chimes again with a new message. Then he holds out his other arm again. "Come on. Be a good sport." Huffing and hoping I sound discontent I give him my hand and help him to his feet.

"You're pretty fast," his tone tells me he's impressed. "Do you run much?"

"Just started today," I say unlocking my phone. Oh, come on, Zel. I have twelve new messages.

"You should do it more often. You're good," Jason wipes a muddy hand across his thigh. "And I think you like it."

My eyes dart up to him, quizzical.

"You were smiling. That doesn't happen much from what I've seen. Not even when you're fawning over Toby."

"Look," I say picking up my notebook from the sidewalk where Jason dropped it. "I need to get home. Just bring these to class on Monday."

As I'm holding the notebook out to Jason, a streak of sunlight breaks through the clouds and splashes across my arm. I'd thought I didn't need sunscreen, that I could wear short sleeves because of the cloudy skies. I hadn't planned on a run around the neighborhood, especially on this street where there are no shade trees. What the hell? Not one blasted tree. Damn it.

I gasp, dropping the notebook and cradling my burned arm. Looking up and down the street, I see no hope for relief. If I'm going to avoid turning into a lobster, I have to get home fast.

"What's going on?" Jason asks, picking up the notebook. "You okay?"

"Low blood sugar," I blurt.

"What?"

"No. I mean, it's this skin thing. I'm super sensitive," I stammer. "The sun. It really burns." Turning, I step into another thin ray of sunlight. "Ouch!" I yell as the ray burns a streak across my right cheek.

"Here," Jason pulls his long-sleeve shirt over his head and passes it to me. Seeing Jason's chiseled chest, I forget about the flaming hot sun for a brief moment. Then another break in the clouds hits me. I let out a string of curse words and yank the shirt from Jason's hands. I pull it on only partway so that it covers my head with the collar hanging loose over my eyebrows. My arms are safely tucked inside the body of the shirt.

Jason steps closer to me, concern written across his face. And, damn it if he isn't even hotter when he's concerned. Or maybe it's the ripple of muscles over his chest and down to a perfect six-pack that has me enamored. Either way, it leaves him looking like a Greek statue. A gorgeously ripped Greek statue.

"Want me to walk you home?" he asks.

"No!" I shout. "I'm just gonna go."

And I do but in the most awkward way possible. *Way to be bold and brave, Kaysee,* I think as I race down the street splashing through a puddle that covers my ankles in rainwater and flecks of mud. When I turn down my street, I look back to see Jason still in the same place. A beam of sunlight shines over his body, accentuating his physique in a way that makes him look like a cologne ad. A shiver curls down my spine.

Back in my house, my heart is racing. I'm totally out of breath. I stand with my back against the door cursing myself for being so careless.

"That boy likes you," Baihe says rounding the corner from the kitchen. She smirks and takes a bite from a pear.

"Jason?" I scoff. "No way. He's hated me forever."

"It didn't look like that to me." Baihe disappears into the guest room she's claimed for her bedroom. She's obviously wrong. There's no way Jason could like me. Besides, I'm into Toby, the hot nerd guy. The one who doesn't make fun of me all the time. The one who has big ideas and hopes and dreams. At least, I think he does. If he'd ever talk to me, I'd know.

Walking upstairs, I pull Jason's shirt off. Its scent lingers over me. I savor the woodsy aroma and replay in my mind the memory of Jason shirtless. My heart picks up pace as I turn on a cold shower to cool my burned skin. Baihe's comment flashes through my mind.

Could Jason really like me? No way. That's ridiculous. It's insane. But lately, weirder things have happened.

11
A WHIRL OF SQUIRRELS

In chemistry on Monday, I can't keep my gaze from flitting back and forth between Toby and Jason. As they measure liquids for our first experiment, I analyze their eyes, their shoulders, the way their hair lays across their foreheads. When Toby scratches his stomach, my imagination explores what he'd look like shirtless. Which then makes me think of Jason shirtless and I nearly drop a glass flask.

"Kaysee," Zel whispers and nudges my arm with her elbow. "Hand me the beaker."

Rolling my head in a circle, I try to release the tension in my neck. I didn't sleep well last night, which is weird because so far, being a vampire has meant that I sleep more than in my pre-vamp days. Oscar said I hadn't made a full transition yet, so who knows? I've stopped trying to guess what ridiculous thing my body will do next. It's just too much to handle right now. Not with the pandemic and school and Toby and Jason and—

"Kaysee!" Zel repeats. "What's going on with you?"

Her question draws a glance from Jason. With a mask and safety goggles on, I can't read his expression.

"I'm fine," I lie as I adjust the straps on my mask. They've been rubbing behind my ears all day. It's a cheap one Mom bought online. It's cute, black with little cherries, like a 1950s print. But it's hard to breathe through and it's way too tight.

"Here," I pass Zel the beaker.

"Nice shirt, Zel," Jason says as he drops saline into his solution with an eyedropper.

Today, Zel has gone with a classic Iron Man shirt. It's looser than some of her others, so I'm pretty sure it's one she took from Heisman. He passed down a bunch of his old t-shirts to Zel when he packed up for college. She has it tied in a knot at her waist and paired with a short skirt and leggings, which makes her look super cute and feminine.

"Thank you," Zel replies with a hint of hesitation like she's waiting for an insult to follow.

"Iron Man is pretty underrated, you know?" Toby says looking up from the lab directions. We all snap our heads at him, making him flinch. "What? He is."

Toby is actually speaking to us. He doesn't have his nose in his phone. It's like he's finally admitted that he's in class. My heart skips a beat when I take in his dark eyes behind the safety glasses framed by his drooping hair. People say he looks a lot like one of the BTS guys, but I think he's abundantly cuter.

"You're right," Zel replies, setting the beaker down to engage in the Marvel conversation. I don't know if Toby realizes that he's opened Pandora's box by mentioning anything Marvel-related in front of Zel. When she's not fuming about her sisters or talking about the popular groups at school, she's identifying the finer points of the Marvel universe. Mostly, she's pointing out Captain America's finer points. And, I agree, there is a lot of Chris Evans to appreciate. But after watching all the movies with her over the years, I'm more of a Star-Lord/Chris Pratt kind of girl.

"Because his was one of the earlier Marvel movies like before Marvel blew up, people overlook Iron Man. But seriously, Tony Stark is the shit."

"Miss Ortega," Mr. Garcia scolds as he meanders past our table. "Language."

"Sorry, Mr. Garcia," Zel coos sweetly.

"How is your experiment going?" Mr. Garcia asks pushing his glasses up his nose and gazing over our lab table.

"Fine," Jason and I say in unison. I glance at him but look away before he can catch me.

"Very well. More chemistry talk, and less comic book talk," Mr. Garcia says moving on to the next lab table.

"We were talking about the movies," Zel says in a hushed whisper.

"Which was your favorite Iron Man movie?" Toby whispers with a glimmer in his eye.

This makes Zel come to life. She passes a test tube to me and leans across the table. "Of the original three or in the entire Marvel universe? Here, trade places," she says to Jason. As she rounds the lab table, she waves him away with her hands.

Taking Zel's place next to me, Jason groans. "Marvel is overrated."

A dramatic gasp escapes Zel. She pulls her safety glasses off and glares at Jason, priming herself for a lecture on the value of Marvel and its contributions to our world. But she's interrupted by Mr. Garcia. "Miss Ortega! Glasses!" he bellows across the classroom.

Zel slips her glasses back on, her glare still on Jason. "I wish you'd blip," she jabs.

"Hey, what does Iron Man do before he takes a bath?" I ask. Everyone looks at me confused. "He gets Stark naked."

Toby and Zel laugh. Even Jason smirks. I've learned over the years that if I can get Zel to break a smile when she's pissed about something, she'll relax a lot faster. She falls into conversation with Toby while I maintain a rigid silence with Jason. We move through the steps of the experiment without talking. At first, I'm totally okay with this. But after a while, I can't stop flashes of Jason standing like a god in a sunbeam from playing through my mind.

"We're done with the Bunsen burner, right? Where does it go?" I ask Jason. He's holding a test tube up to the light and studying the mixing colors of chemicals.

"Cabinet," Jason says with a nod to the end of the table. It's the end of the table where Toby is working.

I straighten my back and toss my hair as I approach Toby. He's completely focused on the experiment now and doesn't see past the beaker in his hand. I've waited long enough, I decide. Time to stop waiting for him to come to me.

"Where should I put the Bunsen burner?" I ask Toby as though I don't know it goes in the cabinet right in front of me.

"There," he says pointing. Oh, come on. He's making this hard. But one look at his profile, his sloping nose, and strong jaw, remind me why I'm doing this. My palms sweat and my stomach flops.

"This one?" I ask pointing at the wrong door. I hate being that girl who plays dumb to get a guy's attention, but I'm all out of options here.

"Let me show you," he says coming around the corner of the table. I blink a few times hoping I look hot. He doesn't notice but stops in front of me. "This cabinet," he points at the one right by my hip.

I laugh knowing I must sound utterly ridiculous. "Oh, right here. Silly me."

When I open the cabinet and slide in the Bunsen burner, he turns away. I panic. "What did you do this weekend?" I blurt. We haven't had a real conversation since the night at the Bluffs. I'm ready to remedy that.

Toby leans his elbow on the table. "Nothing much. Went to see my grandma," he says.

"Oh, that's cool," I say. "Does she like, live nearby?"

I'm an idiot and totally sus. I know it. Something about Toby makes me talk like the stupid lovesick girl I am. But I'm also relishing the attention he's giving me. Toby's even looking me in the eye. No darting glances at his phone. Not one! This eye contact is really exciting. He has really nice eyes with thick, dark lashes.

"Usually, she lives with us, but now she's at our lake house. When people started getting sick, she moved up there to isolate. I spent the summer with her, buying groceries and going for walks with her and stuff."

Aaaaahhhhhh! He's the kind of guy who takes care of his grandma! I knew it! He's perfect. Jason would probably never do anything like this. More likely, he'd just order an Uber and a Door-

Dash. But why am I thinking of Jason? Toby is, as Zel would say, the shit.

"That's so nice of you," I coo.

Shrugging, Toby straightens. "It was nothing. She cooks a lot and has great Wi-Fi, so it was cool and all."

"She sounds great," I say my cheeks stuck in a goofy smile under my mask.

"Five minutes, everyone. Time to write down your observations," Mr. Garcia announces. It totally breaks the moment with Toby. When he steps back to help Zel clean up, the air noticeably cools around me. Under my mask, I'm chewing on my lip as my heart soars.

"Here's your notebook. Thanks," Jason slaps my chemistry notebook on the table making me jump. "Where's my shirt?"

Turning to Jason, I squint my eyes. I had such a good vibe going, and Jason shattered it again. "I'll give it to you tomorrow," I say dismissing him.

"Okay, Wax Lips," Jason says taking off his safety glasses and dropping them in a drawer. His eyes crinkle with a smirk.

"Whatever, Han—*cock*," I retort.

"Real original," he laughs slinging his backpack over his shoulder and heading for the door.

"What was that?" Zel asks watching Jason leave.

I sidle up next to her, clutching my backpack. I feel for the vamp juice that I can't wait to drink. My stomach was flopping when I was having a moment with Toby. I don't know if it was because of him or because I need to eat again.

"Oh, nothing," I say.

"You have his shirt?" Zel isn't letting this go.

"Okay," I sigh. "He loaned me his shirt on Saturday. We were outside when he came to get my notes. The sun came out, and my new skin condition freaked out. He gave me his shirt to cover my arms so they didn't get burned."

"That doesn't sound like Jason," Zel says with a scoff. She's not wrong. The Jason I've known since sixth grade would have just laughed at me burning in the sun. But that Jason was also a foot shorter and had more pimples. *I guess I should be the last person to judge someone for changing*, I think as I take a long swig of my vamp juice.

The whole car ride home from school Doug argues with Oscar. Doug used persuasion on a teacher earlier in the day.

"What's the big deal? You used it too when we registered? Remember? With the paperwork?" Doug whines.

"It's different and you know it," Oscar chides. "You can't persuade people willy-nilly."

"But he was being a germ!"

"A germ? You're a germ," Baihe adds from the front seat.

"Shut up!" Doug yells.

"We don't want another Cleveland," Oscar growls.

Baihe sternly scolds Doug in a long string of Mandarin that sounds particularly biting.

"What happened in Cleveland?" I ask, and three sets of vampire eyes land on me.

"We don't talk about Cleveland," Oscar says then turns to stare out the window at the houses in our neighborhood passing by. And that's the end of that conversation. Tension hangs heavy in the car until Mom turns on the radio to classical music.

When Mom pulls the car into the driveway, she announces, "We're getting pizza for dinner from that new place." I know she's trying to smooth things over but we're too far gone. Even the tried-and-true method of solving teen problems with pizza won't work now. Of course, I'm still not sure exactly how old Oscar, Doug, and Baihe are. They look like teens, but Oscar's already said he's more than a hundred years old.

Upon exiting the car, we're treated to the sounds of another argument coming from the Davis' house. I can't hear everything, but Mrs. Davis is saying something about the lawn. From the garage, Mr. Davis shouts back before the loud rumble of their riding lawn mower drowns them both out. He drives the lawn mower out of the garage, waving at us as if he wasn't just in a verbal throwdown with his wife that was loud enough for the whole neighborhood to hear.

We tromp in the house, dropping backpacks by the front door, and fall into our regular patterns. Doug disappears to the basement. Oscar fills the tea kettle. Baihe slips into the backyard. Heading upstairs to my bedroom, I hear Mom yell, "I'm calling in the pizza now." Only Oscar responds with one of his usual polite niceties.

I close my door and drop onto my bed. In the corner of my room, my art supplies lay in a messy pile. Mom and Dad gave Oscar the tiny bedroom I used as an art studio. Long before that, they took over my studio with absolutely perfect lighting. The sunroom downstairs is their lab now. Now, I've been pushed out again.

The canvas on my easel is blank except for a red geometric pattern. It's inspired by street art from Shepherd Fairy, the Obey guy. It's a weak imitation. I love his work. An article I read online said it was visually evocative conveying a message that is present yet vague and left for interpretation. Not my art. My "art" looks like I'm trying too hard to be something I'm not.

I stand, walk to the canvas, and trace my fingers over the brush strokes. Tacked to the corner of the canvas is a picture of me and my grandparents. We lived down the street from them in St. Louis until we moved to Inman. They were always around. Grandma always cooking. Grandpa always firing up a strange kung-fu movie on the DVD player. They were the first and probably the *only* people who really saw me. Not the person I wanted to be, but the person I truly am. Grandpa gave me my first camera when I was thirteen.

That was the summer I spent with them after we'd moved away. I was desperate to get back and see my best friend, Emma. But in one school year, things had changed. She'd found new friends, new things, and new people to fill her time. I'd pedaled on my bike aimlessly through the neighborhood for a week until Grandpa intervened with an old film camera. It opened my eyes to the world, helped me see it in new ways.

I haven't been back to their house in a long time. We'd planned a visit, but then the pandemic hit. Sighing, I think I could really use some time eating Grandma's veggie pot pie and watching Jackie Chan movies with Grandpa. I'm reaching for my laptop to video call them when I hear a strange noise outside.

From my bedroom, I can see down into the backyard. Baihe has stopped her tai chi moves to stare at the privacy fence separating our yard from the Davis'. The grinding sound of Mr. Davis' lawn-mower has changed. It sounds like the engine is coughing. Being on the second floor, I can just see through the tree branches. Mr. Davis is bouncing his lawnmower near the fence line.

Bouncing? Lawnmowers aren't supposed to bounce, are they?

The machine bucks under Mr. Davis, the engine sputtering. Mr. Davis wears a look of surprise and mystification as he pulls levers and urges the engine to continue forward. The commotion has caught Baihe's attention too. She's pulling a patio chair to the fence and standing on it so she can see over into the Davis' yard.

The back door of their house flies open and Mrs. Davis stomps into the backyard. Wet hair drips over her fuzzy pink bathrobe. I can't hear her words. The sounds coming from her wide-open mouth are lost to the lawnmower engine's grinding and sputtering.

With a heave, the lawn mower jumps forward as the plastic cover over the blade goes flying toward Mrs. Davis's head. In its wake is a burst of debris blowing up in the air and showering Mrs. Davis with mangled pieces of dried leaves and fur.

Oh, no! Doug's squirrels. I burst out laughing. He ran over the pile of Doug's dead squirrels!

"Oh, heavens," Oscar says coming into my room. "What in the world is going on?" I wave him to my side and point out the window.

Mr. Davis' engine grinds and lurches forward again. The blades spit out another shower of leaves, grass, fur, and by the way Mrs. Davis is racing toward her house, also chunks of squirrel bones and entrails. Oscar's laughter joins mine as we watch Mr. Davis yank on another lever and whip the steering wheel.

I bet there are videos on YouTube or something where drunk rednecks pop wheelies on their lawnmowers. But I'm guessing that was not Mr. Davis's intention by the look of panic creasing his face. The lawnmower spins and the front end becomes airborne. Baihe ducks behind the fence just in time to avoid being peppered with mangled squirrel remnants. Fragmented bones pelt the wood fence sounding like hail in a thunderstorm.

When all four wheels of the lawnmower land on the ground with a thud, the engine chokes, shudders, and dies. Mr. Davis' gaze is drawn to my bedroom window where Oscar and I are cracking up like we're at a slumber party and prank-calling boys. We dive away from the window simultaneously, me landing on my soft bed, and Oscar bashing against my desk. As he collapses to the floor in a pile of heaving laughter, his foot catches the leg of my easel and knocks it to the floor.

I lay in my bed catching my breath as small giggles sporadically escape. The energy in the room changes as Oscar's laughter abates too.

"I never thought I'd witness a squirrel massacre like that," I say with another giggle.

"Damn it, Doug," Oscar replies, a smile in his voice.

Leaning up to rest on my elbow, I look at Oscar. "What happened in Cleveland?"

As soon as I say the words, Oscar stiffens. He stands and straightens his shirt. "We don't talk about Cleveland," he says with finality. He moves for the door but stops and turns back. "Kaysee, I need you to stay out of this Cleveland issue. It's for your own good."

I stop him when his hand reaches for the doorknob. "You can't just say something like that and walk away. What do you mean? For my own good?"

"Oh, my sweet, young vampire. You aren't ready," he looks at me with pity like I'm a toddler complaining because he won't let me chew on an electrical cord.

"But, I—"

Oscar stops me by resting his hand on my cheek. "You. Aren't. Ready." And, damn it, I know he's using his amazing vampire persuasion on me and I'm totally pissed that I'm mesmerized into submission. My mouth won't move, and my thoughts go fuzzy.

I stay on my bed staring at my toppled easel unable to really think or do anything until the fog leaves my brain. Sneaking in my door, Pablo jumps onto my bed and curls up next to me. Absent-mindedly, I stroke his soft cat head as I listen to the distant argument between Oscar, Doug, and Baihe that drifts from the basement through my air vent. Random words like squirrel and Cleveland tickle my ears. But I don't care. I sit in my vampire-induced blissful state until my stomach starts rolling begging to feed.

12
No Bites

"We're running out of blood," Mom says with alarm.

"Fast," Dad adds, sighing and rubbing his stubbled chin.

"That's why we're having this family meeting," Mom looks around our kitchen at our vampire quartet.

"Mom, we never have family meetings," I say adding sarcastic air quotes around *family meeting*.

"Well, we do now!" Hands-on hips. Not a good look for Mom. Also, not a good outlook for me. This is DEFCON level 1 of Mom's seriousness. The last time she stood, feet spread and hands on hips looking like she was trying to play charades and her clue was "superhero," was when I asked her if I could take the driving test last spring. Both my parent still insist that I'm not ready to drive. It's too dangerous. And, yes, the irony of my parents working with vampires while I'm not allowed to drive is not lost on me one bit.

It's well after midnight. Everyone in the house has been on edge for the past week.

"What do we do?" I ask because no one is looking at anyone else. Gazes explore outside dark windows or read the back of a cereal box, but no one will make eye contact with another living soul—or half-living soul. "Wait. Mom? Dad? Is it your blood?" I swallow vomit that threatens to emerge at the thought, "Your blood in the vamp drinks?"

"No!" They shout in united repulsion.

Doug laughs over my shoulder as he shovels another handful of Cap'n Crunch into his mouth. Half of it ends up on the floor, which Pablo happily sucks up like a furry vacuum cleaner.

"No," Dad adds. "We had a source, but that's not an option now."

"Why?" I ask, once again annoyed with my parents. "Don't you have a backup plan?"

"The source was the backup plan," Oscar's hushed voice comes from where he leans against the refrigerator. "And that source is no longer available." Through the angry squint in his eyes, I swear he shoots a glance at Doug. Not that Doug notices. He just keeps crunching away.

"We're looking for a new source," Mom says relaxing her arms to her sides. "It just takes time. With all the virus concerns, it's harder to connect with people willing to give up their blood."

"Where do you even find a source?" I ask contemplating ways I could get us out of this situation. For heaven's sake, our survival depends on this.

"Facebook Marketplace," Baihe chimes in. At my incredulous look, she continues. "But there's a code, Kaysee. We don't just go online asking for blood donations. We're not amateurs."

"Okay, so get on Facebook and post something. Have you even tried yet?"

"Yes, Kaysee, we've tried." Mom's exasperation is not disguised. "For a month now, as we've watched our stock dwindle, we've posted. More than we should have."

"Make another account," I say.

"We already have eleven," Doug says during a brief pause from shoveling food in his mouth. "It was my idea to use more than one account. We've had five of them for years, but we added more to get the blood. But, no dice." Another handful of cereal goes down the hatch.

"So, what is the point of this meeting then? To tell us that we're screwed? That we don't have anything to feed our voracious vampire bodies? That we're going to starve to death?"

"There are other ways," Oscar says with foreboding.

"You mean eat people?" I'm absolutely aghast at the idea, my mouth hanging open in shock.

Baihe smirks and nods her head at Doug. "There's always squirrels." My gaze shifts between Baihe's smirk and Doug's triumphant grin.

"Damn it," Oscar stomps. "I said no direct feeding on humans, and for God's sake, absolutely no more animals."

Pablo weaves between Oscar's legs, rubbing against him as though he knows Oscar will protect him from ever being eaten by a vampire, especially Doug.

"We have a plan if things don't come together soon. There's a plan," Oscar adds. By the long sigh he releases, I can tell he doesn't like the plan much.

"And?" I prod.

"There's a blood drive, next week. We can," he pauses searching for the right word. "Intervene. That would help restock us for a few months at least."

"We're going to bust up into a blood drive and demand they hand over the donations?" I ask imagining our ragtag group sauntering into the blood drive with teeth barred and demanding the freshly retrieved goods.

"No, not like that," Baihe shakes her head as though I'm a child. "We'll hijack the blood van." I should be used to hearing outlandish things like this tossed around nonchalantly by now, but this is utterly ridiculous.

"We can't. That blood is supposed to help people," I say.

"Aren't we people?" Doug asks.

"Yes, but no. We can't do this," I say looking across the faces gathered in my kitchen. Doug shrugs and goes back to eating. Oscar won't meet my gaze. Baihe smiles an apology. Dad is tapping something on his phone. Leaning against the counter, her intensity faded, Mom drums her fingers against her arm. She's thinking, I know. She always taps her fingers or her foot when she's trying to solve an impossible puzzle.

"It's our only choice," Mom says with finality. "Our formula isn't perfected yet. We have the enzymes balanced but the synthetic protein mix hasn't proven effective yet."

"It definitely has not," Oscar says under his breath. Lately, he's been looking a little more washed out with a shadow of dark circles under his eyes. I didn't realize before, but it looks like Oscar's been the guinea pig for Mom and Dad's trial synthetic blood blends.

"Until we get the formula set, we must depend on traditional methods," Dad says dropping his phone into his lab pocket. "And no more bites on the Marketplace ad."

A huffed laugh escapes from me, not only because of Dad's unintended vampire pun but just at the ludicrousness of the situation. Junior year was supposed to be my year. The year that set me up for senior year and amazing successes afterward at art school far away from Inman. But this, it just bites. Instead of being that bold girl who captures Toby's heart, I'm a vampire with anger issues who is slowly going to starve to death.

"I'm going for a run," I say turning toward the living room. Grabbing my sneakers from where they lay in a pile of shoes by the front door, I slip my feet in and step into the cool early-October night air. The scent of lingering rain that passed through earlier in the night embraces me. It drips from the trees bringing browned, dead leaves floating to the ground.

As I pound my feet across the sidewalk and grind the wet leaves with my feet, my mind swirls. In my kitchen, being faced with a blood shortage, my stomach had begun to churn. The only way to stop the impending vamp attack was to run and keep running until I felt more like a human and less like a vampire.

Turning corners on my new favorite route, I'm Jason's house. Of all the houses on his street, his is the only one with lights on. Inman is such a boring town, at least it seems so on the surface. I wonder what people would think of our little suburb if they knew there was a pack of blood-thirsty vampires living in their midst.

The thought makes me question what other perilous elements are lurking beneath the surface of Inman.

With my heart thumping against my ears, I almost miss my name drifting across the midnight air. Slowing my steps, I look over my shoulder to Jason's house. I'd just passed it, focused on getting to the trail at the end of his cul-de-sac. It winds through a thicket of woods and connects half a mile away to the trails at the big city park.

Jason stands on the sidewalk wearing shorts and a t-shirt thick with sweat. Using a gym towel, he wipes his forehead, making his hair stand out at odd angles.

"A little late for a run," he smiles but there's a hint of a question in his eyes too.

"I needed some air," I say between breaths. My short run has eased some of my vamp fury, but it's still bubbling under the surface.

"I wouldn't go into the woods this late."

Stepping closer to Jason so I can keep my voice low and not wake the neighbors, my cheeks warm with tingles of defiance. "Why? Because I'm a helpless girl?"

"No," Jason quirks an eyebrow at me. "Because it's a bad idea for anyone to go into those woods late at night. Have you never seen a horror movie?"

A snorting laugh escapes before I can stop it. "I'm fine. Go back to whatever you were doing," I say with a dismissive wave.

"Seriously, Kaysee," Jason says grabbing my arm. My first instinct is to shake him off, slap his hand away. But something about the tiny shock, like a surge of electricity, snaking from my elbow to my shoulder stops me.

Meeting his concerned eyes, I use my free hand to peel his long fingers off my arm. "Seriously, Jason, I'm okay."

"Fine then," Jason steps back, resting his chin in his hand and trailing his eyes over me from my feet to the top of my head. Under his gaze, my heart beats harder.

"What are you doing?"

"Just memorizing what you're wearing for when the police ask in the morning. You know, for the missing person's report they always ask what the person was last wearing." He points at my clothes. "Sneakers. Black exercise pants. Surprisingly thin pink t-shirt."

Embarrassed, I wrap my arms over my chest. He's right, the shirt is pretty thin, so is my bra underneath. I hadn't thought about what I was wearing when I ran out the door. "Shut up, Han-*cock*," I spit.

"Ooh, sick burn there," he rolls his eyes. "Why don't you avoid the woods? You can risk your life another night. I have a busy day tomorrow and don't have time to spend with some cops asking tons of questions."

"You know you're an asshole, right?" I say turning my back to the woods.

"Takes one to know one," Jason snaps the towel on my thigh. The fabric popping is particularly loud in the quiet night, so is my yelp. I swat at him as I trot down the sidewalk. "See you tomorrow. Unless you get murdered," he says with a singsong voice, taunting as ever.

My reply is a particular finger held high over my shoulder when I pass under a streetlight. I know he sees me because his laugh breaks through the night.

He really is an asshole.

13

HOMECOMING & A HEIST

"It's all because someone's stupid ass parents got their stupid ass big mouths involved," Zel spits as she spins on her stool to face Toby across the chemistry lab table. She looks particularly cute today in a tight sweater and jeans. I swear Zel's figure can make any outfit look good. It's not fair that her angry glare and squinted eyes make me think of a heroine in a historic drama. I take in my baggy jeans and long sleeve burgundy shirt with a few holes along the hem. I've had it for three years. I look more like the town beggar, you know like one of the poor on the brink of starvation? Which, considering we still haven't found a blood source, is kind of accurate.

"Over Homecoming?" Toby asks looking like he's trying to solve an equation. He's so hot when he's thinking.

"Dances are kind of lame anyway," I say trying to get his attention.

"No, it's not that," Toby says without looking in my direction. "It just seems overprotective. We would have to wear masks at the dance anyway. Why not have it?"

I gape. What the hell? Toby likes dance?. I didn't see that one coming.

"Yeah, that's what I meant," I sputter, now sounding like the village idiot. My reward is a chortle from Jason. He glances up from the formula he's figuring in his notebook to shake his head.

"Yes!" Zel claps her hands making me jump. "We are not children. All these overprotective parents need to step back and let us do something fun. Everything, like *everything,* has been canceled. Can't we have just *one* dance?"

"Nope," Jason replies robotically. "No fun. No more. Not ever again."

The words "shut up, Jason" roll off Zel's tongue with practiced ease. Her rolling eyes land on Toby before her head swivels back to me. "The Bluffs," she whispers with wide, excited eyes. The blue mask she's wearing highlights her glitter eye shadow making her look like the cartoon princess she's named after. "We should have Homecoming at the Bluffs."

"Bad idea," Jason looks up from his notebook again.

"And why is that?" Zel's hand rests on her hip, ready for a verbal throwdown.

"Um, obviously, it's October. It'll be cold. You girls in your tiny dresses will freeze," he sits back with amusement dancing in his eyes. "But, hey, if you get frostbite and lose a few toes, maybe they'll give you a discount on your next pedicure." Toby laughs and high-fives Jason.

"You think that's all Homecoming is about? Tiny dresses?" Zel turns to me but keeps her voice loud enough for half the class to hear.

"It's just a bad idea," Jason says pointedly.

"No, it's not," Zel turns on him. "We'll have a bonfire, make s'mores. If we tell everyone to wear warm clothes, they'll be fine."

"I still have some tiki torches from the last Bluffs party," Toby says, warming to the idea.

"Yes!" Zel points at him. "Tiki torches. I'm going to talk to Tabitha and the student council girls and see if we can arrange this on the sly." By the look in Zel's eyes, I know there's no stopping her. When she gets an idea in her head, especially one that she can take to the stu-co girls, she'll let nothing get in her way. There will be a Homecoming at the Bluffs, bonfire, tiki torches, and all.

When the bell rings for the end of class, Jason watches Toby and Zel leave together whispering about Homecoming plans. "You know this is a bad idea, right?"

I shrug, "Yep. I know a thing or two about bad ideas. Remember?" Rounding the chem table a shocking thought hits me. Did I just flirt with Jason Hancock? Gross.

Word spreads lighting-fast. In art class, Maddy and Maeve can't stop whispering about Homecoming every time Mrs. Carroll turns her back. They only return to their canvases when Mrs. Carroll finally separates us. She sends me and my easel to set up next to Indigo. With a quick nod, Indigo welcomes me to the corner of the classroom. As she turns, my eyes drift to the throb of her carotid artery. Delicious.

Holy frijoles! I'm losing my mind. I force my gaze back to my canvas where I've penciled an outline for the project I'll likely enter in the district art contest. If I win a first-place prize, I'll get a scholarship for art school. I need to win that prize. It's not only about the money, although that would be awesome considering my parents don't have jobs now. But it's about knowing someone sees that I have something to contribute to the art world.

Studying the pattern of my sketches across the blank canvas, I imagine how the mixed media project will come together. I'm using an idea inspired by the techniques of Shepherd Fairy again. An off-kilter picture frame will embrace the edges of the painting, hopefully making the viewer feel a little lopsided. My plan is to cut a stencil to spray paint a pattern on the center of the piece. But what that pattern or design will be is still eluding me. In this moment, I'm considering something dripping with blood, life-giving blood.

I stretch and crack my back trying to refocus...again. I need motivation. I need inspiration. More than that, I need blood or I'll never be able to get any work done on this piece. Then I'll lose the contest for sure, and I'll never get a scholarship. And that would be even worse than having to live as a vegetarian vampire.

I won't lie. My stomach has been doing wild gymnastics for the last few days. As excitement over the planned secret Homecoming has grown, so has my body's desire to eat itself. At least, that's what it feels like.

Having to ration our vamp juice has made me antsy. I've probably run thirty miles in the past week trying to burn off the vamp energy that makes me daydream about eating all my friends. That's why I know this is our only chance.

"We're going to hijack the bloodmobile," I say, sighing with defeat. "Tell me the plan again." A quick sip of vamp juice helps me focus as Oscar and Baihe start walking through the steps of our heist for the fifth time.

"Doug has looked on the Google to find the blood drive tomorrow," Oscar begins again. He's way too patient with me. Doug isn't. He looks at me like I'm an idiot vampire who isn't smart enough to survive, which is kind of accurate. As Oscar continues laying out the logistics, I take another sip. I've taken to letting the juice coat the inside of my mouth before I swallow. At first, I thought it might trick my traitorous stomach into thinking I was drinking more than I was. Turns out, I am that stupid. My stomach doesn't fall for it, and now it's become like a sick form of torture. I still do it anyway.

"Why do I have to be on the bike again?" Doug huffs, bringing my focus back to the vampire crew crowded in my kitchen. My parents are locked in their lab after saying something about plausible deniability and shutting the door.

"Damn it, man, you know why," Oscar is losing the battle to keep his voice low. "It's your fault we're in this situation. You will be the sacrifice again."

"Can't Baihe do it this time?" Doug whines. He must be serious because there's an open bag of Oreos sitting in front of him, and I haven't seen him touch it once.

"*Dang ran bu*!" Baihe spits the Mandarin words like we'll miraculously understand. "You do it, Doug. Not me."

"Okay, but on a bike? The road rash last time took a week to heal," Doug says resting his chin in his hands as he drops his elbows to the kitchen island. He doesn't usually look this defeated unless he's just had a tongue-lashing from Oscar.

"Toughen up, mate," Oscar replies. "The bike is faster, they won't see you coming."

"Fine," Doug spits as he grabs the Oreo bag and turns for the basement. "See you tomorrow then."

Baihe looks at me with concern. "We've done this before. It'll be fine. Doug knows what to do. Then we'll be set for maybe half a year." Her eyes crease as she smiles. It makes me believe her fully. Or maybe she's just using vamp persuasion on me. Usually, I can tell but not lately. Not when I'm starving to death.

"Okay," I say grabbing an apple and taking a bite. It tastes like ass. All food does now. Swallowing, my stomach lurches complaining about the apple and fighting against its intrusion. It feels like I'm literally at war with myself. "It better work."

The next day I feel like garbage again. No, I feel like dog shit that someone stepped in. Then they tried to scrape it off the bottom of their shoe, grinding it into a patch of grass. Yeah, that's what I feel like. Smeared dog shit. My head hurts. My stomach feels like it's shrinking to the size of a walnut. No matter how many miles I ran this morning, I'm completely on edge to the point that my hands are shaking. I tried to hide it from my mom, but by the worried look in her eyes at breakfast when she passed me the last bottle of vamp juice, I can tell she knows.

Opening and closing my hands like they're exploding fireworks helps a little. As I wait, bundled up wearing all black in the front seat of my mom's dumpy car, I keep opening and closing my hands. Opening and closing.

The night is dark and ominous, with a cool breeze promising rain to come. As Oscar steers Mom's car around a corner, I catch him glancing at me.

"How're you holding up?" he asks.

I reply with a muffled grunt. I don't need to go into the dog shit description right now, I decide. Behind me, Baihe holds up her phone with the map app open.

"The bloodmobile should be turning just ahead," she says. As Oscar presses on the accelerator, anxiety fills the tiny space of our car. It's covering us like a weighted blanket, making our movements and thoughts more difficult to maneuver.

"You sure Doug's got this?" I ask trying not to reveal how worried I am. I mean, really. What are we going to do if this doesn't work out? We don't have any more "supply" left. That means we have to go straight to the source. And the only source I can even consider going straight to is Jason Hancock and his fat mouth. He almost gave away the secret Homecoming in class yesterday when he was teasing Zel about it as Mr. Garcia walked by. I wasn't very excited about Homecoming at first, but the more I think about redeeming myself with Toby at the Bluffs, the more excited I get. I've tried to drop hints all week about not having a date yet. But every time I do, only Jason seems to notice. Then the teasing begins.

"Doug has this," Oscar says with finality. "He's done it a few times before." Something about Oscar's attempt to comfort me leaves me trusting him a little less.

Peering into the darkness punctuated with passing street lights, I look for my old bike waiting on a side street. It was the only bike we had to sacrifice, and the image of Doug riding my hot pink bike with a unicorn-shaped basket and glitter tassels hanging from the handlebars brings a smile to my lips. When we dropped him off earlier, he wouldn't stop complaining and was still yelling and kicking at the bike when we drove away.

"There!" Baihe points out the window. Ahead, brake lights flash on a large vehicle. The bloodmobile slows at a four-way stop. I begin salivating and my stomach growls with anticipation.

"Slow and steady," Oscar says. "We don't want to draw any unwanted attention."

We glide into position behind the stationary bloodmobile, the red light from its brake lights illuminating us in the car. When the lights go out and the vehicle rolls through the intersection, I can tell we're all holding our breath. Oscar turns off the headlights and follows the bloodmobile. I'm clenching my seatbelt as Oscar steers through the dim light only spotted with street lights spread too far apart. So much darkness sends a quiver of dread down my spine.

"Doug should be two blocks ahead," Baihe announces behind me in a hushed whisper. The tall trees along the street look vaguely familiar from when we dropped off Doug.

As the bloodmobile hits a bump in the road, its headlights flash off the reflectors on the spokes of my old bike. "There!" I yell and point.

"Grab the kit," Oscar orders. Behind me, tools jingle from our stash in Dad's old fanny pack.

"Got it," Baihe says.

Oscar grinds his teeth as he stares ahead like he's conjuring something. "Come on, Doug."

The brake lights flash again. The streak of a pink 10-year-old girl's bike with a scrawny vampire wearing all-black races right in front of the bloodmobile. Oscar slams on the brakes in unison with the bloodmobile stopping far enough behind the vehicle so we can still see its impact with Doug.

When I took driver's ed online last summer, we had to watch these videos where they showed us these staged situations of hitting something with your car. Damn It Doug collides with the front grill of the bloodmobile and sails through the air as the bike is crumpled under the vehicle's tires. I'm guessing that the bloodmobile was going at least 40 mph when it hit Doug. He tumbles through the air, his clothes blending into the dark night. All I see are hands flailing and his mouth open in a scream.

Doug lands with a thump fifteen feet in front of the bloodmobile, which is still rocking from the sudden stop. I'm breathing again, heavy and ragged.

"Wait for it," Oscar whispers, his hand resting on the door handle.

"Holy mother of god!" An older man's voice pierces the night as the driver's side door of the bloodmobile flies open. An instant later, a woman with her hair in a bun jumps out of the passenger side.

"Bruce! What did you do?"

"Oh, my god! Oh, my god! Oh, my god!" Bruce repeats as he looks between Doug's lifeless body and the smears of blood across the chrome grill of the bloodmobile.

"Now! Go!" Oscar says, jumping out of the car with the speed and agility of a cat.

I tumble out and trip on my feet as I run to the trunk and pull out a cooler. I lug the large cooler to the bloodmobile that looks like an adapted ambulance with wide swinging doors in the back. Oscar tests the handle and shakes his head at Baihe. She already has the fanny pack unzipped pulling out some thin tools and passing them to Oscar's open hand.

"Hurry," I say. The two bloodmobile workers, Old Guy and Bun Lady are calling out to Doug to see if he'll wake up and urging each other to call an ambulance.

Oscar looks like James Bond as he works the tools and pops the lock. The door swings open and he waves his hand with a bow. I drop the cooler onto the floor of the bloodmobile and shove it forward. It grates across the floor and makes a loud sound that draws Bun Lady's attention. I drop to a crouch on the pavement. Next to me, Baihe is cursing me with her eyes. She holds up her hand and slowly raises one finger at a time. When she gets to five, she signals with her hand like a Navy SEAL and we jump into the back of the bloodmobile.

Oscar slides in behind us with another cooler.

Refrigerators line both walls. The handles don't move when we pull on them. Silent curses fly through my brain. I knew this was a bad idea. Here I thought that becoming a vampire would ruin junior year. Being arrested for hijacking a bloodmobile would absolutely make it much, much worse.

Leaning out the back of the vehicle, Oscar whistles a tune, light and airy like a bird call. In front of the bloodmobile, still spotlighted by its headlights, Doug groans, and rolls to his back. Old Guy and Bun Lady shriek, jumping backward. Oscar and Baihe yank on the refrigerator handles and pop them open. The sound of the locks breaking is masked by more groaning and shrieking from Doug and the bloodmobile duo on the road spurting curses.

When we open the refrigerators, we find them packed full of blood bags. So many blood bags, I almost cry.

"Go fast," Baihe elbows me in the ribs. "But don't throw them or they might pop open."

I'm grabbing five bags at a time, and stacking them in the cooler. Baihe and Oscar move with a synchronicity which demonstrates this isn't their first heist. It looks like it's their hundredth.

"Kid, are you okay? What are you doing riding your bike in the dark?" Old Guy steps toward Doug as though he's a wild animal who'll attack. Little does Old Guy know.

"We need to call an ambulance," Bun Lady insists, her face white with fear.

Doug continues to groan and roll around on the pavement, smearing his blood like a work of abstract art across the blacktop.

"I'm calling an ambulance," Bun Lady says walking backward toward the bloodmobile.

"Drop!" I whisper yell as she turns around. The three of us plummet. I land hard on the metal floor, cracking my knee as my elbow collides with the side of the cooler. It flips on its side and a few blood bags fly out and land on my stomach. I scramble to grab them as Baihe shushes me with a vengeance. Holding the blood bags against my chest I can feel warmth still emanating from the blood. It's fresh. The idea makes me both want to retch and to pierce the bag with my fangs and devour every drop.

The sound of a bird escapes from Oscar again, this time more panicked. In response, Doug says, "Hey, I'm okay. Really."

"Don't stand up!" yells Old Guy. He sounds like he's about to have a heart attack starting a new chorus of "Oh my gods."

"Lay back down!" Bun Lady yells, her feet pounding away from the bloodmobile and back toward Doug.

Oscar and Baihe spring up and grab wildly for the blood bags. Dropping the loose blood bags back into the cooler, I pull myself off the floor and empty the fridge. The cooler is so full that the lid won't close fully. Oscar has already unloaded his cooler and is hoisting it back to the trunk of our car. Baihe yanks on our cooler as I shove it from behind. It takes both Baihe and Oscar to lift it into the trunk. The suspension of Mom's crappy sedan groans when they drop it in the trunk. We slip back into the car as Oscar whistles again.

Starting the car, he puts it in reverse and backs down the street before turning on his lights and hitting the gas. He maneuvers around the bloodmobile and comes to a stop where Old Guy and Bun Lady are practically shoving Doug to lay back down on the ground.

"There you are," I say rolling down my window. My heart drums in my chest. Did we actually get away with this? *Not yet*, I think as I plaster a disapproving look on my face. "Mom's going to be pissed," I say to Doug.

He's standing now and shaking his arm as though he's resetting a bone in his forearm.

"She shouldn't have taken my phone!" Doug says with very believable anger.

Leaning across me, Oscar smiles at Old Guy and Bun Lady. "Sorry to bother, Mum took his phone and he had a temper tantrum. Come on, and get in the car," he orders Doug.

"But, but, but," Old Guy stammers as Doug limps to the door Baihe holds open.

"You're hurt," Bun Lady scolds, her eyes as big as saucers.

"He'll be fine," Oscar purrs, persuading them with his vampire magic. "Rub some dirt in it, walk it off." He chuckles.

They stare wide-eyed, incredulous. "If you're sure," Bun Lady stammers, her eyebrows slowly creeping up her forehead.

"Perfectly fine," Oscar smiles as Doug drops in the back seat and slams the door shut. Before Old Guy and Bun Lady can respond, Oscar hits the gas and sails down the street.

"Walk it off, my ass," Doug grumbles in the back seat as houses and trees fly past.

"Toughen up," Baihe says.

"No, I mean it. My ass. I hit and skidded right on my ass," Doug squirms in the back seat. "I'm going to be digging gravel out of my ass crack for a week."

Laughter explodes from me, partly from relief that we'd succeeded and partly because of Doug's ass. I can't help it. Baihe joins me, tears streaming down both our faces.

"No really," Doug complains. "And I broke my arm and some ribs in case anyone cares."

Letting up on the gas and slowing to a speed much closer to the speed limit, Oscar joins in our laughter. "Brilliantly done, Doug."

"You guys are jerks! I get first dibs on the blood!" Doug sulks behind me in the back seat.

"Yes, you do," Oscar says. "And well-deserved." He glances at Doug in the rear-view mirror with a twinkle in his eyes. "I think this was our biggest haul yet."

14

CANDY CORN

Before me is a smorgasbord of blood. All types, some a shade darker red than others. We'd filled two coolers completely and now have our spoils spread out on the kitchen island. Mom stands near the sink holding a steaming cup of tea but not taking a drink. A horrified look is plastered across her face. She can't hide it. At least Dad excused himself to the lab.

"Dibs on the B positive," Baihe says reaching across the island for a blood bag with a large B+ written on the label in Sharpie. She bites the cap off the end of one of the tubes sticking out the top and spits it in the trash before squeezing the blood into her mouth. Her demeanor changes almost instantaneously. We've all gotten extra pale in the past few days. Dark shadows had grown around Baihe and Oscar's eyes. I think they'd been passing on blood so I could keep up my strength. As Baihe downs the B+, color returns to her cheeks, the shadows under her eyes fade, and she looks like she weighs twenty pounds lighter. Her shoulders straighten from the stoop they'd adopted a week ago.

Doug is on his third bag, and Oscar is finishing his first, but I can't. I just can't. After years of being a vegetarian and only a few months of being a vampire, my vegetarian brain is winning. But my vampire stomach is putting up a fight. It's flipping, clenching, and threatening to eviscerate me from the inside.

"Kaysee?" Mom stands over my shoulder, steam from her teacup drifting past me. "It's okay, honey." She sounds like she is urging me to jump into the deep end of the pool or to take the training wheels off my bike. But this is not like that at all!

"I can't," I whisper as my stomach cramps.

"Love, you need to eat," Oscar says from across the island wiping his lips with a napkin. A red streak is left across the white paper.

"I can't. I don't eat meat. That means blood too," I say with anger rising. I don't need an emotional vamp attack right now. Seriously. It's not the time to get all teen angsty. "Mom, can't you mix up a vamp drink really quick?"

"I'm sorry, Kaysee," she says sitting on the stool next to me. "It doesn't work that way. I have to process the—the samples before mixing the formula with the juice. It takes a few hours."

"I'll wait," I sit back and push the O+ blood bag in front of me across to Doug. He grabs it with glee and begins to devour it like he does all foods: messily and as though he has something to prove.

Resting my elbows on the island, I drop my head in my hands and close my eyes. My mom rubs circles on my back. "Couldn't you drink just a little?"

"No," I say, my voice muffled.

"I could make you drink it," Baihe says playfully. Of course, she could totally kick my ass and force me to drink blood all night long. But from what I've learned about Baihe so far, that's not how she rolls.

"No," I repeat.

"You need the proteins," my dad's voice comes from the lab door. I peek up to see him leaning against the door jamb, his face so tight it looks like it might crack. "You need to drink it, Kaysee. The proteins are what keep you going. They also keep you from losing control."

A groan escapes as my stomach responds to Dad's advice with a violent jolt. "Fine," I say through gritted teeth.

"This is a good one to start with," Baihe passes me a half-drunk blood bag.

The medical plastic is slippery in my hand. Lifting the tube that Baihe opened with her teeth, I look at the floppy improvised straw and close my eyes. The tube on my tongue feels too flimsy and too thick at the same time. Curling my lips around it I suck.

My entire body jolts when the blood hits my tongue. But I barely swallow the sip and choke as it glides a little too easily down my throat.

Coughing, I force out, "What is wrong with this? It tastes like salty candy corn."

Baihe's demeanor drops, her lips falling into a frown. "I thought you'd like it. It was sweet."

With a nod, Oscar proclaims. "Diabetic."

"What?" Still sputtering, I turn to the handsome English vampire gentleman who, as always, looks dashing in simple black clothes. There's something about the waves of his hair that makes my toes curl in a very pleasant way.

"Did you give her a diabetic?" Oscar asks Baihe. She responds with a pouting nod. "High blood sugar, love. It stays in the blood. Gives it a sweet flavor."

"Really?" I cringe looking at the blood bag still in my hands.

"It's not the only thing that holds the sugar," Doug smirks between slurps.

"Doug, gross," Baihe slaps his shoulder hard enough for him to step out of her reach. Then she turns to me assuming the demeanor of a teacher. "Sugars stay in the urine too. And a hundred years ago, before scientific tests were developed, the only way a doctor could diagnose diabetes was by tasting the urine."

"Ew, Doug, that *is* gross," I say passing the bag back to Baihe.

Glancing at me over the blood bag he's sucking dry, Doug chuckles and wiggles his eyebrows at me. His arm still juts at an odd angle, and he has road rash up his forearms. The combined look is strangely entertaining.

"Here, drink this," Mom passes me a purple plastic princess cup. It's one that we've had since I was a kid. Mom only used it when she mixed liquid medicine with juice, the only way I'd swallow medicine until I was ten. A plastic bendy straw sticks out of the lid so I can't see what's inside. "Close your eyes, take a sip. You need this."

"Please, Kaysee. We'll have more vamp juice tomorrow, I promise," Dad adds.

Pinching my nose, I squeeze my eyes shut and lift the drink to my mouth. Of course, I miss and poke my eyelid. Good thing my eyes were closed. I peek out one eye and close my mouth around the straw. In my mind, I'm telling myself that what I'm drinking is anything but human blood. It's cherry juice. It's a strawberry milkshake. It's sweat squeezed out of one of Jason's workout shirts. Disgusting, yes. But so much better than the idea of blood.

"Good job," Baihe says and pats my shoulder.

"Chug it! Chug it!" Doug chants from across the island.

The others join in so that by the time I sip the last drop, everyone is chanting and pounding the countertops. And they're laughing. It's a ridiculous, slap-happy kind of laugh. The kind you have after you've accomplished something as a team.

My laughter comes with a grimace as I lick my lips. Inside my body, things are happening that I can't understand. I probably never will. But it feels like that moment in a movie where the couple finally connects and dances through a ballroom with soft music accompanying their first kiss. It's absolutely glorious!

"Well done, Kaysee love," Oscar toasts me with a fresh blood bag and the others applaud.

Having never played sports outside of PE class, I've never known what it's like to be part of a team. Even in art, it's pretty much a solo adventure. But here and now, in my kitchen in the dead of night, I know what it's like to belong. My vampire crew is my team. We triumphed tonight. I can't imagine where we'll go next.

I may not know where I'm going with my vampire teammates, but I do know, for a fact, that Zel is driving straight for the mall. With the cooler weather, we're not melting in her falling-apart car. It puffs out smoke behind us as she zips between cars headed for the big city. There aren't any decent dress shops in suburban Inman, so we're going 15 miles north to the big shopping mall on the south side of Springfield.

"Pull up my Insta. Tabitha posted a photo of the sweetest dress. I want to hit up that shop first," Zel orders as she tosses me her phone and passes a minivan. The woman driving the car whips Zel a frightened gaze as we zip by.

Unlocking Zel's phone, I open Instagram and begin scanning.

"You should do more on your Insta. Yours is so boring. Just a bunch of art stuff," Zel says.

"And that's how I like it," I reply tapping on the picture of Tabitha in a long, blue dress with sparkly crystals along the plunging neckline. The haughty smile on her face makes me want to sketch her as an evil, blood-thirsty vampire. She fits the part better than I do. "And why do you care what Tabitha's wearing? Aren't you guys on the outs again?"

Zel scoffs. "Psht, we're not on anything. I could care less about Tabitha. I just like her dress."

Once we're in the store and Zel has on the exact dress, but in red, I can see the allure. I adjust my mask straps as I gaze at the dress perfectly hugging Zel in all the right places. If I put that dress on, it'd hang like a wet dish rag.

"Zel, it's—it's just wow," I stutter.

"I know," Zel says with a triumphant glimmer in her eyes. Her hair billows over her shoulders and draws attention to the glittering crystals that dip along the neckline. "Abuelita said she'd make a mask to match too. I'm thinking it needs more bling than this. She'll make you one too, once you pick out your dress."

"I'm still not sure I'm going," I shrug. "My last time at the Bluffs didn't go great. And it's going to be pretty cold."

"Ugh, Kaysee, come on," Zel rolls her eyes. "You have to go. You're going. It's final."

And there you have it. Zel has just transformed from a fun friend to a mean girl in two seconds flat. I hate when she does this. I can think for myself. I don't need her to drag me through the world on her heels.

"Whatever," I stand up, dismissing her attitude with a wave.

She calls after me as I stride through the store, my hands in my pockets where I'm doing the firecracker thing again. This time it's not because I'm starving to death, but I can feel the vamp rage building again. Yes, I skipped breakfast again. I've been doing okay since the heist last week. Mom and Dad had a new batch of vamp juice ready to go the next morning, and I've been drinking a pretty steady stream of it since. It's easy because I definitely prefer their cherry and beet juice concoction over the candy corn diabetic blood.

Feeling my feet stomp against the tiled mall floors helps me release some tension, but I'm longing to run. I pick up my pace and soon find myself outside where I rip off my face mask and sulk my way back to Zel's junky car. My phone blows up with pings from Zel's angry texts, but I ignore it.

When she finds me, I'm leaning against the car with my butt perfectly cradled in one of the dents. With my arms folded across my chest, I pinch my side because my vamp-ness is still not quelled. I wish she'd taken another fifteen minutes.

"Gee, thanks, Kaysee, for abandoning me," Zel huffs as she slings a dress bag into the back seat. She mimics my stance, arms across her chest, fire in her eyes. I know she's pissed. I'm pissed. We're both pissed. So what? It's just another tantrum from Zel.

"Let's just go home," I say reaching for the door handle.

Zel steps forward blocking my reach. "No. Not yet." Her glare could fracture diamonds. Great. She's not just pissed. She's royally pissed.

"Come on, Zel," I try to push past her.

She blocks me again. "For real. We need to talk. You've had a stick up your ass since school started," she unleashes. And I know it's going to be bad because she shakes her hair off her shoulders in frustration, a rare move reserved for ultimate annoyances. "So, like, what the hell?"

"It's nothing, just this skin thin," I say tightening my arms across my chest and pinching harder.

"No, it's not nothing. You have three exchange students living in your house. Three! And one of them is that disgusting guy Doug. Did you know that he's asked me out like a dozen times? That kid can't take a hint. The Chinese one always looks at me like she wants to kick my ass. Now Oscar, he's fine. I'd wrap him up and take him home any day of the week. But, you!"

She juts her finger into my shoulder for emphasis. "You! What is going on? You have done nothing but avoid me and stare googly-eyed at Toby in chem class. Do you even care about Homecoming?"

"No," I say sharper than I intend. My one word hits her hard making her eyes glisten and threaten tears.

"What about me?" A single tear slips down her perfect face. And I'm done. My hands begin to shake as I realize what I need to do. It's time for Zel to hear the truth.

"Zel," I begin, my roiling vamp rage picking up speed. "It's hard to explain. And maybe this isn't the best place." I point to a mom ushering her kids to an SUV a few rows over.

"Yes, it is," she says. "This is as good a place as any. What are you hiding, Kaysee?" The look on her face tells me that she's not letting this go. Just like she didn't let go of planning Homecoming at the Bluffs. That's happening in a week.

"Okay, fine," I huff. It takes me a moment to compose the words. I shake my arms trying to rid myself of the electric buzz flowing through them. "It's hard to say it." I'm stalling, and we both know it.

"Well, just spit it out," Zel taps her foot. "I know you don't have something like an STD, so what is it?"

"Look, you need to just give me a break. You've been a lot lately. And that's hard because now I'm a—" I start but freeze. "I'm a—" The words won't come out. Zel's foot keeps tapping. I glance around the parking lot. No one else is in sight. "I'm a vampire," I blurt so quickly I don't know if she comprehends me.

"You're shitting me," she replies with the biggest eye roll in history. "A vampire? You expect me to believe that?"

Stomping around the car, she opens the driver's door and slides in. The engine fires to life so quickly I actually believe she's going to leave me behind so I scramble inside.

"First, there was the whole I'm in love with Toby thing. I was there for you on that, cheering you on. Then you avoid me and make up this skin thing. Next, you diss Homecoming. Now, you say you're a vampire? What the actual hell is going on?"

I'm buckling my seat belt as the engine rumbles. I'm glad she hasn't shifted into gear yet. Driving on a normal day, Zel is a disaster. I can't imagine what chaos she'll wreak if she drives this angry.

"I never said I was in love with Toby," I say.

Zel turns on me, chin dipped, looking at me like I've lost my mind. And in many ways, I think I might have. "That's what you have to say about this?"

Grabbing her hand, I squeeze her fingers, mostly to keep her from putting the car in gear. "It's true. I'm a vampire." Zel doesn't move. Her glare pierces me. We're having a staring contest, one she's determined to win.

"I. Am. A. Vampire," I repeat emphasizing each word as though she didn't speak English.

"Bull. Shit." She parrots my emphasis bobbing her head side-to-side with each word.

"You don't believe me?"

"I don't believe you." Zel puts that car in reverse.

I reach across and yank the gear shift back to park. The car lurches at the sudden stop. A new puff of smoke billows in a cloud from the muffler. "I am a vampire. I can prove it," I say.

Sitting back, Zel stares daggers at me. "Why are you doing this? Is this so you can get Toby's attention? Because if so, it's a lame attempt."

"No, this has nothing to do with Toby," I sigh in frustration. "It has everything to do with Doug and Oscar and Baihe and my parents!" And I have to stop myself. I don't know how much I can tell Zel. She's always trying to get attention online and IRL. Can I really trust her? I study Zel's gaze. She gapes at me, but I can see the wheels turning.

"This is a new low for you," Zel says with a sigh and backs out of the parking space. She comes uncomfortably close to a giant truck and only misses scraping against its bumper by inches.

"I'm not lying," I say knowing it's a losing battle now. Zel has made up her mind.

"I just never thought you'd be one of those lonely girls who makes up ridiculous stories just so you can get attention," Zel says merging into traffic. With a quick glance at me, she adds, "Like Toby's attention."

It's a proverbial dagger to the heart. The silence that fills her car on the ride home twists the dagger and pushes it farther. I should have known that Zel wouldn't believe me. I don't know why I told her anyway. I wish I could take it back, use vampire persuasion to make her forget. But I haven't figured out persuasion yet.

When she pulls into her driveway, we both sit silently in the car waiting for the other to say something. Neither of us budges. With a pitying look at me, Zel climbs out of her rust bucket car, grabs her dress from the back seat, and stomps into her house. I stay, picking at the cracking vinyl seat with my fingernail as I wait for my blood to stop boiling.

But I know it won't, so I toss my bag in the house and slip on my running shoes.

15
BELGIAN DUCKS

On Wednesday, I make a final stab at getting Toby to ask me to Homecoming, but it's hopeless. I'm still fuming after dress shopping with Zel and ready to plan a night of binge-watching BBC shows. But now Baihe and Oscar have heard about the Homecoming plans and are begging me to go. We're trying to keep it quiet so Doug doesn't find out. The last thing we need is him harassing girls in a large group like that. Likely, someone will kick his ass. More likely, he'll lose his mind and start eating squirrels...or people.

"Okay, I'll go," I say to Baihe at lunch.

A smile fills her face as she squeals and pulls me into a hug. "My first high school dance!"

"Didn't you say you've done this before?" I ask as I sit and pull out my lunch.

"High school, yes. Dances, no," she replies. "Until this year, where we can wear masks and everyone is edgy and different, we didn't fit in enough."

"So, it took a global pandemic to make you fit into high school?" I snark.

"We definitely fit into this global pandemic better than the last one," Oscar sips his vamp juice. "And this dance is a highlight. It's against the rules, lawless. How very American." He winks at me across the table.

Over Oscar's shoulder, Zel steps outside to the picnic tables. She catches my eye and changes directions with a sneer. She's been mad at me before, but not quite like this. As she steps back toward the door, she bumps into Doug. He smiles and waggles his eyebrows in a way he probably thinks is seductive. Instead, he looks like a demented doll from a low-budget horror film. Zel groans loud enough for everyone to hear and shoves Doug aside. Like usual, he brushes it off and moves on to the next girl.

"Still on the outs with Zel?" Oscar asks catching my expression.

"She's ghosting me," I reply and take a bite of my PB&J.

"Give her time," Baihe says knowingly. And I want to believe that everything will be okay. But this is Zel.

Too soon, the bell rings and I'm tossing my lunch back into my bag. I drank a full vamp juice, only because I knew it was the one thing to keep me from going mental. Zel's drama weighs heavy on me and zaps my appetite. I guess a few bites of PB&J will have to suffice. Keeping my head low, I adjust the straps on my mask. They're really starting to chafe behind my ears. It's from another package of cheap masks Mom found online. When they came in the mail, they smelled lightly of cigarette smoke. And the fabric is as scratchy as burlap.

I'm still messing with my mask when Mrs. Carroll sneaks up behind me in art. "Kaysee," she says making me jump and drop my paintbrush. "You've been staring at that canvas all week. How about you get some paint on there?"

Retrieving my paintbrush, I settle back on my stool. "I don't know where to go with this one," I say.

"What about your sketches?" Mrs. Carroll asks. "Use those for reference to guide you. Or maybe free paint on a different project."

Under my mask, I'm biting my lip and jump when one of my fangs catches wrong. "I just want this to mean something, for the judges to see it as worthwhile."

"Kaysee," Mrs. Carroll places her hand on my shoulder and looks at me over her purple, cat-eye glasses. "The best art isn't created to please a judge, it's created because the artist couldn't imagine a world where that piece of art didn't exist. A piece where the artist exposes a part of who they are or shares a message they're dying for the world to hear."

Well, crap. She's right. I stare at my canvas that is seriously lacking any artistic integrity then grab my sketchbook. I dig through the canister of colored pencils and pull out three hues of red. When the bell rings to end the school day, I don't notice until everyone else has left the art classroom. Two pages of my sketchbook are covered in red. There are swirls of lines and jagged edges, soft areas, and those where I pressed so hard I nearly tore through the paper. It doesn't look like anything I've created before. I don't like it at all, but the chaos scrawled across the page definitely reflects how junior year has gone so far.

Unexpected. Unrealistic. Hopeless.

Nothing good happened all day. So, when Mom asks Oscar to go pick up some groceries, I jump in the car without asking for permission. The temperatures dropped throughout the day. Having the heater on fogs the windows. Of course, I draw a heart with my finger on the glass. Then I wipe it away with my palm leaving a dripping mess.

At the grocery store, we keep our heads low and our masks tight. The fluorescent lights give the store a green shine. When we walk past a tall display of little chocolate-covered donuts, I grab three bags. Doug will eat two of them for sure. And everyone in the world knows that little chocolate-covered donuts can solve nearly all of life's problems. I doubt this bag will make it home.

"Oscar, what's your thing?" I ask as we load groceries into the trunk.

"Whatever do you mean?" He glances at me quizzically taking a donut from the bag I'm offering him.

I sigh. These vampire emotions are the worst. I want to run. I want to eat people. I don't know how I can live like this. "Your thing, you know, like Baihe and kung fu and I have running. What do you do to deal with the vampire rage?" A whole donut disappears in my mouth.

"My dear, I'm English," Oscar replies with a devilish grin. "I don't have nearly as many emotions as you Americans do."

"Okay, I get that. I've watched enough BBC dramas to know you would rather be stabbed in the eye with a hot poker than show any feelings in public," I tease following him to sit in the car. "But even you have vampire rage. Instead of eating your way through a whole village, what do you do to calm yourself?"

Oscar sighs as though he's weighing his words and snags another donut. Pulling out of the parking lot, he drives in silence for a few minutes. I'm worried that I've hit a sore topic when he finally responds.

"At first, I did, as you said, eat my way through a village. Through quite a few villages in fact." The tone in the car instantly becomes somber with the weight of misery in Oscar's voice. It carries both pain and regret in his clipped words. "I found another vampire who did the same thing. We teamed up for a few years until I realized how much of a monster I'd become. I didn't stop until after I'd discovered that my mother had died alone."

"Oscar, I'm so sorry," I say.

"I moved past my mother's death by traveling Europe, using persuasion to get money when I needed it," Oscar explains with a wave of his hand. "I saw some brilliant places. Anytime the rage to eat came, I'd walk away from town and spend time in the countryside feasting on animals until it passed. Since then, I've tried a number of activities and hobbies. Some lasted longer than others, but eventually, I'd need to reinvent myself. Then I met Baihe, and having her as my project helped more than needlepoint or eating Belgian ducks ever could." His smile reappears. Humor is his tool once again. Oscar never really opens up much about his past. He always spins the conversation into something to make me laugh.

I lean over and nudge his elbow. "If I ever need some needlepoint done, now I know who to ask," I jest licking chocolate off my fingers.

"I'm also quite good at cheesemaking, archery, and fencing," he replies straight-faced.

"But can you make cheese while fencing?" I laugh.

"Absolutely," Oscar says pulling the car into our driveway.

We're still giggling when we get out of the car. I look up and catch Zel's eyes. She's standing by her garbage can at the curb. We obviously caught her taking out the trash and now she's frozen like a rabbit hoping we don't see her.

But I do. And she sees me too.

Her lips tighten and she tips her chin higher as she walks right past me into her house. No words. She doesn't even look at me again. Like I'm the trash waiting to be sent to a dump, Zel leaves me gaping on the driveway.

There are so many names that I want to call her, colorful words that drift through my mind. But it's Zel. This is what she does. She always comes back around, we make up and go back to life as normal. At least, that's what we've always done before. In the back of my mind, an inkling of dread blossoms as I wonder if we'll be able to make up and get back to normal this time. Or have I completely ruined our friendship?

16
SUCK-FEST

I want to go to Homecoming as much as I want to have my fingernails pulled out one at a time. It's going to suck royally. I know it. Everything has sucked lately, why wouldn't Homecoming too? I'm only going because Baihe is grinning like a kid getting a king-size candy bar on Halloween. So, I stuff down my disappointment at not capturing Toby's attention and plaster a smile across my face.

Oscar bumps the car over the uneven ground, a few choice curses escaping when he hits a deeper hole. "Whose idea was it to have this dance in the wilderness?" he grunts.

"Zel," I grunt back and grab onto the door to brace myself for another lurch.

"It's going to be magical," Baihe coos from the back seat. "And look, they have lights!"

Ahead, strands of Christmas lights hang from a few trees along the edge of the Bluffs party area. It's bathed in their soft light along with rows of tiki torches glowing in the darkness. It does look beautiful, but I won't admit that to Zel. At least, not yet.

Once we survive the drive across the field, we park and the three of us pull ourselves out of the car. Oscar looks dapper in a dark blue suit. He's accented it with an ascot tie, shiny brown shoes, and a long, deep mocha-colored trench coat that clings to him in all the right places. When he runs his hand through his mass of curls making them even more unruly, the look is complete. For a moment, I wonder if I should give up on Toby and go for Oscar instead.

Stepping next to Oscar, Baihe is a vision in a red traditional Chinese dress. Slits up the sides flap around her legs exposing her thighs with every step. Her hair is pulled into a stylish knot, and the only thing out of place with her ensemble is Dad's coat sitting on her shoulders. The old, rust-colored puffy coat hangs nearly to her knees. But she still looks amazing and garners a few head turns as she and Oscar enter the soiree.

I lean against the car, watching, and wrap my arms over my chest. Music thumps, reverberating off the rocky bluffs and across the river basin. There's probably two hundred people milling around, drinking, dancing, standing off to the side chatting. I scan the crowd looking for Toby. *Maybe he didn't come*, I think as my heart forces me to study every guy I see.

After a few moments of scanning for my hot crush, I find him. Seeing his hair, black as the night sky on a new moon, swaying in rhythm with The Weeknd's *Blinding Lights* makes my heart skip a beat. There he is. And he's dancing. I didn't know Toby Chan liked to dance. I've never cared for dancing, but Toby might change my mind.

As I step away from the car, I stand up straighter and adjust my dress. Yes, Baihe convinced me to dress up for Homecoming, but only a little bit. I'm wearing a sapphire blue dress I got at the thrift store a few years ago. There are little trails of red roses along the long sleeves, and the full skirt brushes against my knees. I shiver, but not because of the cold. I'm prepared for that wearing my winter long underwear under the dress. Sure, the monochromatic purple stripes don't go with my dress or Mom's old insulated winter boots that I snagged, but I was going for comfort, not style.

Toby bobs in time with someone else. I can't see who it is through the crowd. With every step closer to him, I feel lighter and heavier at the same time.

The music changes into a slow 90s ballad, and all the other dancers on the floor pair off. Arms wrap over shoulders and around waists as the crowd moves like a wave in the ocean to the music. I push past a couple whose hands are roaming all over each other and catch sight of Toby's date.

Holy shitballs! "What the—"

My potential curse rant is stopped short by someone who grabs my arm and spins me around. I trip on Mom's clunky boots and stagger, latching onto thick arms to keep from falling. Unfortunately, those thick arms are connected to a smiling Jason Hancock. He must see the murder in my eyes because he places his finger over my lips and says, "Don't say anything you might regret."

My first thought is to bite his finger, that jackass. Instead, I purse my lips and swallow my hatred for him and now for Zel too.

"How could she?" I rage whisper. "She knows I like Toby."

"Do you honestly want my opinion?" he asks. Couples swirl around us, the music driving them to see nothing but the person in their arms.

"No!" I spit. Like, really. I'm so pissed off that when I speak, trails of spit are spraying out like a water sprinkler on high. "You don't know anything about this." I wave my hands toward Zel and Toby. What infuriates me most is that they don't notice me. Not at all. Not one bit. And, holy shitballs again, she's laughing at something he said, shaking her long hair so that it floats seductively over her shoulders. Her shoulders that are covered in a suit jacket the exact same color as his pants.

Jason's grip on my arms tightens. "Down, Kaysee," he gently commands.

"Don't talk to me like I'm a dog!" I shake out of the prison of his arms and take two big strides toward my crush and my ex-best friend.

"Stop!" Jason full-on grabs my waist, lifts me up, and places me back where I'd been standing. "What are you going to do? Scream at Zel? Make a scene? Punch her in the face? Actually, I might like to see a full-on girl fight." He lets go and gives me a little shove in their direction as a mischievous smile plays across his lips.

I stop myself short, watching Toby and Zel spin. As she turns, she catches my eyes. I freeze. My heart aches seeing her in his arms. Her wide eyes look guilty as hell as she stumbles. Of course, she's wearing strappy high-heeled shoes. Jason was right. She's going to freeze, or maybe even break an ankle.

As much as I hate her footwear and the guilty look she wears, what I hate most is that she doesn't exude an ounce of remorse. Not one bit. Before a tear can pour from my eyes, Jason has his hands on me again. This time he's gentle, comforting. I don't protest when he lifts my hands to his shoulders and rests his on my waist. I'm not exactly moving in time to the music, but my body responds to the slow rhythm and love-angst of the squealing guitar.

I'm so totally pissed. But I'm also embarrassed, horrified, and hurt. Zel really did it this time. And she obviously doesn't even care how I feel.

Leaning in, Jason whispers into my hair. "See, we'll dance together and make Toby so jealous he'll be begging you for a date within a week."

I scoff. "That sounds like every plot to every teen movie on Netflix."

"Every one?" he asks, scrunching up his eyes as he thinks. "It must be effective then, right?"

After finishing rolling them, my eyes land on Jason. In the soft light, a smile lifts his lips. His dark, wavy hair grazes his eyebrows. I swallow thoughts I don't want to think and turn my gaze back to Zel and Toby.

"Nope," Jason takes my chin and pulls my face back to his, but this time he's leaning in closer. Too close, in fact. "They won't believe it if we don't sell it." The scent of laundry soap and breath mints fills the small space separating us. I bite my lip and hold his gaze. I hadn't noticed before that he has a cluster of freckles below his left eye. They remind me of a Jackson Pollock painting.

The moment the song switches to BTS's K-Pop some girls shriek with delight. The spell is broken. I step away from Jason and turn to Zel. To my surprise, she's striding toward me, dragging Toby behind her by the hand. She looks ready for a fight. Toby looks like he's scared she actually will kick my ass.

"I thought you weren't coming," Zel snaps.

"I never said that." I step closer lowering my voice. We've caught some people's attention. As much as I wanted people to see me this year, to be bold, having a catfight at Homecoming isn't what I had in mind.

"Yes, you did. At the mall." Zel yells. "Now you're here trying to ruin *my* Homecoming."

"Whatever," I turn my back on her. Who does she think she is? I've known for years that she wanted to control the world, but seriously? Where does she get off trying to control me too?

"He asked me two weeks ago," Zel continues. Her voice is rising, bouncing off the boulders along with BTS singing *Dynamite*. It's like the music is fueling Zel. "I knew you'd be mad. That's why I didn't tell you. I was thinking of *you*, Kaysee."

"Bull. Shit!" I turn on her. "When have you ever thought of me? When?"

"I think of you all the time," Zel withers slightly.

"You could have said no," I say nodding at Toby. As Zel has puffed up with indignation, Toby has collapsed inward. His shoulders droop, and he doesn't notice when his suit jacket falls off Zel's shoulders. Zel stares at me, her mouth shaping words that don't come out. She looks like a fish out of water. "You could have said no," I repeat and turn away again.

"Go ahead and run away," Zel says, her initial fervor dwindling. "Hide somewhere. That's all you've done this year anyway. Ditch me for those weird exchange students again, why don't you? And take all your lies and secrets with you."

Her voice fades as I walk away. I contemplate flipping her the bird, but it wouldn't do any good. She's right. I have been hiding.

Keeping secrets. The truth settles in and sparks my vamp rage. It courses through my arms, my legs, vibrating with my slow heartbeat. It feels like a thousand soldiers fighting against my veins.

Zel's right. Toby wasn't interested in me. I was an idiot to think he ever would be. Rage overpowers me. I can't catch my breath and have to stop next to a truck. Resting my hand against its tailgate, I force myself to breathe in and out. I'd rather just stop breathing and run a hundred miles. I'm so angry and humiliated and a million other emotions too.

"Kaysee, love," Oscar is at my side, his hand on my shoulder. "Are you okay?"

"No!" I snap, leaving a dent in the truck with my pounding fist.

"We can go home," Oscar says. "I'll gather Baihe."

"Don't," I grab his arm stopping him. "Look at her, she's having a blast." Across the muddy grass, Baihe is shaking her tiny hips to Dua Lipa. A cluster of guys and girls dance around her, all smiling with joy.

"Kaysee?" Jason steps between some cars. "You okay?"

"No!" I repeat. "Oscar, go on back to the party. I'm just going to wait in the car." Like I did the last time I came to the Bluffs. He must feel the bitterness I'm oozing because he doesn't move an inch. "Really, just go."

"I can give her a ride home," Jason offers with a smile. "This shindig is pretty lame anyway. Kaysee and Zel already provided the only worthwhile entertainment."

"Are you okay with that, love?" Oscar's gaze passes with caution between me and Jason.

"Fine, it's fine. Okay." I sigh and turn to Jason. "So, where'd you park?"

"This way," he nods, and I follow. We step through the rutted earth in silence. His hands are shoved into his jeans pockets. They're nice jeans, not ripped or wrinkled. He has a thin winter coat zipped up to his chin hiding anything he's wearing underneath. Like me, he's wearing heavy boots.

"I'm up here by the road," he says pointing ahead. The final leaves of autumn drift down from the trees, floating around us in colors of bright yellow and fiery orange. Breaking through the trees comes a lonely pair of headlights down the highway and around the curve toward the bridge.

Lights flash on a well-worn, scratched, and dented green truck when Jason presses a button on the fob in his hand. I slip into the front seat and pull the seatbelt over my shoulder. My blood is still pounding with rage spreading like a sickness through every cell of my body.

"So," Jason says with a dramatic sigh. "That was—well, it was something."

"Everything sucks. Zel sucks. Toby sucks. Homecoming *really* sucks. And being a—" I stop myself from saying vampire. "Being with you sucks. You suck too."

"Me? What did I do?"

"It's just your general nature. You suck. Since sixth grade, you've always sucked. You still suck today."

"Seeing how upset you are, I'll let that one slide for now."

We bump the short distance to the highway, Jason's truck handling the uneven ground much better than Mom's car did. Or Zel's. "See that's the problem with Zel," I rant. "She's everywhere. Next door. In school. She's been my best friend for years, so there's not much that happens in my life without her. Now, she's being such a jerk, I just want to punch her gorgeous face."

Jason laughs. "Please do. She's too pretty anyway. Plus, if you sell tickets, you'll make so much money that you won't need that art scholarship."

"How do you know about the art scholarship?" I sit straighter.

"You and Zel talk a lot," he shrugs. "I can't exactly mute your chatter."

"Eavesdropping, huh?" I slouch back against the seat. "Now I want to punch you."

"You want to punch me?" he smirks.

"Yes, one hundred percent. You suck, like Zel. You both deserve to be punched."

"Wow, this hostility. I didn't know you had it in you," Jason smacks his lips like he's thinking. "There's only one cure I know of for an angry Kaysee." He signals and turns off the highway.

"This isn't the way home, Hancock."

"Just trust me," he shrugs.

"Yeah, famous last words of every serial killer ever," I huff.

"Seriously, trust me. I know a thing or two about wanting to punch the lights out of something." His voice rings with a level of honesty I didn't expect. An honesty that I didn't know he had. Intrigued, I settle back and focus on my breathing as street lights pass creating a calming rhythm. But it's not working. Not at all. I feel like I'm about to jump out of my own skin when he finally pulls off the road and into a parking lot.

17
BUNCHES OF PUNCHES

"Punch it," Jason stands in the corner of a well-used 24-hour gym next to a blue punching bag. The aroma of sour sweat leaves me cringing and grateful that I have on my mask to filter out some of the smell.

"Give me your hand." He holds his palm out and I reluctantly rest my hand on his.

My heartbeat hasn't stilled, it thumps against the inside of my skull, but touching Jason's hand sends a sizzle up my arm. I'm trying to decipher the meaning of the sizzle when Jason begins his lesson.

"Curl your fingers, but keep your thumb wrapped outside your fingers and keep your wrist straight," he folds my hand into the correct position. "Thumb wrapped, not inside your fingers, so you don't break it when you hit. Same thing with the straight wrist."

"Got it," I lift my clenched fists for him to approve.

"You don't have gloves on, so go easy at first." Jason steps to the side, leaving me to face the punching bag. I focus on a small crack in the blue vinyl and let my fist fly. When my knuckles make contact, a vibration shoots up to my shoulder. The bag swings from its hook, its movement mockingly slow and unaffected by my rage. I'd intended to knock it across the gym.

"Whoa, Rocky, take it down a notch," Jason stands behind the bag and holds it steady. "Not so hard this time. Find your spot. Focus. And go. Try again."

Taking in a deep breath, I find the crack on the bag again and punch, this time with less vehemence. My fist makes contact with a solid thud. Jason holds the bag to keep it from swinging and shifts backward with the force of my punch. His eyes find mine. They crinkle with a smile. "Again."

I don't think most people smile when they attack a punching bag with the force of a raging PMS hurricane, but I do. I grin like a drunk and I laugh with glee when I knock Jason off center. All my frustrations and disappointments, my pain at having my world stolen from me by Damn It Doug, all of it flows out of me and into that bag.

"Okay, stop a minute," Jason says out of breath. "Let me see your hands."

"They're fine," I reply, running my fingers through my hair hoping that I hide my skinned knuckles. I could feel the flesh slowly peeling off them with each hit. It wasn't completely gone, or there'd be blood streaks on the bag. I just need a few minutes for my vamp powers to work and heal them.

"No, really, this bag can be murder on knuckles. The first time I came here, I didn't use gloves either. A lady at the front desk insisted on bandaging my hands because I was leaving drips of blood everywhere."

"Geez, what made you so mad?" I ask deflecting again as I stretch my arms behind my back. "Some guy on the football team tick you off?"

"No," he shakes his head, and even though his face is masked, I can tell his smile has disappeared.

"Okay, then I know, jilted by a girl?" I playfully slap him on the shoulder. Holy frijoles, he's solid as a slab of rock. I shouldn't be surprised by this. I've seen him working out in his garage lots of times...usually without a shirt.

"It was my mom," he whispers, his voice nearly lost amidst the clanking of weights from two beefy guys in the free-weight area.

"Your mom?" I ask surprised by his stoicism. I don't like it. Seeing him like this makes me realize that I've grown to really like playful Jason and his smirks. I need to lighten the mood. "What did she do? Take your phone away?"

He doesn't respond right away, as though he's debating something with himself. With a sigh, he meets my gaze, looking deep into my eyes. His scrutiny unsettles me, so I give another quick jab at the bag. The force barely affects him, but it pulls him out of his head.

"She died." The sadness on his face invades his shoulders making them droop as his eyes fall to the floor. He looks so, well, so broken. This is not the Jason I know. The Jason I know is the one always tossing insults with a smile. The one who never talks about his family. And realization hits me.

"I'm sorry," I say feeling totally lame because what else are you supposed to say? A dismissive smile passes over his face in return. "I don't remember hearing about this. When did it happen?"

"It was just before you moved here," he shrugs and shakes himself off. After brushing his hand across his face, the mischievous smile returns to his eyes, which I notice for the first time are the color of milk chocolate. "It's nothing. Long time ago now. It was just hard because it took so long. Cancer."

"Hey," I say resting my hand on his shoulder. "It still sucks, no matter how long ago it was. You want to take a few hits on the bag? I'm learning that punching something really hard makes you feel a lot better about sucky things." I drop my hand noticing that the skin on my knuckles is still red, but it's mostly healed already.

"Yeah, that's a good idea. You might want to step back a little, I'm going to bring some heat." And Jason is back, the Jason I know. Joking. Smiling. And when he slugs the punching bag, it sways on its chain much more than it did from my measly hits. Jason dances around the bag goofing off pretending to be a boxer, but when he punches, he throws his full force into the hits. It's hard not to appreciate how his muscles fight against the constraints of his thermal shirt. I shouldn't be surprised. He's a football player or was one before his knee was blown out. I hear his brothers were big in sports too. They're older, so I've never met them. But everyone talks about the three Hancock boys as if they're Olympic-level athletes.

Taking turns, we throw punches at the bag until we're both sweating, panting, and our knuckles are red and speckled with tiny purple bruises. We ditched our masks since no one else was in our corner of the gym. They were getting sweaty, and it was harder to breathe through them as our punches grew in force and speed.

I slump onto a bench next to the wall. All my rage is gone leaving me feeling drained. I'm so tired I couldn't care one bit about Zel and her drama. Even thinking about Toby doesn't make my heart hitch. I'm totally spent.

"Next time, we bring gloves," I say.

Jason drops onto the bench next to me, his chest rising and falling quickly as he catches his breath. He holds up his hand to display his raw knuckles. "I agree. To the gloves and to a next time."

When he turns to face me, I can feel the air between us. It's thick, crackling with a surprising anticipation. My energy returns the instant our eyes lock. I hadn't ever noticed just how thick his eyelashes are, and now it's all I can think about. Jason. Eyelashes dark as espresso. A thin scar by the edge of his lip.

He shifts, leaning closer, his lips nearing mine. And I freak out and fly from my seat so fast I trip on a seam on the foam mats covering the boxing area. "I should get home," I say way too loudly and catch myself before I plummet to the floor. The weightlifting guys look our way, one of them pulling out an earbud and cocking his head in our direction.

"Sorry," I say waving and tromping in Mom's boots for the door. Fresh fall air greets me outside. I let its coolness waft over and through me and wait for Jason next to his truck. Stretching my arms, I enjoy the soreness from our workout. It takes Jason longer than I expect to find me. He doesn't make any excuses, just unlocks the truck doors with his fob and climbs in the driver's seat.

The night envelopes us in darkness and silence as Jason guides his truck toward our neighborhood. Turning off the main road he breaks our silence. "I'm glad the punching helped."

"Yeah, thanks for taking me." I struggle for words. The space separating us isn't filled with electricity now. Instead, it's more of an awkward swirl of regret and mystification.

"Thanks for what you said about my mom," he replies turning onto my street. "I don't like talking about her cancer much, but that's why I want to go to medical school."

Like the punching bag, I'm hit with a surprising force. "What? Medical school?" I ask aghast. I hadn't thought much about what Jason would do for a career, but I always assumed he'd aspire to the level of a used car salesman, not a doctor.

"I know, it sounds ridiculous," he shrinks into his seat and guides his truck up to the curb in front of my house. "It's just that I saw how hard the docs worked with my mom. But there was this one doc who was a total jerk about things. He had no empathy. Like he's never met someone with cancer before. And he's a cancer doctor. I remember meeting him and thinking that I could do better than him."

"That—that's terrible," I say.

"Exactly," Jason turns to face me. "The next doctor was amazing, the kind of doctor I think I could be."

"Wow, I'm shocked," I say with a smile.

"I know, I know," he shakes his head. "No one thinks I can do it. Even my dad keeps telling me to do something easier like become an athletic trainer."

"No, that's not what shocks me," I say. "I think you could be a doctor if you really want it and work your ass off for it. What shocks me is discovering that Jason Hancock has a heart." I punch his arm, making him smile.

"Yeah," he laughs. "Don't tell anyone."

"Your secret is safe with me," I say and slip out of the car before the electric crackles return because I can seriously feel them building. Jason sits in his car and only drives off after I've opened my front door with my keys.

Before stepping inside, I scan my knuckles. Small rosy patches are all that's left. This vampire healing stuff is pretty freaking amazing. I step inside cautiously trying not to wake anyone up. The dash clock in Jason's truck had said it was almost 1:00 a.m. I'm greeted by the soft flicker of the TV in the living room. Oscar and Baihe are lounging on the couch. She has a blanket pulled up over her Homecoming dress, obviously asleep because she doesn't move when I come in.

"You're home late, love," Oscar says as I sit next to him on the couch.

"Yep," I say, motioning to the tv. "What are we watching tonight?" Onscreen, people in drab period clothes saunter down a dirty industrial street.

"The BBC at its best, *North and South*," Oscar says pausing the show.

"You don't have to turn it off," I say. "Don't let me interrupt, I can catch up."

"I need an interruption," Oscar says and stretches his arms over his head. No longer wearing his dapper Homecoming outfit, the t-shirt shifts with his movement revealing his trim, muscular arms. They aren't quite like Jason's. Oscar's are leaner and less bulky. And, what in the world? I'm comparing hot guys' arms now. This is something new. Another element of lunacy to add to my vampire repertoire.

Studying my expression, which is wide-eyed with my mouth ever so slightly hanging open, Oscar drops his arms. "What thoughts are running through your head tonight?"

"Arms," I blurt. "No, that sounds stupid. It's just your arms are nice, I was thinking. And my arms kinda hurt."

Shifting to face me directly, a flash of concern covers Oscar's handsome face. "Did something happen, love? Do I need to, as you Americans say, open up a can of ass whoop?" He flashes his vampire teeth menacingly.

"No!" I yell, making Baihe stir. "No, nothing like that. I left Homecoming with Jason, and he took me to a gym where we punched a bag."

"That sounds mildly exciting." Oscar relaxes back into the plush sofa.

"How was Homecoming after Zel's drama?" Asking the question, I'm hesitant to hear the answer. In my mind, I'm imagining Zel and Toby in each other's arms, dancing and kissing all night long.

"Doug showed up," Oscar replies with a side glance.

"Oh, damn, what did he do?"

"Oh, he was up to his usual bag of tricks, chasing girls who didn't want to be chased and such," Oscar pauses and I know that Damn It Doug did something Oscar doesn't approve of. Every time Oscar talks about Doug with a sigh or a pause, I know he's building up to something catastrophic. "Doug is such a knob. He showed up with a friend," Oscar uses air quotes. "Together they caused quite a kerfuffle. If the dance hadn't broken up because someone said they heard the police were on their way, I truly believe Doug might have had his nose rearranged...again."

"Crazy," I cringe. "Not surprising, but crazy."

"Yes, dear. And you should know that the bloke who tagged along with Doug was another vampire."

"Here? In Inman? I thought we were the only ones."

"We were," Oscar sighs. "But Damn It Doug has a few friends who occasionally show up."

"Like in Cleveland?" I know I shouldn't ask this, but curiosity has been killing me.

"We do not speak of Cleveland. But yes. This was one of Doug's associates from Cleveland. His name is Jeff."

I snort with a laugh. "Jeff the evil vampire?"

"Yes," Oscar emphasizes the word. "Absolutely, Jeff the evil vampire. He's not too bad in the grand scheme of things, but he is certainly someone not to trifle with."

"I get it. Damn It Doug is running around with Evil Jeff," I say still smiling because the whole thing sounds like an early reader book for kindergartners. Damn It Doug and Evil Jeff are on a race. Stay out of their way or they'll eat your face.

"Kaysee, this is serious," Oscar pulls me back from my frivolous thoughts. "You need to be cautious. No one knows you're a vampire, and that's a good thing. You might have noticed that we are not what most people imagine when they think of vampires. We've already tried being blood-thirsty killers, and we don't want that anymore. But we're definitely not the norm, my dear. If you see anyone odd, do tell me as quickly as you can."

"Okay, I will," I say, all silliness dissolved. Glancing at the drape-covered front window, I'm now imagining Evil Jeff lurking in the shadows outside. "These evil vampires wouldn't do anything bad to my family would they?"

"It's not likely, but one can never tell," Oscar runs his hand through his wild hair. "But they might have a grudge against me and Baihe."

"Cleveland?" I ask.

Oscar nods. "Cleveland." He turns off the TV and heads for the stairs. "Good night, love. Sweet dreams."

"'Night," I reply and add. "Sweet dreams of killer vampires."

18

VAMPIRE CONFESSION

Over the next few weeks, the weather changes from cold to hot then back to cold again. It reflects the mood in our house where Damn It Doug has been pushing limits every chance he gets. We expected him to eat all the chips and cookies in the pantry. We didn't expect him to suck his way through 27 blood bags in two weeks. We still have 64 bags left, but he made a big dent in our supply.

On Monday, I had to stop him from persuading Mr. Kent, the math teacher. I only caught him because I forgot my water bottle in class and had to go back at lunch to get it. There I found Damn It Doug standing over Mr. Kent, who was staring blank-eyed at his computer. Doug was whispering into his ear as Mr. Kent typed on his keyboard. I grabbed Doug by the arm and pulled him out of the classroom. He ran off and cut the rest of classes that day, but when he dragged himself home, Oscar was waiting. They holed up in Doug's room again to shout at each other. Oscar emerged from the argument, took a blood bag to his room, and didn't come out until the next day.

Yesterday, Baihe let it slip that Doug's been doing a lot more that I don't know about. "He goes through phases," she'd said with a shrug before Oscar joined us at lunch. The two of them are being very tight-lipped, and I don't like it at all. But I've learned that I need to let things cool down for a bit before Oscar will be willing to divulge much of anything.

"Why do you even keep Doug around if he's so much trouble?" I cornered Baihe before her kung-fu class. She's been taking classes at the rec center for a few weeks.

She lifted her bag on her shoulder and replied in her matter-of-fact manner. "He makes the documents on the computer. Without him, we wouldn't have a way to move around freely. No one can go anywhere these days without a passport or driver's license. Plus, he's kind of like that stray puppy you feed once who keeps coming back. After a while, he just belongs to you."

And, so it's Friday now. Outside, dark clouds roll across the sky as rain pelts the windows of the chem lab. The glare from the fluorescent lights cuts into my head leaving pain streaking beneath my skull, the beginning of a migraine for sure. After sitting down at our empty lab table, I take a quick swing of vamp juice. I'd skipped it at breakfast and rage is starting to build.

Rage at Doug.

Rage at the stupid lights.

Rage at everything basically.

"I can't believe the heaters are broken again," Toby says dropping his backpack on Jason's empty stool. He shoots me a sheepish look. We've barely talked since Homecoming. Not that I wanted to anyway. What am I supposed to say? *Hey, Toby, so Homecoming was even more embarrassing than dousing you in soda, but we don't need to be awkward about it, right?*

But I can't keep my eyes off him and his heavy sweater, one that an old man would wear, but on Toby, it somehow looks charming. The beige, knitted sweater buttoned up to his throat highlights the rich caramel undertones of his skin. Visions of caramel frappuccinos dance through my head. But thinking of coffee drinks makes me think of drinking. That makes my mind ponder what's throbbing under that sweater buttoned around Toby's neck. Would his blood taste sweet too?

"Kaysee, are you okay?" Toby eyes me as he sits.

"Sweater!" I blurt way too loud and hella awkward. "I mean, I like your sweater. That's what I was thinking, why I wasn't talking. Your sweater. It's nice, and cool I guess."

To my utter and complete surprise, Toby Chan laughs at me, and not in the way you laugh at someone who just squirted chocolate milk out their nose. He laughs at me like I'm amusing in a cute way, the way guys always laugh at Zel. For the second time in two minutes, I'm struck silent.

"Zel said you were always making odd jokes," Toby says laying out his chem book and notebook.

"Zel?" I ask. It's odd to talk about her with Toby. It wouldn't have been a few weeks ago, but after the Homecoming drama fiasco, I feel my heart sink hearing Toby speak her name.

"Yeah, Zel," he says. "She told me some stuff at Homecoming."

"Oh."

"Actually, have you heard from her? I keep texting her but she's disappeared." His eyes tighten ever so slightly as he speaks. Like someone just told him he couldn't keep the cute puppy he found. I feel sad for him. Of course, I'm still pissed that he took Zel to Homecoming, more so that she actually went with him. The level of her betrayal is still hard to believe. But the poor guy has probably never experienced Zel's wrath. It makes me feel bad for him.

I shrug hoping it looks nonchalant. "Zel just does that," I say. "She's hot and cold. When we were in middle school, Abuelita told me she had such a fiery personality because Zel's mom ate too much spicy food when she was pregnant with her."

"Abuelita," Toby chortles. "Zel told me about her too."

"Toby," I say reaching my hand across the table to rest it on his. "Zel just does this. It's part of the package. She's fiery. Not everyone can handle that."

His fingers shift beneath mine, but he doesn't pull his hand away. A tiny sizzle tickles my skin where it touches his. What's surprising is how subtle the burn is. It doesn't flame and devour but ripples with warmth. I embrace it. It's the first time I've made physical contact with Toby like this. Having our shoulders crash together after I doused him in cola doesn't count. And the happy tingles erase thoughts of him and Zel at Homecoming.

"Thanks, Kaysee," Toby says before slipping his hand away to open his notebook. We work through the lab assignment chatting about silly things. His grandmother, who is a germophobe hasn't handled this pandemic well at all. How my parents are virtually mad scientists. I leave out the parts about them making blood substitute products for vampires. I'd hate to scare the guy when I've just gotten his attention.

Neither Zel nor Jason show for class and I'm in heaven. Just me, Toby, and a bunch of chemistry stuff. I bump into him and make skin-to-skin contact four more times. Yes, I counted each one. This forty-five minutes of chemistry class has been the best forty-five minutes of junior year, by far.

Later, when I get home from school, I find Zel waiting in my driveway, I worry that the day is about to take a 180. Even Baihe hovers by the front door as Zel approaches me. But I refuse to let her steal my joy again.

"Hey," Zel says with a half-smile. Her hands are in her pockets making her look demure, the opposite of the raging Homecoming monster she'd been before.

"Hey," I reply leaving the single word to hang in the air.

Zel sighs and blows out a puff of air. "Look, I was a bitch."

"Yeah, you were."

"Come on, I'm trying to apologize here," Zel huffs. "So, yeah, I'm sorry. You've just been so weird lately. And there you were dancing with Jason."

That worked? I think so loudly the words nearly escape my mouth. What surprises me more is my next thought, that I can't wait to tell Jason. What the hell? I must need more vamp juice.

"Anyway," Zel continues. "I just hate how things have been. I've even ghosted Toby until we could talk. All day, I've been at the restaurant and kept thinking about what an ass I was. God, I do this all the time, don't I?"

"Yeah, you do," I say with a smile.

"Don't rub it in," Zel says pulling her hands out to wrap her arms over her chest. "Look, it's freezing out here. Can we go in your house to talk? Jasmine is doing everything she can to ruin my life right now. She'll be hanging around eavesdropping."

"Sure, but first," I set my backpack down and hold my arms open. Back in seventh grade, we went through a rough patch. Zel's parents had just opened the restaurant and were never around. Abuelita was there, forcing us to hug after every fight. Zel steps into my arms, her head resting on my less-than-formidable cleavage and her arms wrapping around me. We stand silently just holding each other and releasing the hurts we've caused. In the quiet, my stomach rolls and I know what I have to do.

"Come on in," I release Zel, retrieve my backpack, and head for the front door. "You know how I've been weird lately? Well, I have something to show you."

Zel and I drop brief hellos to my parents who are huddled in the kitchen with Oscar. I don't let their concerned faces bother me as I lead Zel to my room and close the door.

"Sit down," I say pointing to my desk chair as I plop on my bed. Pablo is waiting for me, giving me a typical disappointed cat face. When I rub his chin, the disappointment fades into a purr.

"I tried to tell you this before, but it didn't come out right," I start, measuring my words, trying to find the best way to come out to my best friend that I'm a blood-thirsty vampire. "Things have been weird this year. I know I've been off."

"You told me it's the skin thing. I get that," Zel says morphing into a supportive friend. She must be really sorry for blowing up at me. Or she's embarrassed. It's hard to tell with Zel.

"It's more than that, Zel." My hands drift to my mouth as though my body is trying to stop me from saying the words. If I do, Zel has the power to destroy everything, including me. But I carry on. "You didn't believe me before, but I really am a vampire." I smile and flash my sharpened teeth.

"Not this again," Zel sighs and stands.

"No, really, look," I smile broadly, fully displaying my sharp teeth, and lean deep into her personal space for her to see.

"Kaysee, this is stupid. Why are you doing this?"

"It's not stupid. It's real. I was bit by a vampire. Now I'm a vampire. Look at my teeth. Remember the sun allergy thing? And do you wanna guess what's in those protein drinks I always have with me?" I'm standing now, blocking her exit.

After performing the single largest overly dramatic sigh in the history of mankind, Zel squints at my teeth.

"Really?" she asks, obviously not convinced. Why would she be? She's always believed more in superheroes than the supernatural.

"Yes, really." I point at my deadly canine teeth.

"Fine," Zel pulls out her phone, unlocks it, and snaps a picture of me before I can stop her. "But I'm going to prove to you that this is not real. I'll show you, your teeth are like those crazy people, like *Vampire Diaries* fanatics who get their teeth sharpened. You can't be a vampire."

"But I am!" I'm shrieking in frustration.

"But you're not!" Zel pushes past me and stomps for the stairs. "I should have known. You've fallen too far off the rails. You're making things up. Why?"

I'm on her heels trying to grab her arm. "Zel, stop. I'm not lying. I promise."

She rounds on me, her eyes flashing with both hurt and anger. "Just cut it out, Kaysee. I'm your friend, or at least I thought I was. I thought we could apologize and move on, but you won't give up on this vampire nonsense." At that I catch my parents' and Oscar's heads pop up and turn our way. I didn't want them to know I'd told Zel. This whole thing is backfiring. Part of me wonders why it even matters if Zel believes me or not. But deep inside, I know I need someone else in the world to share this with.

"Fine! Come here," I grab her arm and drag her to the kitchen where I yank open the refrigerator door and pull out a blood bag from the top shelf. "You don't believe me? Then watch this." I tear off the top enclosure and start sucking on the blood. It tastes very salty with a hint of taco seasoning. Gross. But I keep gulping, my free hand raised begging Zel to question me again.

"Are you done yet?" Zel taps her foot where she stands like a statue next to Oscar.

"I'm literally drinking a bag of human blood in front of you, and you still don't believe I'm a vampire?"

"Oh, honey," Mom butts in. "Don't be silly. Zel didn't think you were a vampire." She laughs pathetically.

"You're right, Dr. Fehr, I didn't think she was a vampire. And I still don't. That's just some of that juice stuff you drink all the time. And, having it in a novelty blood bag is just disgusting. Did Doug put it in there?"

"Are you kidding me?" I spew, a spray of blood exploding from my mouth. "You are so damn stubborn."

"Perhaps I can be of assistance here," Oscar says stepping to Zel.

"She's lying," Zel replies.

"No, she's not," Oscar responds, his voice calm and matter-of-fact. "She's a vampire. And every vampire needs to have someone they can share their secret with. For Kaysee, that's you. With your close friendship, I'm surprised she didn't tell you sooner."

A series of grunts and pfts escape from Zel expressing her utter disbelief.

Oscar steps closer, his chin dropping and his eyes unblinking. I'd hoped it wouldn't come to this, but sometimes his persuasion is the best cure. "She's a vampire. I'm a vampire. We're both vampires."

Zel is mesmerized but still unbelieving. "What about Kaysee's parents?"

There's a smile in Oscar's voice now. "No, they're not vampires. They're helping us, but they're not vampires."

"But you are?" Zel asks, the tension on her face relaxing.

"Yes," Oscar replies with a nod.

"Baihe?"

"Her too," Oscar says.

"Doug?"

"Yes."

Zel shrugs as realization takes hold. "That one makes sense. He's a weird dude."

"He's the reason I'm a vampire," I interrupt. "I shouldn't be but there was an accident."

Zel turns to me, looking closer at the blood bag and my blood-stained teeth. "Holy. Shit," she draws out her exclamation. Eyes sparkling, she closes in on me. "You're a vampire. Oh my god, I have so many questions."

Instantly, we're twelve years old again. I'm feeling good after downing an entire bag of blood, a little guilty and disgusted but physically my body is rejoicing. Zel is like a kid in a candy store. At one point, Baihe sneaks through the room but disappears when she notices the rapidity Zel is peppering me and Oscar with questions.

And I learn a few things, things I hadn't thought to ask about. That whole having to be invited inside if you're a vampire? Totally not a thing. Oscar explained that one witch in the 1500s cast one spell on a vampire guy who was basically stalking her. He couldn't come in her house unless she invited him. Well, that incident spurred the legend. Oscar says that witches used to cause a lot of trouble.

"But now with the internet and modern science, their tricks aren't so fascinating," he explains. We're clustered in the living room with one of the *Twilight* movies playing muted on the TV. Zel had turned it on for inspiration. Turns out that a lot of stuff from that movie is totally wrong. "And with social media," Oscar continues, "anyone can do a simple science experiment on TikTok and the world is amazed."

"So, there's no more witches?" I ask.

"Oh, there are some," Oscar takes a handful of popcorn from the oversized bowl on my lap. "But they prefer to stay in the shadows nowadays. And if you ever meet one, definitely get on her good side. I had a mate last century who learned that lesson the hard way."

"What happened?" Zel asks with eyes wide as the moon. I swear she hasn't blinked in an hour.

"Let's just say that after a cocktail from this particular witch, that bloke's cock had a new tale to tell. And it didn't end well." Oscar winks conspiratorially which makes Zel gasp and giggle.

As Bella and Edward live out their sulking teen angst on screen, Oscar continues with tales of his past and run-ins with other vampires. Most are pretty funny. One vampire got drunk then tried to bite into a whole watermelon. When his vampire teeth got stuck in the rind, another drunk vampire thought it'd be a good idea to just split the watermelon with a sword.

"Now between the two of them, they only have three ears," Oscars laughs doubled over.

Oh, that's something else I learn, vampires can heal but aren't like starfish. We can't grow back body parts that have been cut off.

As the second *Twilight* movie starts, Doug traipses through. He's been wearing the same clothes for three days as though he wants to punish us with his odor. He and Oscar are still fighting. Doug listens in for a bit but wanders off to the kitchen then back to his dungeon.

Around midnight, Zel pulls out her phone. "Oh, no. My mom's called like fifteen times." She taps away and drops the phone back down. "I told her I'm staying the night," she says picking through the half-popped corn at the bottom of the bowl.

"I just can't believe all this," she says again with awe.

"Me neither," I snort laugh.

"I'm sorry I was such a terror. I thought this was all about Toby," she settles back into the plush pillows she'd gathered on the couch. "That's the only reason I got him to ask me to Homecoming."

"You tricked him?" I gasp. "That's horrible. I can't believe you did that."

"Yeah," Zel grimaces. "I thought if you saw him with me, you'd be jealous and finally do something. Maybe you'd come up and tell me to back off because you've got the hots for him."

"You thought I'd do that in front of half the school? Do you remember who you're talking to?" I laugh feeling anxious even imagining myself calling Zel out the way she did to me. "Oh, man. I might be a vampire, but you are pure evil."

"And then you were dancing with Jason." Accusation floods her face. "What was up with that?"

"It was his lame idea. Thought it'd make Toby jealous," I reply.

Zel tosses a piece of popcorn at me, and it lands in my hair. "You should have been there with Toby. That guy is so your type. All he wanted to do was talk, talk, talk. Talk about science. Talk about politics. Talk about climate change. Ugh. I'm more interested in a guy who likes to take action."

"Sorry it was so terrible," I say putting the popcorn down on the coffee table and pulling my throw blanket over my chest. With the drop in temps and the teachers whispering about an ice storm, I know winter is definitely upon us.

"I wouldn't say it was terrible," Zel turns her gaze to the TV screen in contemplation. "He was interesting. Like I learned some stuff about solar power versus wind power, but something was just missing."

"Like his tongue down your throat?" I jest. To which I am rewarded with a pillow to the face.

"Hey, now, I only did that with that guy freshman year. And only because Tabitha said I had to try it. What was his name?"

Zel and I talk into the early morning hours. We make up for all the time we've missed when she ghosted me, for which she's appropriately self-deprecating. Like so many times before, I am quick to forgive. We don't talk anymore about Toby or Jason but about pretty much everything else. And I have my friend back. I drift off on the couch as she's telling me something about colleges she's been looking at. And when I wake up in the morning, she's left a note next to a new bottle of vamp juice.

"It's good to have my friend back," she'd written. "Even if she's a murderous vampire now. So, drink up, and don't you even think about eating me. –Z"

19

HOT DINNER WITH NAI NAI

Just when I thought my junior year was a total dumpster fire, all of a sudden Zel and I are getting along better than ever. Doug is keeping his head low. And Baihe is kicking ass in her kung-fu classes, which I've started going to with her.

Best of all, Toby Chan is talking to me. And not in the way that some guys just grunt and nod in a conversation. He's asking me real questions and talking about almost everything. Yeah, some of it is boring video game stuff that I don't understand. I find myself grunting and nodding mindlessly, but I perk up when he talks about his family. His grandmother sounds a lot like Abuelita. Toby calls her Nai Nai, the Mandarin name for his dad's mom.

After I learned that he spoke Mandarin, I begged Baihe to teach me some words and phrases. Of course, I can't pronounce anything right yet, it's those tones! Seriously, Mandarin is HARD. But I've nearly mastered a simple hello and how to say "How are you?"

They're almost exactly the same, but I'm counting every little a win.

The only thing that's strange is how quiet Jason's been in class. All week he's mostly kept his earbuds in and his head in his notebook. But, whatever. That's just Jason, and it means he's not pestering me.

"Hey, Kaysee," Toby says as he approaches our lab table.

"Hey," I reply trying to sound suave while also trying to hide the fact that I'd watched every step he'd taken across the classroom like a cheetah watches a gazelle.

"Did you hear that a bunch of the football guys got sick after some party?" Toby asks.

"Really?" I ask even though everyone's heard about it.

"It was their end-of-the-season party," Jason grumbles as he drops onto his stool.

"Why aren't you quarantined?" I ask Jason.

He puts his earbuds in, "That's not my crowd anymore."

"He's in a mood," I whisper, awkwardly leaning closer to Toby across the lab table. I steal a glance at him remembering the ride home from homecoming when he'd actually acted like a normal human. That Jason disappeared that night. We're now stuck with grumpy Jason.

"Yeah, he said his dad's on him. Something about college," Toby shrugs. "Hey, is Zel going to be here?" *Now, who's awkward*, I think. Toby's words and stance are stiff as he asks me about Zel.

"Um, no, she's quarantining too. One of the cooks at Burgers & Burritos got sick, so they shut down the whole restaurant," I say. "Being stuck at home with her sisters is making her *crazy*."

Now that we're on speaking terms again, Zel regularly blows up my phone with complaints about Ariel and Jasmine.

"That's good. I mean not good for her because of the quarantining, but good for me. For now." Stuttering Toby is instantly my favorite Toby. Something about his hesitance is super hot. Maybe it's the way his glance keeps darting away. Or maybe, it's the way he's come around the table and is standing right next to me. Like, right next to me. His spicy scent is making my knees weak. I just wish I could see his shy smile, but at least with masks on, he can't see my goofball grin. Because I think something is about to happen!!!

"Good for you how?" I ask, feeling like a true seductress for the first time in my life. My heart is fluttering, and my stomach is dancing.

"Well, you and me, we've been talking a lot lately. And that's been, like, really good. I kinda wanted to ask you about something. It's probably good if Zel's not here," he says fiddling with a pen. "I mean, you know Zel. She can get a little excited."

A very unattractive snort-laugh escapes, making my mask flutter.

"So," he continues, dancing around his words. "I was thinking you might like to come have dinner at my house sometime. I mean, usually, I'd ask you out to eat somewhere, but most of the restaurants are only doing takeout right now, so my house could work, right?"

"Yes," I yell as I leap from my stool. Toby jumps back probably remembering the whole cola crotch incident. It doesn't help that a few people in class already have their phones up ready to record another embarrassing incident to share with the world. "I mean, yes, I'd love to," I say in a normal-person kind of voice.

"Cool, give me your phone," he says holding out his hand. "I'll put my number in there and we can work out the deets." I fish my phone out of my pocket, unlock it, and hand it over as the bell rings to start class.

When Toby returns my phone, I go back to my stool and scroll through my contacts to make sure Toby Chan's number is really, truly in my phone. And it is! Excitement to match a Fourth of July celebration explodes over my body. I have to hold myself back from breaking into a celebratory dance.

But a glance at Jason is like a fire hose dousing my fireworks display. He's watching me like someone might watch an animal at the zoo. Not as in, oh this is a fascinating animal specimen. More like, oh, why is that monkey throwing its own poop? What a weirdo.

Whatever. I open my laptop and start typing notes to share with Zel. As class starts, I'm formulating all the comebacks I should be throwing at the stupid look on Jason's face. But I keep them inside because even though Jason revealed he's a real human being, he's also a jerk. And today he's not allowed to ruin the bubbles of elation bouncing through my entire body.

"Don't wear that shirt," Zel's voice comes from my laptop as I hold up another possible outfit for my date with Toby. "It's too formal. This is a date at his house, not a job interview."

"I think it's cute," Baihe grins. She's lying across my bed amidst the piles of rejected clothes. "But it makes you look like a banker."

"That's a 'no' then," I toss the shirt on Baihe's face and am treated to one of her infectious laughs. "Maybe I should wear the black dress." I pick up the long-sleeve dress and hold it up again.

"No!" Zel yells. "You've had that thing since freshman year. I veto the old black dress."

"Ugh," I groan. "This is impossible!" I flop into my chair and Pablo jumps into my lap. He's been giving Baihe the side-eye since she took over my bed. Scratching under his chin sets off a comforting purr that rumbles across my thighs.

"Go back to the green dress," Zel commands over the video chat.

"It's too short," I protest.

"Well, wear leggings," Zel retorts.

"And you'll be sitting at a table to eat, so no one will really see anything, right?" Baihe adds.

"I guess," I admit with reluctance. "The green dress is good, but the neckline is a little low for my taste."

"Then his eyes will be on your boobs and not your vampire teeth," Zel says.

"Good point!" Baihe jumps up and grabs the dress. "Put it on so we can see." She thrusts the dress into my hands and pushes Pablo off my lap. He yowls in protest before slinking out of my bedroom. I slip into the bathroom and pull on the dress.

"It's too much boob," I say returning to Zel and Baihe. "And that sucks because I don't have boobs."

"Stand in front of the camera," Zel says. "I can't see."

I stomp over to display myself to Zel and fidget with the neckline of the dress. Baihe stands next to me, looking at my image in the corner of the computer screen.

"*Hen piaoliang*," Baihe says with dreamy eyes.

"I think it's perfect," Zel nods with approval.

I sigh, not fully on board with this dress. "But my boobs."

"Your boobs are not a problem, Kaysee," Zel replies. "You're so used to hiding yourself under old t-shirts and thrift store jeans that you've forgotten that you are a teen girl and that you do certainly have boobs. Flaunt that rack!"

Still pulling at the neckline, I'm checking to make sure nothing inappropriate will show when Doug steps into the room. "Did I hear boobs?"

"Go away, Doug," Baihe launches a discarded shoe at him.

The thick-soled combat boot hits his stomach, making him groan and bend over. "You were the ones talking about boobs. What's the big deal anyway?" "You were the ones talking about boobs. What's the big deal anyway?"

"Kaysee has a huge date, and you're not helping," Zel yells over the computer.

"Out, Doug," Baihe orders. "Don't you have somewhere else to be?"

"Okay, okay." Doug holds his hands up in defeat. "I actually do have some friends to meet up with."

Baihe closes in on Doug. "You are staying out of trouble, right?"

"Yeah," Doug scoffs.

"Pinky promise, no trouble," Baihe holds out a pinky.

Doug rolls his eyes but links his pinky with Baihe's. "I promise, Mom. No trouble."

With Doug retreating down the stairs, I ask Baihe something I had been wondering. "How old are you anyway?"

Baihe shrugs and scrunches her eyes in contemplation. "I guess I'm 76 now."

"What?" Zel's voice erupts from the computer. "How old were you when you became a vampire?" Now that she's in on the whole vampire secret, Zel has shown random spurts of curiosity about our lifestyle.

"I was sixteen," Baihe says, coming to adjust the dress on me.

"So, how did it happen?" Zel asks.

"No one has asked me that in a long time," Baihe replies. "My father told me many times that even though our culture favored boys because they carried on the family name, that girls carried a place in a father's heart. There was a famine. We were all starving. There was no food, and when my sister died from the hunger, my father became desperate. My two brothers were married and away, so I was the only child left. He cried so much after she died, then he disappeared. Mama worried because she didn't know where he'd gone, just that he was desperate. Two days later, he returned with a strange man. Baba said he only had enough money to pay the man to help me, not him or Mama. The man took me into the house while Mama and Baba waited in the garden."

Baihe shrugs. "So, he was a vampire and bit me and I didn't die like my sister."

"Whoa," Zel says, her eyes wide and glistening.

"I'm so sorry, Baihe," I pull her into a hug.

"It's okay now. Long time ago," Baihe says nonchalantly, but I can see the tension in her eyes.

"What about your parents?" Zel asks.

"Oh, they died too. Everyone was starving. I knew it would happen," Baihe states before turning to me and changing the subject. "Now, we need to practice your Chinese."

I groan as Zel laughs. "Hopefully, she's better at Chinese than she is at Spanish."

Baihe walks me through the few Mandarin phrases she thinks I'll need to know as she adds makeup and curls the ends of my hair. Time moves quicker than I expect, and before I know it, it's almost time for Toby to pick me up. Zel and Baihe decide which jacket I should wear before Zel's battery dies on her laptop and she's disconnected from us.

Walking downstairs to wait for Toby I ask Baihe to remind me of Chinese manners. "Never stick your chopsticks in your rice bowl, lay them across. And be ready to take off your shoes when you come in."

"Baihe, do you think this is all still relevant, the phrases and the etiquette?"

"*Wo de keai*, the Chinese have a 5,000-year history, not much has changed in the last 76."

I am so glad that Baihe coached me. The first thing Toby did when we walked into his house was take off his shoes. He told me I didn't have to, but since I'd painted my toenails for this exact situation, I slipped off my ballet flats and placed them next to his pristine white Nikes.

The one thing Baihe didn't prepare me for was the fact that this wasn't just a dinner between me and Toby. Oh, no. Toby's mom, dad, and Nai Nai are all smiling at me politely over their rice bowls and tiny cups of hot tea. They nod at me as Toby talks about chemistry class and school stuff. I'm so relieved when he avoids the cola crotch incident.

When Toby's mom compliments the color of my dress, I reply with, "*Xie xie.*" I'm rewarded with an approving nod. I drop a few more *xie xies* and some *hao des* throughout the conversation, and everything is going super amazingly awesome. I even catch Toby scooting his chair closer to mine after going to the kitchen to refill the teapot.

Unfortunately, I failed to notice how hot the fresh tea is and take an exuberant sip of the liquid that is roughly the same temperature as the center of the sun. Fighting to keep it together, my whole body cringes in response. My tongue is scalded, and I'm pretty sure that if I look in the mirror right now, it'll be covered in blisters.

"Kaysee, are you okay?" Mr. Chan asks tilting his head.

"Um-hm," I mumble and shovel rice into my mouth as I wait for my vampire abilities to start healing my tongue. I know it's stupid, but as I chew the rice, I'm willing my body to heal because there's maybe a small chance Toby might kiss me tonight. And my tongue might be called into service then. I don't really know. I've never Frenched a guy before. Actually, I've only kissed one guy before, and I found out later that he did that as part of a dare. Pathetic.

"Anyway," Toby draws out the word as he watches my chaos. "So, Nai Nai made all the food tonight with some traditional recipes. I hope you like it."

"Oh, yes," I reply, my tongue still searing with pain. Some hair falls in my eyes, so I push it back as I'm talking, but in my typical clumsiness, I bump my eye and feel something fall in and immediately attach to my eyeball.

Nai Nai gazes at me across the table. She's totally put together with a tidy pink cardigan and her short hair styled to perfection.

"I like the rice," I continue with a new lisp, compliments of my scalded tongue. "I've never had plain rice like this with Chinese food before. Usually, we get Chinese food from a restaurant and it comes with fried rice."

Okay, this is bad. I'm rambling and this thing won't come out of my eye.

"Oh, interesting," Mrs. Chan says in a way that I know she's not interested at all. I need to do whatever I can to bring this back. In my mind, I'm trying to piece together the Mandarin words and phrases Baihe taught me.

I take a deep breath and meet Nai Nai's gaze. "*Wo xihuan chaofun*," I say slightly slurring due to the first-degree burn on my tongue. "With Toby, *wo xihuan chaofun*." My eye is fluttering like I'm winking suggestively at Nai Nai as I use my chopsticks to point between me and Toby. Everyone around the table is frozen, staring at me like I just turned into the Hulk. I stare back trying to piece together what the hell I just said.

Wo—I.

Xihuan—like.

Chaofun—fried rice.

I like fried rice. Baihe taught me how to say "I like." And she taught me how to say "fried rice." I swear that's what I said. I like fried rice. I'd like to eat fried rice with Toby.

"Chan Gang," Nai Nai begins using Toby's Mandarin name. "Perhaps your friend would like a ride home now."

"I'm so sorry, did I say something wrong?" I turn asking Toby who is now sporting a shade of red I've never experienced, not really a blush, more like he's been punched in his whole face.

"What did I say?" Tripping over my scalded tongue, I'm still blinking from the eyelash in my eye. By the silence that follows I know that I've really botched it. I won't need my tongue anymore tonight. Not for kissing nor for talking.

Mrs. Chen clears her throat. "What you said did not mean what you thought," she says. "Translation can be difficult with idioms and such, but you've just informed Nai Nai that you enjoy engaging in sexual intercourse with Chan Gang."

The world stops.

No one moves.

The room is completely silent.

No one will look at me.

And my body is flushing from every pore. There is no way to talk or apologize my way out of this, so I jump up, grab my jacket and shoes, and race outside before I put on either of them. I drop to the first step on the stoop outside Toby's house to slip on my shoes and slide my arms into my jacket. The rush of cold almost-winter air cooling my embarrassment is all I feel until Toby pushes open the door and slams it into my arm.

"Sorry," he mumbles jingling his car keys in his hand. That's the last word I get out of him. On the drive home, we sit silently listening to an NPR music special where a guy plays the cello in a way that sounds like a wailing cat. As the strings screech into my ears, I plan all the ways I can make up for this disaster. And, just how many ways do I come up with? None. Zero. Not one thing can make up for me telling Toby's grandmother that I like having sex with him. I'll never live this down. Never.

As I shut the front door behind me, I find Baihe and Oscar watching more BBC shows, I think that maybe it wasn't so bad. Baihe listens when I tell her what happened but only responds with cringes. At least Oscar tries to make me feel better.

"Buck up, love. I'm sure it wasn't all that bad," he tells me.

But it was that bad. And, as I pull the covers up to my chin and Pablo nestles against my legs, I wish I'd only burned my tongue and then stopped speaking for the rest of my life.

20

THE PATRON SAINT OF VAMPIRES

It's been two days and my tongue still burns. I swear I'm never drinking Chinese tea again. The low-hanging clouds and quickly setting sun reflect my dour mood. I'd made it through my first few classes without anyone saying anything to me, so I'm thinking that Toby didn't share our dinner disaster with anyone. But walking into chemistry class, my whole body is stiff with tension.

Zel is still in quarantine, and only Jason sits at our lab table. His nose is in the chem book so he doesn't notice when I sit across from him. A few minutes after the tardy bell rings, I relax a smidge. Toby isn't in class today. It's like a gift from the gods that I don't have to look him in the eyes.

Jason and I work through the lab experiment with little communication. He seems as depressed as I feel. Part of me is curious why he's down today. But I remind that part of me that I hate Jason and should be celebrating his sadness. And then yet another part remembers his puppy dog eyes when he told me about his mom's death.

As we're cleaning up, there's a ruckus at the back of the room. Some girls hover over a phone squawking. This is exactly the drama that Zel loves, the newest bit of online gossip. Fleetingly, I think I should text her to see what's up, but just as quickly I remember her phone was taken away. She got in a big fight with Jasmine, and her parents said she had to give up her phone for a few days. Being in quarantine has been rough on Zel. She's going stir-crazy, especially since she doesn't have any symptoms. She only has two more days, which I know will stretch on forever without her phone.

Jason races out of class just as the bell rings, his limp more pronounced than normal. Continuing through my day, there's more of a buzz through the halls. It's the same energy everyone has before a big vacation. But Thanksgiving break is still a few days away.

Finishing my day in art class is my favorite. I've found a line for my art piece that weaves throughout the canvas in an abstract, unbalanced manner. I'm planning to use color differentiations to bring the overall picture together.

"Did you see the Insta post?" Maddy asks breezing past me after grabbing a new paintbrush from the supply station. Mrs. Carroll has kept Maddy, Maeve, and I separated because we tend to cause distractions in the typically quiet class. Next to me, Indigo's eyes pop in my direction.

I follow Maddy with my eyes, shaking my head. Is this what everyone is so excited about? Her mask moves as she mouths a response. I swear, these masks are a pain. I glare at her and point to my mask. She rolls her eyes and lifts her paintbrush. In the air, she spells out three letters. Z. E. L.

Oh, no, I think as I whip out my phone. Indigo leans closer trying to see my screen. I pull up Instagram and tap on Zel's page. She hasn't had her phone since Saturday after my date, so I have no idea what she could have posted. But there it is. Posted this morning. It's me. Actually, it's my vampire mouth with my vampire teeth prominently on display. The photo is cropped in so far that you can't see anything more of my face. But, holy hell, my teeth are on full display with the caption "Real vampire in Inman?"

I'm suddenly super, immensely grateful to be wearing a mask. No one can see those same vampire teeth as my jaw gapes open. I put my phone to sleep and drop it in my pocket. I can't focus on my painting now. Damn it! I started this school year so focused. Toby. Win the art contest and get an art school scholarship. But that plan is now a raging dumpster fire. Toby probably never wants to talk to me again, and my hands are shaking too much to hold my brush. If anyone finds out that I'm the vampire in that picture, I have no idea what will happen.

"Nothing is going to happen," Oscar says after I've shown him Zel's picture for the twentieth time.

"You promise? You promise that no one is going to show up on our front lawn with pitchforks and torches ready to kill us all?" I ask talking at warp speed.

"That only happens in the movies," Baihe smiles.

"Happened to me once," Doug chimes in from the pantry. "It was in North Dakota though, like thirty years ago. I doubt they'd do that here."

"See? Even Doug agrees," Baihe says reassuringly as she leans across the kitchen island and clasps my hands.

"Here they'd show up with drones and shotguns," Doug pops his head out of the pantry. "People are real second amendment around this place, and a few shots from a big ass shotgun is nearly as effective as a stake." He shoves a powdered donut into his mouth leaving a white powdered sugar ring around his mouth and sprinkled across his Star Trek t-shirt.

"Don't ever listen to Doug, love," Oscar says with a sigh. His demeanor is calm, but his tight jaw betrays him. "What did Zel say about the picture? Can she take it down?"

"She thinks Jasmine got ahold of her phone, found the picture, and posted it," I say. After an hour on video chat with Zel, we determined this was the most likely scenario. Jasmine is at the mercy of her 13-year-old hormone rages and does stupid stuff like this to Zel all the time. Half of our conversation was Zel planning multiple forms of revenge on her sister. "Her parents still won't give her the phone back until tomorrow, and she forgot her password, so she can't log in on her laptop. She said she'll take it down as soon as she can."

"So, all we can do is wait," Oscar says reaching for a donut from Doug's bag.

Baihe points at my phone. "Are there many comments? Maybe people haven't really seen it." Oh, sweet Baihe. She actually believes what she's saying. Her innocence is endearing.

I tap open the app on my phone, pull up Zel's profile, and suck in a breath. "Baihe, here's some advice for surviving high school. Don't look at the comments. There's over a thousand on Zel's picture."

"This always happens," Doug says with a sneer. "We find a good place to live, we get discovered, then we move away."

"Wait!" I shout. "I'm not moving away. That's my picture, my teeth. But this is my house, my school, my friends. I can't just move away!"

"Calm down, darling," Oscar rests his hand on my shoulder and smiles. "We don't always move away. Sometimes we can stay. Of course, we might need to eat a few people to hide witnesses." He nudges my shoulder to be sure I know he's joking.

My lips pull into a smile at his dark sense of humor. "We're not eating anyone," I say.

"Aw, man," Doug pouts, shoving another donut into his mouth. A ping sounds from Doug's pocket. He pulls out his phone and swipes a few times before bolting for the front door. "I'm going out. Don't wait up," he chuckles slamming the door shut behind him.

"We can just deny it," Baihe shrugs. "It's fake. Everything on the internet is fake right? So is this picture. We make up a story with Zel and say the whole thing is fake. Then we keep our heads low, our masks on, and wait for it to die down."

Her idea sounds like it might work, maybe it will all be okay. But I know the people in this town. They go crazy when a new restaurant opens, so I'm absolutely sure they're going to lose their shit with a rumor of a vampire. I really, really hope Baihe's right and that I'm absolutely wrong.

♥

Damn it. I was right. By the next morning, Zel's picture has officially gone viral. Over 21,000 likes and the comments keep coming. Packing my stuff for school I feel like I'm preparing for battle armed with a mask and two bottles of vamp juice. Once I'm walking the halls of school, things seem normal. The scent of pumpkin spice floats through the air as everyone scuttles down the halls. A zap of electricity crackles around me, a foreshadowing of something really, really bad on the horizon.

And I just can't do this. I make it through my first classes nervously fidgeting with my mask and regularly scanning Zel's pic to see if there's anything identifying there. It's a close-up shot of my mouth. Luckily, I don't have a noticeable scar or wacky teeth that could tip people off.

When it's time to go to chemistry class, I just can't summon the energy to face Jason or Toby. They're perfect reminders of all my failures this year. Instead, I veer toward the girl's bathroom and hunker down in a stall. People come and go until the tardy bell rings and I'm treated to the peaceful silence only interrupted by the faint trickle of water running through the pipes.

Taking out my phone, I unlock it. The picture is there filling my screen again. Wild fantasies float through my mind of being hunted as a vampire. They all end with me burned at the stake, Joan of Arc-style.

"No way," a girl says as she clops into the bathroom with a few other sets of feet.

"Yes, my cousin knows what he's talking about," comes Tabitha's voice in response. Her self-entitled lilt is unmistakable. "He's part of this internet sleuth group, and they copied the picture and blew up the background."

I bite my lip to hold back a multitude of curses as I look at Zel's pic again. There it is. Behind me, there's part of the wall of my room. It's totally out of focus and just looks like a fuzzy wall blob. But I know what's on the wall and how it might bring everything crashing back to me.

"But it's just a blur," another girl says, someone whose voice I can't place. "How can they see anything there?"

"Technology," Tabitha responds, drawing out the word to imply that the other girl is a total idiot.

"Who cares?" the first girl says, her words slurred like she's putting on lip gloss as she speaks. "It's just Zel anyway. That loser will do anything to get attention."

When the trio laughs, my instinct is to burst out of the stall and do something dramatic to stand up for my best friend. She might not be the best best friend in the world, but she's mine, and I'll defend her to the end. My slow heart picks up its pace as I ball my fists.

"You're right," Tabitha says. "She thinks people will like her because of her brother, but she is no Heisman. Oh, he is so hot." She trails off as the bathroom door closes behind her.

Evil bitches. Here I am a bloodthirsty vampire, and these girls are so much more evil than me. I sit on the toilet seat boiling with anger and fear. I'd love to suck those girls dry. But they'd probably taste terrible, like artificial sweetener and spray tan. I take a big swig of vamp juice and collect my thoughts because I might be in some real trouble soon.

♥

"I will kick their *pigu*," Baihe says at lunch after I tell her about the conversation in the bathroom. She sits taller and scans the lunch tables, her eyes squinted with focus.

"No, that's not the point," I say and finish the last drops of my second vamp juice. I'm out for the day, which is reckless on my part. I usually get the vampire jitters in the afternoon. But the thought of eating my PB&J or other food just turns my stomach. It looks like Mom and Dad's vampire blood drink is the only thing that will satisfy me right now.

"I'll still do it," Baihe says.

"Let her finish, love," Oscar rests his hand on Baihe's calming her.

"There's something in the pic," I say taking out my phone for the millionth time. "See, here in the background."

"There's nothing to see," Oscar says.

"No, not like this. It's blurry," I reply, my stomach knotting again. "But Tabitha said people online were trying to bring it into focus, and if they do, they'll see my art certificates pinned on my board here." I point to the white area of the blurry part. "They're awards I've won and have my name clearly on them. If someone can bring that into focus, well, we'll be—"

"Toasted," Baihe says.

"Toast," Oscar corrects. "We'll be toast. Bloody hell, we're buggered."

"What do we do?" I ask Oscar praying he'll have another of his brilliant solutions to all things vampire.

"We lay low. We keep our mouths shut. We hope it passes," he replies with an unconvincing tight-lipped smile.

I hold on to that advice as I go through my next classes and walk into the art room. I am instantly comforted by the scents of clay and tempera paint. My jaw relaxes a smidge, tight from literally keeping my mouth shut all afternoon. I also keep my head ducked, because I might as well keep that down too.

"Kaysee?" Mrs. Carroll's voice makes me jump from surprise. She's behind me wearing a strange expression, her eyes flitting around the room. "Are you okay? You don't seem like yourself today."

"Fine," I blurt. "I'm fine. I have my period, so I'm a little off, that's all." Fun fact: vampires still have periods. They're different, but still there. I guess you can't get rid of that curse even if you are cursed with immortality.

"I also noticed that your work isn't progressing," Mrs. Carroll continues ignoring my awkward menstrual talk. "Do you think you'll have it ready for the contest?"

I glance from Mrs. Carroll to my canvas that, as she said, isn't progressing. Really, it's a train wreck of abstract slashing colors. "When's the deadline?" I ask.

"January 15 to be considered for the spring show. They moved the date earlier because there's been so many more entries over the past few years. It takes a while to judge them all," she says.

"Okay, yeah," I fumble. "I'm sure I'll have it ready by then."Mrs. Carroll peppers me with questions about my choices and my artistic vision for the piece. I make up a bunch of BS because, unlike Indigo who has already created three freaking amazing paintings, I have no idea what I'm doing. It's as though Doug biting me not only took away my humanity, it also took away my artistic abilities.

I catch Maddie, Maeve, and Indigo all sneaking glances as Mrs. Carroll says something to me that I think she means to be inspiring, but it's just a muddled mess of words to me. When my stomach rolls and I find my eyes focusing on her pulsing carotid artery, I know I need to take a break.

"So, Mrs. Carroll, my period," I whisper. "I kinda need to go to the restroom."

"Of course, Kaysee," she whispers and motions for me to leave.

This bathroom stop is much less interesting until the principal comes over the school speaker system.

"Attention students, faculty, and staff," she clears her throat. "Due to the rising number of ill students and the high number of required quarantines, Inman High School is going to follow the advice of the local health department and transition to virtual learning. Everyone should take your laptops and chargers home today so we can all transfer to online school starting tomorrow, November 17, and continuing until January 3 when we return from Christmas break. If you have questions, email your counselor."

Whoops of joy erupt from classrooms as I walk back to the art studio. I add my voice to the commotion because a long break where I can hide in my room for weeks is exactly what I need. When

I find Oscar and Baihe after school, their eyes are smiling over their masks.

"Someone must have said prayers to the patron saint of vampires," Oscar says joining in step with me headed to the car pickup line. I let out a laugh that releases some of the tension in my stomach. I'm still vamp-hungry, but the stress of being outed as a vampire fades slightly.

"Hey, Kaysee," Jason says from behind me. Turning, I find him half running, half limping. "You missed chem class."

"Yeah, so?" I snap.

"Whoa, don't bite my head off," he snaps back. "I was going to give you the notes."

"Can you text them to me?" I ask, licking my lips because in the air between us I can sense his quick pulse which makes me want to devour him. "I have to get home."

"Sure," he shrugs.

"Thanks," I say shoving my hands in my pockets. "Gotta go."

I quicken my pace to catch up with Baihe. Looping my arm through hers, I say, "I think a nice long break is going to be fantastic."

21

NINCOMPOOP

Okay, virtual school sucks balls. But it's better than being discovered as Inman's newest vampire. Zel got out of quarantine the day after school shut down and got her phone back the next day.

"Damn," she says staring at her phone. "This is legit viral. There's like 52,000 likes on here. And I have all these DMs. Looks like most of them are from creepy old guys though." Zel scrolls through her phone sitting on my bed next to Pablo.

"But you're still going to delete it, right?" I ask spinning side to side in my desk chair. Zel doesn't respond. "Zel! You're deleting it, right?"

"Um," Zel's eyes flick up to meet mine. "Well, yeah, I want to, but this has been shared and copied all over. Even if I take it down now, people still know about it." She goes back to skimming through her phone as I mentally curse all social media and technology.

"So, I'm screwed," I drop my head back and sigh. "You know someone will find out about me."

"Yeah," Zel says absentmindedly.

"Zel!" I toss a teal-colored pencil at her, feeling a sick sense of joy when it bounces off her forehead.

"Kaysee, what the hell?" Zel drops her phone.

"Zel, I'm telling you that people might show up at my house any minute with the sole purpose of killing me, and you can't get your nose out of your phone," I huff furious at her selfishness.

"I know, sorry, but I have this message," Zel holds up her phone. "It's from Brittany Bell."

"The reporter?" I ask.

"Yeah, and it looks real, not like some poser. She wants to interview me about the picture." Zel's eyes widen with excitement. Seeing the same look on her face as when she's with the popular crowd makes my guts ache. I haven't told her about Tabitha and the girls in the bathroom. It would crush her.

"But you're *not* going to do it," I command. Zel bites her lip. "Oh, come on, Zel. She's the trashiest reporter around. Remember that story she did smearing that murder suspect guy last year? People destroyed his house and broke the windows on his car. And he ended up being innocent."

I'm standing and pacing now. "What do you think people will do if she reports on the Inman vampire?"

"I hadn't thought about that," Zel whispers.

We sit in silence. The only sound that enters my bedroom is Doug's muffled voice talking on the phone in the backyard. The orange hue of a November sunset warms my room. But it's not a comfort. My only comfort right now is that I don't hear an angry mob marching down my street.

"Damn it, Doug!" Oscar yells, slamming the fridge door as I step into the kitchen.

"What?" Doug feigns innocence as believably as a Kardashian saying they've never had plastic surgery.

"You know bloody well what!" Oscar slams his hands on the island making everything on it jump. A package of Nutter Butters crashes to the floor. I yelp in surprise, causing Oscar to turn and face me.

"Everything okay?" I ask questioning if I should find Baihe to help Oscar. He doesn't show this level of annoyance much, so seeing it now, I'm quite shocked.

"Doug's done it again," Oscar says shaking his head. His wild hair dances with the movement, but instead of looking hot like he usually does, he looks like a mad scientist about to lose his shit. My eyes shift to Doug, and I pin him with a questioning glance.

"What? It's no biggie," he shrugs. And I know this is a lie because he's not eating anything. He has to be pretty off-kilter to not be stuffing his face. "I just had some extra blood."

"Some extra blood?" Oscar steps to Doug, looking ferocious. "You ate 20 bags. That's not just some extra blood, you arse. It's all but our last three bags!"

"You didn't?" Baihe gasps from behind me. The commotion must have lured her to the kitchen. "Doug?"

"Yeah, whatever," Doug shrugs and scoffs. "I needed some extra for a friend passing through. I thought you guys wouldn't mind because it'd mean he wouldn't need to eat people and leave a big mess."

"But twenty bags?" Oscar asks his anger dissipating to defeat.

"Okay, there were a few friends. We had a little party at the park. They ate and left," Doug replies looking like a dog with its tail between its legs. "It's really no big deal. Geez."

Oscar lifts his head and turns to Baihe, who's come to stand next to me. "You know what this means."

Baihe shakes her head. "I'll check the bloodmobile schedule."

We have to wait a full week for a good bloodmobile to hijack. Baihe finds one about half an hour away from Inman. The others were too close to try again. We're all hungry. Which means we're all on edge too. Every day we wait, we have to carefully ration the last three bags. Mom and Dad give us some of their blood substitute, but it just makes us all sick. And I don't mean a little sick, I mean lifeless next to the toilet barely able to lift our heads so we end up puking on the floor sick. It was disgusting and humiliating, but mostly disgusting.

At least being sick kept me from looking out the front window every ten minutes. I swear someone is going to show up at our door with a wooden stake or a machete any minute.

I'm so jittery from being sick and paranoid that I decide to volunteer as the sacrifice for the heist. I know, it makes no sense whatsoever. But I'm truly afraid that because my hands are so shaky and I'm so jumpy I'll drop something or bump into a cabinet and botch the whole heist. This is the last blood drive before Thanksgiving, so this has to work or we might starve...or have to murder someone. And, damn it, if I'm not willing to have a cow murdered so I can eat a greasy hamburger, I'm sure as hell not going to murder a human to eat their blood.

"I'll drop you off in a few blocks," Oscar says steering the car down the darkened street. It's only 5:15 p.m. but the street lights are all on because thick clouds have drowned out the setting sun. It gives the town a creepy Halloween vibe.

"Sounds good," I say tightening my shoelaces. Because my bike was destroyed on the first heist, I'm just going to pretend that I'm jogging and run in front of the bloodmobile.

"We can still make Doug do it," Baihe says from the back seat. Doug winces when she punctuates her sentence with a punch to his arm.

"No, I got this." I take out my old phone from 8th grade and plug in some old earbuds. I took out the SIM card and wiped the memory on the phone just in case I drop it when I get hit. I wince every time I think about what it will feel like to be creamed by a bloodmobile.

"But, Damn It Doug—" Oscar starts.

"It's fine," I say stopping him. "Trust me, I need to do this." Oscar and Baihe have babied me a lot. It's time I toughen up and take on my new role.

Shortly after Oscar drops me off, I'm hitting a good stride when I hear the rumble of the bloodmobile turning down the street. *Make it believable*, I'm telling myself as I pick up my pace. The bloodmobile is cruising down the street quicker than I expect.

"Oh, no," I grumble as I push my legs, racing faster for the mobile that I'm positive is now speeding. Just when I think I'm going too slow and will miss the impact, the bloodmobile hits a pothole and veers slightly, slowing down. I'm two strides in front of it when it makes impact.

There are few people in this world who can accurately describe what it feels like to be hit by a speeding bloodmobile. If their experiences are anything like mine, then they'd agree that it hurts like hell! When the vehicle careens into me there is an immediate sound of cracking and squishing mixed with my blood-curdling scream. Then I'm flying through the air, weightless like a bird. That doesn't last too long before I crash into the street, pavement tearing my skin and rocks carving my flesh. There's a new mix of cracking and squishing when I hit and roll to a crumpled stop.

I hurt everywhere.

My deep groan escapes into the silent night. With the sound of two doors opening and footsteps on the pavement, the heist begins. The driver and his co-worker exchange curses and accusations as my body begins to regenerate. It sounds like these two really don't get along because they quickly move from questions about what happened to insults about each other's families and something sketchy that happened at a Fourth of July bar-be-que.

I've managed to shift onto my back and stretch out my leg that must have been broken in five places. The sensation of my bones knitting themselves back together is almost more painful than being hit by a speeding vehicle. I continue groaning as Oscar had directed. It was supposed to cover up the sound of him and the others emptying the bloodmobile. But my groans are totally unnecessary. The driver, with his spiky blonde hair, looks like he's maybe 22 years old, and the lady, with thick black braids, won't stop arguing. They haven't paid an ounce of attention to my broken body spotlighted in their headlights on the pavement.

Beneath me, the street is cold. Gravel from a nearby driveway is peppered across the cracked pavement. My gaze drifts to the few leaves clinging to the tree branches that stretch across the roadway. I wish I had my camera. Their brownish-yellow color against an inky black sky is captivating.

"What's going on?" an old man in a Vietnam veteran hat and holding the leash to a tiny Yorkie asks from the sidewalk. I was distracted and hadn't noticed his approach. He points his cane at me, a plastic bag in his hand swaying from the weight of the dog's poop in it.

My eyes go wide. We hadn't planned for witnesses. Through the windshield of the bloodmobile, I can see Oscar emptying a shelf, dropping blood bags into the cooler at his feet.

Groaning louder, I add, "I think I'm okay." The Yorkie barks and tugs on its leash nearly pulling the old man to the ground.

"If you're okay, then why are you lying in the middle of the street?" the old man snarks.

"She just—she was there, and we were here," the bloodmobile guy stammers. "It's really nobody's fault."

"I'm sure I'll be fine," I shift feeling where my bones are still broken and twisted. "I was such a *nincompoop*!" I yell the last word, the code word Oscar suggested we use if anything went wrong. A slight jolt of the bloodmobile confirms they've heard me. Oscar's head disappears from view as he jumps out the back door.

"Girl, you'd better stay still," the old man says standing over me jabbing his cane at my mangled leg. "Are you doing the drugs? That why you keep trying to move?"

"I'm fine, really," I say sitting up. The Yorkie cocks its head mimicking the puzzled looks on the faces of Blonde Guy and Braid Lady. "It just grazed me really."

"But you went flying through the air," the blonde guy says drawing his finger in front of him to imitate my flight.

"Trick of the light," I scream, not intending to actually scream. But standing on my leg sends a bolt of pain straight through my whole body. Wiping my hand across my face, it comes away smeared with blood. Damn, I must look like something from a horror film. When the old man takes a step back he looks like he's having PTSD flashbacks to Vietnam.

"This will all be fine," I say knowing I'm not convincing anyone with my fake smile especially when I wince with the sensation of the broken fingers in my left hand pulling themselves back into place.

"We should call someone," the bloodmobile lady says. But she doesn't move to reach for her phone or turn for the vehicle.

"Oh, here's someone now," I wave my hand at my mom's car as Oscar drives up to the scene.

"Whoa, gnarly," Doug smirks through the lowered window with an appreciative nod.

From the driver's seat, Oscar leans across him, "Oh, dear. We told you it wasn't a good idea to play with that fake blood." Oscar is fumbling which makes his efforts at an American accent falter. "Sorry, chaps, for the trouble. Our sister here is not all there," he crosses his eyes and twirls his finger next to his temple.

"Um," I stammer, trying to play along with this change of direction. Oscar was supposed to pull up and say that I'd gone for a run and that Mom had sent him to find me. But apparently, now I'm mentally deranged and covered in fake blood. Okay, let's go with it.

"Victoria," Oscar scolds me. "We told you to stay out of the Halloween box. This was a bad, a naughty idea, Victoria."

"Sorry?" I say, adding a grunt and shrug.

"So, this is all fake?" the old man asks.

"Yes, completely fake," Oscar replies flatly.

"You kids have no sense of decency," the old man pokes his cane at me. "Come along, Mitzi," he says to his dog, "we've got somewhere else to be." He walks away mumbling complaints.

"Let's go, Victoria," Baihe says opening the back door of the car. I walk over, my bones still cracking in places that make me groan with each limping step. Falling into the back seat, I let loose a few choice curses.

"Did you get the blood?" I ask wincing as I situate myself. Baihe pulls the seatbelt over my shoulder and clicks it in for me as Oscar speeds away.

"No more accidents for you tonight," she says with a smile.

"We got it," Doug answers me.

"We got about half of it," Oscar corrects, returning to the sharp lilt of his English accent which perfectly projects the full level of his annoyance.

22

HAPPY VAMPSGIVING

Doug is totally pissed. He's ranting and raving about how unfair it is that Mom and Dad locked the fridge where they store the blood. There's no calming him. Eventually, he snags freshly made vamp juices and a few bags of chips and hides out in his room for a few days.

Mom and Dad keep trying new formulas on the vamp juices using their synthetic blood. Because we're all still in virtual school and home all the time, we've become guinea pigs. Our routine includes school work and giving reviews on sample A versus sample B. Then sample C and sample D. This continues for the few weeks leading up to Thanksgiving to the point where we've tasted through samples BB and CC. Mom and Dad are so focused, they nearly forget to buy food for Thanksgiving.

But Oscar saves us all again with one of his many skills, cooking. He guides me and Baihe in making the biggest spread I've ever seen. And it's all perfect.

We sit at the table altogether, one odd vampire family. The turkey is perfectly baked. There are homemade rolls and stuffing and cranberry sauce. Potatoes and green beans round out the meal, and four different pies await us in the kitchen. To complete the perfectly set table and perfectly cooked food are goblets at four of the table settings filled with thick, red, delicious blood.

I sigh, allowing myself to relinquish my vegetarian ways for one meal. But only one meal. Besides, Oscar also added spices from an old recipe he'd learned for mulled wine when he lived in Germany. The accents of cinnamon and vanilla with the added sugar nearly take away the salty taste of the blood. I sip mine slowly enjoying the feeling of the warmth that fills my body and the strength that pours over me.

We fill our bellies and share stories in the flickering candlelight from the centerpiece Oscar created. And I feel like this house is more of a home than it's ever been. Usually, we go to St. Louis to see my grandparents for Thanksgiving. My parents always end up in the guest room with their laptops as soon as the last bite of Grandma's pumpkin pie is eaten. My heart feels full seeing Mom and Dad laugh about the stories Baihe shares of all the bad haircuts she's had and even Doug's stories of the many, many ways he's had to find his way out of a tough spot.

We end the day curled up on the couches binge-watching *The Great British Baking Show*, Oscar frequently commenting on the bakers' techniques. Zel comes over for a slice of pie, and for the sake of Thanksgiving and how great I'm feeling after drinking the mulled blood, I don't mention that she hasn't taken down my picture yet. Baihe orders me to sit on the floor in front of her so that she can whip my hair into an intricate braid. Next, she braids Zel's luscious hair making her look like the princess she's named for. When Zel slips out to go home, Doug slides out the door behind her with a wave and a look that tells me he's up to no good.

Finally, somewhere around midnight, Oscar and Baihe are asleep on the couches as Paul Hollywood gives a lucky baker a coveted handshake. I pull their blankets up over their shoulders and whisper a goodnight to each of them.

Playing with the end of my braid as I walk up the stairs, I stop and peer down at my family. "Happy Vampsgiving," I whisper across the darkened room feeling my heart fuller than it's been in a very, very long time.

The Saturday after Thanksgiving, the skies are thick and gray, perfect for a run. I slather on sunscreen just to be safe before pulling my long sleeves down to my wrists and grabbing a ball cap.

The crisp autumn air fills my lungs with the scent of fallen leaves as I run. A cold breeze stings my cheeks and my lungs. But I keep going because it just feels so damn good to move. My body has become accustomed to my feet pounding the pavement. The muscles in my legs rejoice with each stride.

As I'm finishing my 10-mile route I turn out of the woods and down Jason's street. Yes, I did this on purpose. He's been invading my thoughts lately in weird ways. Like when we were watching the baking show, I wondered what he would think of a bread sculpture this lady made to look like a soccer field or what he'd think of my hair styled into the braid. Each time, I tried to brush it off, clear away the invasion. But he kept finding his way back.

When I catch sight of him loading something into his truck, I'm embarrassed to find myself smiling. I slow to a walk and cross the street to his house. "Hey, Jason," I say stopping on the sidewalk to stretch my legs.

"Wax Lips," he replies dropping a cooler into the bed of his truck. He leans against the tailgate. "How far did you run today?"

"Only ten miles," I say with a shrug trying to ignore how his biceps are straining against the sky-blue sweater he wears and how said sweater highlights the color of his hair. It looks like rich caramel drizzle on a mocha dark chocolate cake. The idea makes me lick my lips. Damn it, I have to stop watching so many baking shows.

"What are you doing today?" I ask stumbling over my words.

"Hiking," he crosses his arms over his chest. "I'd ask if you want to come along, but you're probably too tired after ten miles."

"Psht," I say with a smiling shrug. "I've run up to 25 miles. And the weather is nice after all the rain yesterday."

"So, are you saying you willingly want to go hiking with me?" Jason quirks an eyebrow and smirks. And what the hell am I doing? I have no idea. But since he told me about his mom, I can't help wanting to see that side of Jason again. I can't explain it. There's just something about him, like a puzzle I thought was of a mean grizzly bear but turns out it's of a fluffy unicorn.

"As long as you promise not to murder me and leave my body in the wilderness to be eaten by wildlife, then yes. I think hiking sounds great."

Jason smiles and nods at the passenger door. "Hop in then. I promise that if I murder you, I'll leave your body in plain sight to be found quickly, but not too quickly. I'll need a head start for Canada."

I climb into the front seat and fasten the seat belt. "I need to stop by my house to grab my phone and let my parents know what's up. Where are we going anyway?"

"Busiek State Park," Jason says backing his truck into the road. "It's about 20 minutes from here. I'm thinking of doing a trail that's just over four miles, then heading back."

"But no plans for murder today?" I tease.

He scoffs. "Not unless I *really* have to."

After a quick stop at my house, I have my phone, more sunscreen, a vamp drink, and a thick hoodie jacket. Sitting next to Jason, I don't know what to say. He obviously doesn't either because he silently watches the road after giving me an awkward look when we stopped at a red light. Seeing the cord dangling from his radio, I pull out my phone and plug it in.

"What kind of music do you like?" I ask pulling up my playlists on my phone.

"Almost anything really," Jason says turning onto the highway.

"So, you're saying you're a Swiftie, big fan of T. Swift?" I tease him. After years of him pestering me, I'm finding a lot of joy dishing it back.

"No, stop!" Jason says as I play the first few beats of *Shake it Off*. He reaches for my phone, which I pull away. "Anything but this. I've heard it a billion times." He's laughing playfully, his eyes crinkling with mischief.

I hit the random button on my phone and Chris Martin's somber voice fills the truck.

"Turn it off," Jason says, his jaw suddenly tight. "Put on something else."

"I thought you said you liked anything," I say. "What have you got against Coldplay?"

"Just turn it off," Jason repeats, all playfulness evaporated. "For real, this guy's voice is grating."

"What is it?" I prod. "Chris Martin does have a strangely high-pitched voice, but the music is good."

"Kaysee, just turn it off. Bad things happen when I hear Coldplay," Jason says. "Please put on something else." I stop the track and turn to Jason. "Okay, you can't just say something like 'bad things happen when I hear Coldplay' and not explain," I say. "Spill. What's your deal with Coldplay?"

"Kaysee," Jason sighs my name.

I nudge his shoulder with my hand, and yes, I also notice how awesome his muscles are. "Jason," I sigh his name in return. "Is it something with your mom?"

He takes his eyes off the road to give me a quick glance, and I know by the sadness overshadowing him that I've hit a nerve. It reminds me of how his eyes softened the night of Homecoming. Seriously, what is it with guys? Can they not just talk about their emotions without someone having to drag it out of them?"

You can tell me," I press. "I won't reveal your secrets to anyone. Whatever's said in the truck stays in the truck." I smile when he looks my way again.

He stares silently ahead for a few minutes before pounding the steering wheel twice. "Mom listened to Coldplay a lot," his words tumble out. "She was listening to them when she got the phone call that the tests showed cancer cells. She was listening to them when she went into the hospital the first time. She was listening to them when…"

I lean across the seat and rest my hand on his that's gripping the steering wheel like it's his lifeline. "When what?" I ask.

"The night she died. She asked Dad to open up her bedroom window so she could see outside. She had me put on Coldplay, again. *A Sky Full of Stars*, that's what was playing when she died. See, bad shit happens when Coldplay music is played, so just turn it off."

"That's really, it's tough. I'm sorry," I say.

Sniffing, Jason says, "Don't be sorry. Just put on something different."

"Okay, how about one of my favorites?" I ask feeling like I'm asking a wounded animal to let me help heal it. Jason replies with a grunt, and I pull up Lizzo. When her flute joins the thumping bass rhythm Jason smiles and taps his hand on the steering wheel in time with the music.

By the time Jason pulls his truck into the parking lot at the park, we're both grinning and singing too loud and a whole lot off-key. But, we're both smiling, and I find that I'm actually having a really good time with him. What worries me the most is that I haven't thought about Toby once.

"Come on, the trail's this way," Jason says tossing me a water bottle and slinging his backpack over his shoulders. I skip a few steps to catch up with his long strides as we leave the parking lot. After crossing the bridge over a swiftly flowing creek, we're enveloped by the forest.

The trail is rugged, well-worn. Rocks and roots create an uneven pathway, but I welcome it. I'm on an adventure in the woods where the bare winter trees are intermingled with tall evergreens. The scent of their needles is thick and mixed with decomposing leaves.

I think I've found my new favorite smell. When I breathe it in and feel the magic of nature fill me, I forget that I'm with Jason.

But that doesn't last long. "Take my hand," he says standing below a small rock shelf. The trail is partially washed out, so we have to jump a few feet from the rock to continue.

"Thanks," I say grasping his hand. And there it is! Zing! It shoots through me, igniting tiny pleasure sensors through every part of my body and settling in a joyous celebration deep in my stomach. I'm so distracted that when I land in the mud below, I slip and have to fling myself into Jason's arms to keep from falling.

He doesn't let go immediately. Maybe the chorus of zinging, pleasurable tingles has found him too?

"Sorry," I say stepping out of his arms. He lingers behind me a few steps, which I am totally okay with. This way he can't see the smile overtaking my face nor the tension in my eyes as I internally battle these strange emotions. "I brought my phone to take pictures," I say changing the subject away from the delicious heat growing between us.

Our hike continues through the trees and along the creek flowing high from the recent rain. Jason humors me each time I stop to take a picture. I capture one of a thin strip of sunlight reflecting off the creek at a perfect angle. I need to print that one out in black and white.

The trail takes us up a long incline where the pathway narrows with each step. Below us is a growing valley where we can see some of the treetops and the birds flittering between them. Of course, I stop for another picture when I catch a few cardinals chasing each other through the branches.

"We're going to be here all night if you keep taking pictures of every leaf you see," Jason huffs. But he huffs in a way that I don't believe he's truly annoyed.

"I'm not taking pictures of every leaf," I say turning to him. "Just when something striking catches my eye."

Jason smiles, shaking his head and resting his hands on his head. From my position below him, he looks like he's floating in the clouds. I snap a picture of him with a smirk.

"Like what you see?" He wiggles his eyebrows as he shifts into a trashy pose turning to stick out his well-shaped ass. "What about this?" Moving again, he lifts the edge of his shirt revealing his amazingly well-toned abs. And, hell yeah, I take a picture of that! He doesn't stop until I have 12 pictures of him trying, and totally succeeding, at looking sexy. Really, this is fodder to light up Instagram and get everyone's minds off the whole vampire in Inman thing. Almost.

Laughing as he moves from his last trashy pose back to his usual stance, Jason says, "Now that we're done with that. Let's get a move on. The sun is setting much earlier today, and I don't want to get stuck out here. Come on, Ansel Adams."

"You know who Ansel Adams is?" I ask falling in step behind him.

"Well, duh, of course I do," he laughs and stops. He turns to me and leans closer. "You did that project on him freshman year in history class." Turning away, as though he's talking to the trees, he adds, "You'd be surprised how much of you I remember."

Mystified, intrigued, and confused all at once, I let Jason get ahead of me on the path. Because, seriously, what was that?

I drop my phone in my pocket as we descend the hillside and the trail loops us back toward the parking lot. My hands need to be free to grab on to trees and rocks so I don't fall on my ass and slide down the hill. After running this morning, my muscles quiver on the steep path.

As we return to the bottom of the hill, I catch sight of the parking lot through the trees. For a moment, a fleeting thought invades my mind, *I don't want this trail to end.* That fleeting thought is enough of a distraction that I don't lift my leg high enough to step up on a rock shelf and catch the toe of my sneaker on the lip. I crash onto the shelf, and my shin is smashed against the sharp edge of the rocks. The crack is audible, so is my yelp of pain as I land in the rocky mud.

His face full of surprise, Jason turns back to find me face-first on the trail. I lift my hands and discover thin tracks of red mixed with the mud on my palms. I question whether I should try to move my leg, and immediately regret it when I do.

"Kaysee!" Jason yells when I cry out in pain. He's on me in two quick steps, reaching out tentatively. "Are you okay?" His hands hover over me like he doesn't know where he can touch me that hasn't been injured.

I groan as I roll to my back, leaving my leg to dangle at an odd angle. I hope Jason doesn't see it. I know it's bad, but I can also feel my vamp powers working.

"Are you okay?" he repeats.

"I need my juice from the truck," I stammer through the pain. "Go get it for me." This request serves two purposes. 1) It'll give me a few more minutes to vamp heal. 2) I learned from getting run over by a bloodmobile that if I can feed, I'll heal much faster, and I'll be less of a cranky monster about it.

"I'll be right back," Jason says before sprinting for his truck. I take the moment to breathe and focus on a beautiful evergreen next to me. It stretches for the sky, skinnier than others nearby, and the scent of its needles that soften the ground next to me calms my tense muscles.

Breathe in. Breathe out. Scent of evergreen.

Breathe in. Breathe out. Scent of evergreen.

"Here," Jason thrusts the bottle at me. I shift to sit up and wipe my free hand on my pants to clear the mud. The scrape on my palm is nearly gone already. A few chugs of the vamp juice, and I can feel my body feeding off its energy. I jump when the bone in my leg cracks back into place.

"What the hell?" Jason startles. "Was that your leg?"

"It's nothing," I say trying to tuck it under me, which is impossible because it hurts like a mother.

"Let me see," Jason commands, reaching for my pants. I try to squirm away, but he pulls them up from the ankle to reveal a myriad of colorful bruises across my shin. Blinking, I think I see them move like clouds. "Kaysee, this is bad."

"No!" I scream. "It's not bad. It's fine. I just bruise easily." I chug the rest of my vamp juice. "Just give me a few minutes."

"I'm carrying you to the truck," he says very alpha male-like before taking me into his arms. I squeal as I'm crushed against his chest. The scent of the woods, clean soap, and pure animal magnetism intoxicates me making a very unladylike groan escape from somewhere deep in my throat. Tipping his gaze to meet mine, a thick wave of his hair falls into his eyes. And, holy frijoles, I have to hold myself back from reaching for it. Probably it's the concern etched across his eyes that keeps my impulse at bay.

Each of Jason's steps jostles me against him. He's not exactly graceful picking his way down the last hundred yards of the trail and up and over the bridge. I hold in a gasp when he slips and my very broken leg bashes against him. An apology is written across his face, and I kind of like the look.

Just before he sets me gently onto the tailgate of his truck a moment of panic races through me.

What. The. Hell. Am. I. Doing?

Like, really? What the hell am I doing? I'm drooling over Jason Hancock. What's worse is that I'm enjoying the whole ordeal. I'm screwed. I bite my lip reminding myself of the many reasons why I hate Jason.

"Let me see it again," Jason reaches for my leg.

"Really, it's fine," I block his hand.

"Quit trying to be so tough," he lifts my pant leg again. The bruising is already fading, and I'm pretty sure that I felt the bone shift fully into place when he was carrying me. "I think you need to see a doctor."

"No, just chill," I rub my leg, massaging my calf. "This is an old bruise." The lie slips easily from my tongue, and I think Jason believes me.

"Let me get you a rag to clean your hands," he says walking to the driver's door. He comes back with a bottle of water and an old gym towel.

There's mud caked to the knees of my pants and up the sleeves of my hoodie. I peel the hoodie off since the clouds are still thick overhead. Jason pours the water over the towel and passes it to me.

My hands clean up quite well. The only remaining injury is thin white scratches where my skin had already knit together. Thank you, vamp juice. Jason nods approvingly seeing the skin unbroken.

He turns his attention to my leg again. It's definitely not 100%, probably not even 70%. But if there's something I learned from my experience being plowed over by a bloodmobile, it's how vampire healing works. Based on the heat rushing up my leg, I know that the bone has healed and that the tissue will soon follow. Bones are like that. They heal quick. It's the tissue damage that takes forever to stop swelling and bruising. I'm feeling lucky today that I didn't sprain my ankle. That'd take a full day to heal.

"You say these bruises are old?" Jason looks at my leg skeptically.

"Yeah, a few days ago, I tripped at home. I was on my phone and missed a step on the stairs." I'm learning through my vamp experience that adding small details to lies makes them more believable. But don't go too far or you're in too deep and will sink into the deception.

Tenderly, Jason runs his fingers up my shin. His touch sends a wave of tingles over my healing flesh. The mixture of sensations of pain and pleasure balance perfectly. It's like the perfect blend of dipping Wendy's fries in a frosty. I bite my lip again.

When his eyes meet mine, I can't breathe. I'm captured in his gaze and freeze, both wanting and not wanting what might be happening. He licks his lips and whispers my name. "Kaysee," drifts on the breeze, the only thing separating us.

And, oh I want to wrap my arms around him and pull his lips to mine with more intensity than I ever thought possible. But I remember my teeth. My strange healing. The picture on Instagram.

I sigh, leaning back, away from him. "Jason, I can't." It physically hurts to say the words. The disappointed shadow that crosses his face is like a knife to my heart.

"Yeah, sorry," he says stepping back leaving a rush of cold air between us. "Toby, right? Yeah, I shouldn't have—" He stops short and stares at me. I realize that when he looked at me before, he always saw me, who I really am. This look is shrouded like he's put on a mask to hide his feelings.

And just like that, the shivers of pleasure are gone. They're replaced with layers of questions topped with regret like whipped cream on a shit sundae. Jason turns his radio to a country station for the ride home. We don't talk, and I hate how many silent car rides I've had lately with boys who tug at my heart. I hug my hoodie like it's going to protect my troubled soul.

When he drops me off at my house, I steal a quick glance at him wishing we could go back to the easy banter we'd shared. But we can't because I ruined that.

Oh, shit, I think watching him drive away. *I want Toby, not Jason.* But do I really? I'm so confused.

23
Just Call Me Kaysee

I dream of Jason. Of him standing in a beam of sun. Of him jokingly lifting his shirt to show off his sexy six-pack. Of his fingers trailing up my shin. He's there every time I close my eyes. I wonder if this is part of my vampire emotional chaos or what. It lasts for weeks, weeks when I ignore the two texts he sends me and change my running route so I won't go near his house. I just can't handle this right now.

I'm beyond relieved when Mom and Dad pack us up to head to Grandma and Grandpa's for Christmas. It's a welcome reprieve from all the bad news with the pandemic ramping up with the weather turning colder.

Oscar, Baihe, and Doug leave to "visit friends" for Christmas in Mom's car. I want to ask about the friends they'll visit but know that Oscar won't reveal anything. He and Doug have been fighting a lot, so he's really tense.

And time with my grandparents is exactly what I need. The eight days spent wrapped in their hugs, being stuffed with Grandma's cooking, and nights in the dimmed living room watching old kung-fu movies with Grandpa is the normalcy I crave. I'm a new person when we load up to head back to Inman.

During the four-hour drive, I scan through the pictures on my camera. There's a great one of Grandma rolling out pie crust and one of Grandpa wearing a large leaf as a hat and smiling like a kid. I make a mental note to print them. I have a new idea for my art project.

When we get home, it's 6:00 p.m. on New Year's Eve. I send a quick text to Zel to tell her I'm back. The restaurant closed early for the holiday, so she's at a family party. We've welcomed the new year together every year since I moved to Inman. She replies a fraction of a second later with a heart emoji.

Mom puts away the leftovers Grandma insisted we take as I lug my bulging backpack to my room. I find Pablo curled up on my bed. He meows a welcome to me, and I treat him to a thorough petting. Oscar and the other vamps are supposed to be back tomorrow. I've kind of missed my crazy crew and can't wait to see what details about their trip they'll share with me.

Zel makes it to my house just before midnight. She brings some of Abuelita's cookies and a bottle of sparkling grape juice. And, even though it's freezing cold, we wrap blankets around us and sit outside on the patio to watch the stars as we count down the end of the year.

"This year has been a bitch," Zel says brushing cookie crumbs off the bright red blanket wrapped tight around her.

"Yep," I reply sipping sparkling juice. "A pretty shitty year."

"Here's to saying goodbye to a pandemic and hello to a fabulously vampirey new year," Zel raises her glass.

I clink mine against hers and take a sip.

"How's the art project coming?" Zel asks.

With a shrug, I say, "It's a collage. And you're in it."

"Ooh. Who else?"

"Oscar, Baihe, even Doug," I shake my head with a smile. "And Jason too."

My whole body cringes when Zel screams loud enough to wake the dead. "Kaysee! Why would you put him in there?"

I sigh, stalling to gather my words. "It's just—he's just." Pausing, I scan the stars hoping they'll inspire me in how to respond because I don't know what's going on with my own brain lately. "He's just been around. He needed to be in it. I tried to keep him out, but he kept finding his way back in."

"Hm," Zel says studying me. "Is there something you're not telling me?"

"No," I shake my head, "because I don't even understand it myself."

With her gaze stuck on me, I can tell Zel is weighing her next step. She knows me better than anyone, which means she knows it's not the time to push me on this issue. What am I supposed to tell her anyway? About the dream I had where Jason kissed me and my body tingled happily all the next day remembering it? She wouldn't get it. Zel doesn't pine over guys, she just goes for them.

Looking at her phone, Zel says, "Ooh, it's almost time." My love life is forgotten as we watch the footage of a surprisingly empty Times Square and the ball slowly dropping.

"Happy New Year, Zel," I say pulling her into a hug.

"Happy New Year, Vampire Kaysee," she replies with a giggle.

"You can just call me Kaysee," I chide her. "Speaking of, you took down the pic, right?"

"Well," Zel stalls, shoving another cookie in her mouth. "I was going to, I promise. But it was out there. It was copied everywhere. And I got like 3,000 new followers. I couldn't just take it down. Plus, you know that no one will track it back to you."

"Zel," I whine cringing. "You said you'd take it down."

"I know," she grimaces. "I'm really sorry."

"Fine, but if an angry mob bent on killing vampires shows up at my door, I'm sending them to your house."

Zel laughs and hugs me again. "Deal."

I'll be honest. I'm kind of freaked out to go back to school. The press of people in the hallways is smothering, so is my mask. But I'm keeping my mask on for sure now. The buzz on Zel's pic has slowed down, but she's still getting likes and comments every day. I'm scared to death that someone somewhere is going to figure out that the pic is of me. *Zel really needs to delete it*, I think biting my lip against the frustration that has been bubbling for days.

"Where's Jason?" Zel asks as the tardy bell rings in chem class.

"I don't know," I say with a shrug trying to hide the fact that I've been checking my phone nonstop, looking for a text from him. I could've replied to his texts, but I waited all break, so it feels weird now.

"Surgery on his knee again," Toby says to Zel. "He asked me to get the lab notes, said he'll be back in a few days."

My heart drops. I didn't know he was having another surgery. And it hurts that I didn't know that. Maybe I need to take a jog past his house again.

"That's hilarious," Zel laughs and slaps Toby's shoulder.

"What?" I ask.

"Toby," Zel giggles. "He just made this awesome joke about *Guardians of the Galaxy*."

"Goggles on," Mr. Garcia announces rounding our table. Through the rest of class Toby and Zel talk Marvel Universe. I zone out letting my mind drift to my newest concept for my art project. I printed a small stack of photos last night and can't wait to incorporate them. And it's easier to distract myself with art than to dwell on Zel's confessions about late-night video chats with Toby. She hasn't said much, but she's dropped lots of hints. I think she's trying to get my blessing. Ugh, my mind is so freaking confused.

When class ends, Zel and Toby continue their conversation all the way out the door. And I'm lurking in the shadows again. With Zel and Toby gone, I'm invisible, like a snap from Thanos has blipped me away. And I am so totally, completely okay with that. No one will slaughter the vampire they don't see.

In art, I pull out my snapshots and spend class figuring out how they fit onto the canvas. On some of them, I tear the edges or rip the photo so that it's a unique outline. They mix together moving in unison to create a whole picture. When I stand back and look at the moments from my life with my friends and my family, my eyes linger over Jason's picture.

He was about to kiss me that day we went hiking. I know that. And I had really wanted to kiss him. But I knew I couldn't. Just as I know it was a good thing I scorched my mouth and didn't kiss Toby either. For now, it's best I don't kiss anyone.

But I'm still thinking of Jason when I take a midnight jog through the neighborhood and find myself in front of his house. There's dim light coming from a window upstairs, but everything else is dark.

I wonder if he's awake. I wonder if he's okay after the surgery. I wonder if I've invaded his thoughts the way he's invaded mine.

"I'm screwed," I whisper as I break into a jog again. I have to run an extra two miles to settle my chaotic mind and insane heart.

When I get home, Oscar is awake and reading in the living room chuckling as he turns the pages. "You're out late," he says lowering his book.

"Yeah, I needed to run," I sit next to him and glance at the cover of his book. It's some kind of European history book.

"Oh, how far you've come, sweet little vampire," he smiles at me like a proud father.

"Not far enough for you to tell me what you did for Christmas." I've been trying to get info from Oscar and the others, but they're all tight-lipped. The mystery is kind of killing me.

Oscar sighs and squints as he takes me in. I feel like a puppy being chosen from the shelter wondering if I measure up to his expectations. "All I can say is one word," he whispers leaning closer. "Cleveland."

"What?" I yell.

"That's all you're getting," he stands. "I'm off to Bedfordshire."

"Oh, come on," I plead. "What happened in Cleveland?"

He mimics locking his lips and throwing away the key. And it's the sexiest thing I've seen him do yet. I give him a head start before I move for the stairs and my bedroom. When I get to the top of the landing, I hear a key slip into the deadbolt on the front door. I've already turned off all the lights, but even in the shadows, I can see Doug's skinny silhouette slithering through the house. That guy. I have no idea what he's been doing out so late, but learning that they went to Cleveland for Christmas, I know I need to keep my ears open for any kind of madness Doug might stir up.

24

VAMPIRE RAVE

It's almost Valentine's Day. We've been back to school for weeks, and nothing has changed with me and Jason. He keeps ignoring me and going out of his way to avoid me. At first, I thought it was just because of his knee. But the crutches are gone and so is the clunky brace, so he should be over that. I try to justify his aloofness in so many ways, but they all come up short. T

here's only one reason he's acting this way. Me.

On the flip side, Toby and Zel have merged into this weird couple that oddly clicks. They're different in so many ways, but they both have this underlayer of geekiness that meshes well.

I'm happy for Zel. Really, I am. I wasn't at first, but I am now. Seeing them together shows me how bad Toby and I would have been together. His hot nerdiness wouldn't have blended well with my artsy mediocrity. Still, it stings to see them together. I mean, they're not totally, officially a couple yet. That's coming soon though, I know that as sure as I know I'm ready for another vamp juice.

I've developed quite the drinking habit with all the stress weighing on me. That and a running habit. I'm averaging 80 miles and

25 bottles of vamp juice every week. Mom and Dad had a break-through with the synthetic protein, so they use less human blood in each drink. The formula is nearly perfected and ready to market.

It was a difficult day last week when I had to put the finishing touches on my art project. The pictures had come together well, but the painting was rushed. And I'm nervous about the judges seeing it because one of the pictures I used was the corner of my teeth pic. It's the blurry part of the background that no one would recognize, but I know it's there and that's what matters.

Zel finds me at lunch as I suck the last drops of my third vamp juice for the day. I don't even taste them anymore, just open up and down the hatch. "We need to talk," she says, her tone worrying me. She looks around to see if anyone is eavesdropping.

"What's going on?" I ask leaning closer.

"Remember how that reporter kept DMing me on Instagram?" Zel sighs. "Well, she got my phone number and just texted me asking for an interview."

"You said no, right?" My voice screeches. The only good news I'd had lately was that all the chatter around school about the Inman vampire has nearly died. People still pester Zel and ask who was in the pic. She sticks with her practiced answer, always said with a smirk and a hair flip. "That? Ha. I ripped that off the internet. No one believes vampires are real, right?"

Zel stares at me, her eyes wrinkled. "Oh shit. We're screwed," I drop my head to bury my face in my arms.

"I told her no," Zel rubs my back.

And you know what? It doesn't matter one bit that Zel said no, because guess who is waiting with her news crew on the street outside Zel's house after school? Yep. Brittney Frickin' Bell. And I have no escape because Zel drove us to school today. Oscar, Doug, and Baihe are crammed into the back seat with blankets pulled across them because, of course, the heater is broken in Zel's car. Zel and I look ridiculous wearing Snuggie blankets, a Christmas gift from her parents so we could stay warm in her car. A better gift would have been a new car. But I digress.

Seeing the Channel 10 news van, Zel slows the car to a crawl. "What do I do?"

"Act normal," Oscar says from behind us, his voice tight. "Just park and act natural."

"Aw, hell, she's gonna know. We gotta bail," Doug whines.

"No, Doug," Baihe urges. "Just stay quiet. Everyone put your masks on."

Brittney Bell eyes Zel's car as she pulls into the drive. All of us have our masks covering our vampire teeth, but they can't hide the heavy weight of guilt we wear.

"Zel," Brittney Bell sings as Zel gets out of the car. "So glad I found you. I'd like to talk to you about the picture." She smiles, but like a tiger about to eat a fawn.

"I have nothing to say," Zel waves her away as she brushes by Brittney Bell. I'm huddled with my vampire crew and lingering dangerously close, anxious to hear what happens.

Dropping his arm over my shoulders, Oscar says, "Have you decided about signing up for the track team?" His words are light, but his eyes scream at me to keep moving.

"Oh, track," I reply, blood thumping in my ears. "Maybe. You?"

Oscar laughs and we both steal a glance at Zel and Brittney Bell. Brittney isn't backing down. She's followed Zel to her front door, her cameraman filming each step. It takes Zel shouting at Brittney

Bell to get lost using some very colorful language for the reporter to get the hint. Brittney Bell's luxurious locks of blonde hair flutter in the breeze created by Zel slamming her front door.

She shakes it off and turns to catch my eyes. "You," she shouts, stalking forward. "Would you like to comment on the Inman vampire?"

"N-n-no," I stutter and shrug looking like I'm having a seizure.

"You?" she turns on Oscar.

"No," Oscar focuses on Brittney Bell, his eyes squinting. And I know exactly what he's doing. "There's no one here to help you. You'll leave now and not bother us again."

Brittany Bell's eyes have glassed over. She's transfixed by Oscar.

"And you'll stop eating meat," I add, squinting my eyes. Brittney Bell turns her gaze to me, confused. "Stop eating meat. You're a vegetarian now." Oscar pulls me into our house before I can ruin his work. Man, I still need to work on my persuasion skills.

Baihe and Doug wait by the window, peeking through the drapes. "Are they gone yet?" Oscar asks.

"No," Baihe shakes her head. "Just out there talking."

"We can't have another Cleveland," Oscar slumps on the couch.

"Will someone please tell me what the hell happened in Cleveland?"

Oscar drops his head in his hands. "We don't—"

"Speak of Cleveland," I cut him off. "I know. But isn't it time?"

"I'm going to my room," Doug cowers away.

"Stay in tonight," Oscar commands.

"Oh, come on, grouch," Doug complains.

"Damn it, Doug," Oscar punches the couch cushion. "You will stay in tonight."

"Whatever," Doug retreats to the basement. The echo of his door slamming shakes the floorboards.

"Oscar, it's time," I say. "If something bad is happening, I should know."

"She has a point," Baihe says sitting on the loveseat. "And the reporter just left."

Oscar looks between us, considering his next move. From the lab, comes the clink of beakers and the whir of a machine. Mom and Dad are still working. As if reading my mind, he glances at the lab doors.

"Okay," Oscar acquiesces. "But this stays between us. You can't tell anyone. Not Zel. Not Toby. Not *anyone*."

"I promise." Worry grips me. So far, Oscar has presented me with the Disney version of vampire life. He tends to dance around the darker elements, the more HBO gritty side of vampirism.

"A few years ago," Oscar begins, "we were living in Cleveland. We had a very nice apartment and jobs. We looked like normal humans. We'd been there eight years with no problems, but we knew it was almost time to move. People started commenting on how we didn't age. But Doug didn't want to leave."

"Damn it, Doug," Baihe whispers.

"Why?" I ask.

"He'd reconnected with some old friends," Oscar says. "See, when Doug was first turned it was by a really bad vampire."

"Evil Jeff?" I ask.

Baihe laughs. "Oh, way worse than Jeff."

"He turned Doug as a joke, it was a game with his crew." Oscar continues, his demeanor exuding exhaustion. "They'd hunt people and see who could scare their prey the most. It always worked best on young teenagers like Doug. He was only fourteen."

"And Doug ran with that crew for about twenty years," Baihe adds. "He learned a lot of really bad habits."

"Like what?" I ask not sure I want to know the answer.

"Their favorite was what they called a Saturnalia," Oscar explains. "In the 70s, they changed it to a 'rave.' They'd find a large group of people and tear through them one after another. They didn't do it to feed, no they'd just drink enough blood to kill them but not turn them and move on to the next. They did it to toy with their prey, to terrorize them."

"Only to kill," Baihe says. "They'd kill as many as they could and always try to raise their scores."

"That's disgusting," I whisper. I don't want to imagine what that looked like, but my mind is playing out horrific images of carnage.

"Doug reconnected with the crew's leader, Hans," Oscar says. "Hans wanted him back for some reason. He seduced Doug."

"And there was another rave, their biggest," Baihe says. "I had to kick Doug's ass to get him in our car to leave."

"Forty-eight people," Oscar straightens. "Forty-eight people died in the rave. We had to flee. We were on the move for a few years, never staying anywhere for more than a month."

"We saw some beautiful places," Baihe smiles trying to lighten the mood. "Then we connected with your parents."

"If Hans finds Doug, it'll all be ruined." Rubbing his hands over his face, Oscar breathes out the tension. "We have to keep him out of trouble until the artificial blood formula is set."

"I don't want to leave again," Baihe says.

"Can't Doug just tell them to piss off?" I ask.

Oscar scoffs. "Hans is a drug to him. Doug's like his son, but the kind of son who's willing to do anything to please his dad. It's an unfortunate relationship."

"Okay," I puff air through my lips. "Let me get this straight. We have to keep Doug away from Hans—"

"And Jeff," Baihe adds.

"And Jeff," I nod. "And we have to keep Brittney Bell off our asses long enough for Mom and Dad to finish the formula. Because if we don't, either there will be a huge massacre by Hans and his crew or we're outed as vampires and the villagers show up with pitchforks."

"Figuratively," Oscar says. "Doug was right, they'd likely have guns."

"We can do this, right?" I grimace.

The only response I get is a forced smile from Baihe and Oscar shrugging. They don't fill me with confidence, so I just make for the kitchen. With a bottle of vamp juice in each hand, I lock myself in my room. Even Pablo can't make me feel better tonight. We're beyond screwed.

25
SHITS & FANS

"Are you trying out for track?"

I lift my eyes to meet Jason's across the chem lab table. It's just the two of us today. Zel and Toby are both out sick. I wasn't surprised because Zel has given unnecessarily detailed reports on their kissing history that began with a box of chocolates on Valentine's Day.

Squinting with skepticism, I clumsily ask, "Huh?" This is the longest sentence Jason has said to me in months, which leaves me dumbfounded.

"Track, are you trying out for track?" He asks again setting down an empty beaker.

"Why are you asking?"

"Because you and Zel have been acting more jittery than normal, and I thought that asking about track would help me ease into the conversation where I ask what's up with you guys." Jason leans across the table.

"Why do you care about me or Zel or track?" I snark. "Like, really. After weeks of ignoring me, why do you care now?"

"Look," Jason holds his hands up defensively, "I know things ended weird on the hike. Your leg was so gnarly looking. And then I thought you wanted to— but you didn't, and I judged that situation wrong, okay?"

"So, are you saying you're sorry?" I ask. I probably should be the one apologizing. At first, I didn't want to because I didn't think I needed to. Now, I don't know anything. He almost discovered that I was a vampire. I had to ghost him, especially after the picture was posted and with Brittney Bell harassing Zel and Doug out all hours of the night. Relief tugs at my heart seeing the ice melt between us.

Jason smiles his ungodly handsome smile. "Yeah, I am. I'm sorry. I was confused and thought you needed time. Then you wouldn't talk to me, so I thought that was what you wanted."

"So, our friendship has been an endless loop of Coldplay songs?" I ask, a smile hidden by my mask.

"Whoa, I wouldn't go that far," he chuckles. "There'd have to be some serious shit hitting the fan for that to happen."

"Shit and fans? Not part of this experiment," Mr. Garcia passes our table. How does he always do that? He must have superpower hearing abilities. "Back to sodium chlorate, please."

As Mr. Garcia continues on to chide another chem group, Jason winks at me. Good gracious, it is my new favorite sexy thing he does. Memories of the dreams I had over Christmas come back in a flash leaving a crimson blush creeping up my face.

"So, we good?" Jason asks passing me a test tube.

"Yeah, we're good," I reply. My fingers brush his, and he holds on to the tube a second longer than he needs. Does he feel the zip of electricity zinging between us too?

It's amazing what a difference a week can make. Zel and Toby are back to school. Jason and I are talking again. Honestly, we're flirting a good bit too. There's been nothing more from Brittney Bell. Her last news story was on the benefits of vegetarianism, so maybe my persuasion abilities are improving. Best of all, not one angry villager has shown up at my house with a pitchfork...or a shotgun.

I feel so damn good that I show up at track tryouts. Oscar joins me amidst much grumbling. "Kaysee," he'd whined after school, "I'm not much of a sportsman. I'm more of a sword fighter or candle maker, not one of those blokes that runs in circles on purpose."

"Come on," I'd yanked his arm. "You've been moping around the house waiting to catch Doug doing something sinister. Just try out. You might like it."

"Kaysee, I do not like this," Oscar now grumbles next to me. We're sitting on the hard bleachers next to the track as a fine mist fills the air and soaks into our clothes. I nudge his shoulder, then follow the coach calling for distance runners to line up at the starting line.

I've never played school sports before. Dad insisted I play soccer when I was a kid, but I didn't like all the aggressive running for the ball. Instead, I just picked flowers in the grass or looked for insects to save from being trampled. Now, here I am lining up to try out for track.

Running a mile is a walk in the park after all the running I've done since becoming a vampire. I'm hardly out of breath when I cross the finish line ahead of all the other girls. I'm rewarded with a gentle pat on the shoulder from Mrs. Kelsey, my freshman English teacher who coaches the girls' distance runners.

It takes me a while to find Oscar after my race. Not finding him in the bleachers or near the track, I think he's abandoned me to go home alone. Then I catch sight of a group of guys in the grassy side field. Oscar is holding a javelin and laughing with a tall blonde guy.

"Kaysee, my dear," Oscar says as I walk up. "Have you met Greg?"

"Yeah, we've had some classes together," I reply recognizing Greg as a friendly guy from last year's biology class.

"Hey, Kaysee," Greg gives me a head bob.

"Greg throws the shot put, those balls," Oscar says with a gleam in his eyes. "He thinks I'd be good with the javelin."

"Yeah, you have the build, strong shoulders," Greg says. And is it me, or did something just pass between these two guys?

"Okay," I say. "You ready to go home, Oscar?"

"Right-o. See you at practice," Oscar says passing unnecessarily close to Greg.

Once we're out of earshot, I can't hold it in anymore. "So, Greg, huh?"

"Yes, Greg, is an interesting bloke. A good conversationalist is hard to find in the States," Oscar quips.

"Yeah, but you and Greg? I didn't know you, um, leaned that way." I slide into the front seat of Mom's car dropping my backpack at my feet.

"My sweet Kaysee, I am merely embracing the character of my namesake," Oscar says starting the car.

"Explain please."

"My mother was a seamstress working at a theatre in London in the late 1800s. It was the height of the career of the infamous Oscar Wilde," Oscar says. "My mother took the secret of my father to her grave, but she made many insinuations that I was the progeny of the famous playwright."

"Oh," I say as understanding hits. We'd studied Oscar Wilde in sophomore English. I remember it well because one of the really religious kids threw a fit because Wilde had been openly homosexual. No one else cared. His plays were easier to read than Shakespeare's.

I hadn't thought vampire Oscar would be so similar to human Oscar, but it makes sense. Being a vampire and being over a hundred years old makes it more difficult to make assumptions about such things. It makes me wonder what people will think about me in 50 years.

26

THE REAL INMAN VAMPIRE

"I have a crazy ass idea, just hear me out," Zel says. We're sitting on the couch in my living room passing a bag of Oreos back and forth. Zel brought them. Cookies don't last long around Doug.

"I'm listening," I say licking icing from the cookie I've dismantled.

"We should start a Twitter account for the Inman vampire." Zel smiles.

"Why?" I ask. "I thought that whole thing was over now."

"Nope," Zel sighs dropping her gaze. "Some guy who had a small part on *Vampire Diaries* shared it. Turns out he has a cult following, and it's blown up again." The smile is gone replaced by hesitation and regret.

"How blown up?" I ask with a cringe.

"One hundred thousand likes," she pulls a pillow over her head as protection from the Oreo I chuck at her.

"Zel!" I shout. "You said you'd delete it."

"I know, I thought it was done. But now Brittney Bell is messaging me like ten times a day and the pic is still all over Instagram. That's why we need the Twitter account," she nods her head as though the gesture will convince me to join her plan without question. "It's a different platform. It'd be a way to redirect and maybe even prove it was all fake."

"Oh, Zel," I collapse back onto the couch feeling my world crumble, yet again. Why wouldn't she take the pic down months ago? *She's just Zel being Zel again*, I think as I rub my hands over my face.

"It'll work," Zel pleads. "I know it will. We can build interest."

"By adding fuel to the fire?" I stare her down. She has lost her mind.

"Not adding fuel to the fire, fighting fire with fire. It's redirection, like a magician." Zel stands and paces. "We can blow it up. Message the *Vampire Diaries* guy. Once it's huge, we can say the whole thing was fake. It'll at least get Brittney Frickin' Bell off my back."

"I don't know," I say imagining the million different ways this could go terribly wrong.

"Look, I set up an account." Zel plops on the couch next to me and passes me her phone. It's simple, just the infamous picture of my teeth and a name: The Real Inman Vampire.

"I'll have to talk to Oscar," I pass the phone back as my stomach churns tossing the Oreos and threatening to make them reappear. "Give me the login info. I'm changing the password now. I need to have total control over this, including shutting it all down."

Late that night, after installing Twitter on my phone, I show Oscar the profile. Like me, he doesn't like the idea at first. But when I explain that this would be the way to control the narrative, he perks up. Turns out Oscar and Baihe have avoided social media saying it was a waste of time. But for this purpose, it might prove worthwhile.

So, we go live. Zel screenshots the profile page and shares it on Instagram. I post my first official vampire tweet, choosing to keep it simple.

People say I'm not real. What do you think? I include a new picture that Baihe helped me take. We crop it close so that really all you can see is my teeth and the edge of my lip. While I do worry that someone will still track it back to me, I'm also really excited. Because for once, I'm free to be myself without having to hide anything. And I feel in control of the chaos around me.

I'll be honest. I'm enjoying tweeting as The Real Inman Vampire way more than I should. I'm careful, obviously. The tweets are vague but also have just enough information that people are drawn in. The profile has been live a little over a week and I have 20,000 followers. I've even had a few DMs from Brittney Bell.

The only bad thing is that I'm getting some really weird DMs and comments too. I show them to Oscar and Baihe. They warn me these people might be real vampires too. And vampires, in general, don't like anyone openly discussing the lifestyle.

Keeping up with Twitter has taken my mind off the art show coming up in two days. I'm nervous as hell and have been running like a maniac. I'm outside so much I'm always out of sunscreen. So, I'm stressed, excited, and peeling from a sunburn.

In chemistry class, Jason keeps turning my way when I scratch at the flaking skin on my arms. Yes, it's gross, but I wore a long-sleeve shirt to hide that I'm shedding like a snake.

"Stop scratching," Zel commands. "Let's talk about what you're wearing to the art show on Saturday." She squeals and claps her hands.

"Just my black dress, I guess."

"Ooh, not that one," Zel winces.

"Dude," Toby says looking at his phone. "Did you all see this new tweet? The shadow picture."

Biting my lip, I savor the smirk creeping up my face. I know exactly which tweet pic he's talking about. I took it last night. There was a full moon, so Baihe and I went to the playground at the old elementary school. We climbed up on the playground to take the picture of me silhouetted against the moon with the sign for the school in the bottom corner. There's no doubt that it was taken in Inman. The pic only shows my head, and I wore an old, black Halloween wig as a disguise.

"Let me see," Jason looks over Toby's shoulder and scoffs. "Huh. Looks like something Kaysee would take."

My heart stops beating. I freeze.

"Let me see," Zel jumps into action. She glances at the tweet and rolls her eyes. "That's too dark for Kaysee. She does stuff with shadows but also with lots of color. Right?" Her eyes bore into me.

Summoning my courage, I turn to Jason. "That doesn't look like my photos at all."

"I'm just saying, anyone could have taken that picture," Jason says. "Anyone in Inman or from somewhere nearby could have snuck on the playground. This whole vampire thing is stupid anyway. Don't people have better things to do?"

"Yes," I agree. "It is stupid."

"If you really want to see Kaysee's work, you should go to the art show on Saturday." The level of suggestion that drips from Zel's tone is impossible to ignore. She adds a wink to Jason across the table. I haven't really confided in her about everything with Jason. Sure, she sees the flirting and knows I'm crushing on him. But I still don't know if I have anything with Jason. All we've had is one almost kiss and a fair amount of flirting. I don't want to tell Zel how my stomach flips when I see him because I might jinx everything.

But the idea of him wanting to see my art is extremely exhilarating. "Yeah, it's in Springfield at the art museum. Doors open at 5:00." Nonchalance isn't one of my skills but I'm putting all my effort into it now.

"Okay," Jason says, his eyes crinkling with a smile. "Sounds like a blast."

♥

Hell has officially frozen over because my parents are actually going to my art show. I tell them that Oscar can drive me. But they insist, like really insist. Mom gushes about how sad it is she missed my other art shows. I really want to believe she's filled with remorse. I do. But I've been crushed so many times in the past when she and my dad couldn't see beyond the experiment they were working on at the time. They didn't see me. I wonder if they really do now. I hope so.

Sitting in the back seat with Oscar, I scroll through Twitter checking for activity. There's more comments and retweets mixed with some trolls. I just don't understand how people can be such asshats online.

"Here we are," Mom says as Dad pulls his SUV into the parking lot. I spot Zel's car instantly. She said she'd bring Toby. My nervousness levels up having so many people here for me tonight. The only thing that soothes me is the scent when we step inside the museum. Clay and paint and muslin canvases fill my nostrils. It helps my hands stop shaking.

"Here!" Dad finds my piece. It's hanging next to Maeve's painting and Indigo's mixed media 3D experiment. It's my first time seeing Indigo's finished work, and it's remarkable. I'd heard her explain to Mrs. Carroll that she was making something to be seen and touched by the blind. I understand when I see her walking in holding a woman's hand. The woman carries a white cane that she taps in front of her with every step. I never knew. Indigo's mom is blind. The sadness that she's never seen any of the art that has won Indigo so many awards creeps into my heart and gives me pause. There's more of a story to Indigo than I'd allowed myself to see.

"Kaysee, this is beautiful," Mom says giving me a side hug. She's going a little overboard, maybe making up for lost time. Zel and Toby find us and we walk through the displays together. There are some remarkable pieces here. I'm looking at an abstract multicolor sculpture of a cow when I hear my name.

Shifting my gaze, I find Jason looking handsome as hell with a big smile directed at me. I'm so glad that masks weren't required tonight, because that smile is the most exquisite thing I've seen all day.

"Hey, glad you could come," I say. I'm quite aware of the fact that Zel convinced me to wear a cute jean skirt and very form-fitting top. Thanks to Baihe my hair is in a loose fishtail braid that drapes over my shoulder.

"I saw your art," Jason says walking to me. "Did you have to use *that* picture of me?"

"Yes, yes I did," I reply smiling back. "Thanks for coming."

He takes my hand setting off the tingles across my palm. "I like being around beautiful works of art."

A laugh escapes before I can stop it. "Did you practice that line?" I tease.

"Give a guy some credit," he winks. And I melt. It's like my bones have turned to liquid. Electrical sparks zip through my body making me tingle all over.

"Ladies, gentlemen, and artists, please make your way to the lecture hall for the awards ceremony," an announcement comes over the speakers.

"Oh, Kaysee," Mom runs up to me jumping with excitement. "Come on, let's go."

Since Mom and Dad haven't met Jason before, I make quick introductions as we follow the flow of people to the auditorium. When Jason sits next to me, I can't ignore his knee pressed against mine. And I think that maybe things are finally looking up for me. I started the school year with my eyes set on Toby, but my heart had other ideas. My next goal was to win the art contest. Now, it's time to check that off my list.

"Calm down," Zel says in my ear as she rubs my shoulders. She sits behind me with Toby and Oscar. Waiting is killing me. The presenters go through all the categories and take forever to get to mixed media, my category.

Like, seriously, I'm so nervous that when Jason takes my hand to stop my fidgeting, I don't feel one single spark. There's just a thin layer of stress sweat between our skin.

"And now the awards for mixed media," the announcer, an old professor from Missouri State University, drones. Next to me, Mom takes my other hand.

I need to win the scholarship. I need to win to get out of this town so I can find a place where I can fully be myself. These are the things I've told myself since eighth grade. My breath hitches realizing how different this year is, how I'm now surrounded by friends and family.

"Kaysee Fehr," the professor says my name.

"What?" I shake my head, my thoughts snapping back to the room.

"You won," Mom beams.

"And second place goes to Demarco Hughes from Central High School." The room fills with polite clapping. "First place and the $10,000 scholarship to an art school of the artists' choice goes to Indigo Clement from Inman High School."

"Wait, what?" I turn to Mom.

"Go get your prize," Zel urges me.

I turn to Jason. "What did I win?"

"Third place," he says standing to let me pass.

"Third place?" I ask, my stomach dropping.

"Yes, go get your trophy." Jason rests his hand on the small of my back and pushes me forward. I scan the room as I walk to the small stage. It's packed like people forgot we were living in a pandemic. There's even a thick line of people standing against the back wall.

Stumbling to the stage, realization sets in. Indigo beat me again. And worse than that, I got third place. No art scholarship. No ticket out of Inman for me. I feel like an idiot for even thinking I could win.

I pull my mask from my pocket and slip it on as I approach the stage. I keep it on to hide my embarrassment when they have the winners stand together for a picture. Indigo and the second-place winner stand with me and three honorable mentions. Everyone on the stage is happy except for me. My nervous energy is morphing into disappointment which is quickly shifting into anger. Vampire rage is brewing in my gut. I seriously have to get out of here.

Rushing off the stage, I push past people and run outside. Pacing, I rip off my mask struggling to catch my breath. My blood is boiling. This can't be happening. I was supposed to win, not lose to Indigo *again*. Not come in freaking third place!

Yelling in frustration, my voice echoes off the marble walls. The doors open behind me, and Zel tumbles outside.

"Kaysee." Zel's voice drips with pity.

"I just—I just need a minute," I wave her away trying to compose myself. If she hugs me, I'll lose my shit, so I need her to keep her distance.

"Are you okay?" She asks.

Before I can form an answer, the door opens again and Toby steps out sheepishly. "You guys need anything?"

"No. Just leave me alone." My eyes sting. Blinking, I attempt to keep the tears inside. I do not want to cry. I do not want to cry. I will not cry.

"Hey, what are you guys doing?"

A seething dread pours over my body when my eyes land on Doug and some people I don't know striding toward us from the parking lot. An arrogant smile plays on Doug's mouth, his arm resting across the shoulders of a short girl in a tight dress. Her hair and makeup are so odd they look like they're from a TikTok tutorial gone wrong. Two guys wearing jeans and dark hoodies stand on either side of them, and they seethe with malice. My fingers tighten around the small third-place trophy in my hand.

"Damn it, Doug," I shout. "What are you doing here?"

"Oh, us?" Doug smiles. "We're just here for the art." His friends snicker.

"Ooh, Doug," says one of the guys. He has a snake tattoo peeking from his sleeve and wrapped around his hand. "What a bitch. Want me to take her out?" He bares his teeth with a wicked grin.

"I can handle her, Jeff," Doug replies.

"You can't go in there," I tell them, rage building inside me to a level that I might just Mount Vesuvius his ass. "Go home, Doug. And take these guys with you."

I steal a glance at Zel and Toby and discover Jason slipping outside. He eyes the scene, and caution shrouds his face. And, oh my god, I do not need this right now!

"Doug!" I shout, stepping down the stairs as his friends hiss at me. "Go home," I command, a slight quiver in my voice.

"I think the one over there," Jeff nods at Zel, "would taste like orange blossoms." Zels' eyes go wide.

"You can't stay here," I glower at Jeff. "Leave. Now."

Doug advances on me. He's so close I can smell Doritos on his breath. "Hell. No," he says with a smirk. This is obviously some kind of power play, a vampire pissing contest. "You've been hanging around Oscar too much. You have no idea what life can really be like for us. The strength. The power." The girl on his arm giggles.

"Kaysee?" Zel whimpers behind me. My best friend cowers with Toby. Jason stands next to them looking like he's ready to kick some serious ass. I can't let Doug hurt them, or my parents, or anyone inside. No one here deserves to die, especially not at Damn It Doug's hands.

"Doug, you and your friends need to go. Now." I say through clenched teeth.

"Or what?" Doug puffs up, and the girl on his arm hisses at me.

"Or I will become your worst nightmare. Not only will I kick your ass, I'll kick their asses too," I say feeling all my vampire rage fill each word. "And I will burn all your computer equipment and make you watch it go up in flames as I drive a stake through your selfish, black heart. You seriously picked the *wrong* day to piss me off."

"Bitch," Jeff steps forward challenging me.

Blood races through my veins. I can't keep this up much longer. If I hadn't been so furious about the contest, I would have backed down with their first hiss. But rage is fueling me now, so I widen my stance and stare down Jeff.

Jeff studies me, looking deep into my eyes before shaking his head. "I'll get you, later. And I'll enjoy watching every drop of your blood drip from your body." He licks his lips and turns toward the parking lot. "Come on, Doug. Bianca, Tony, let's get outta here."

Falling into his usual slouch, Doug takes a step back. A smile overtakes his face but doesn't hide his indignation. "Fine," he spits. "Probably wouldn't be worth it anyway, a bunch of artsy-fartsy people. They always taste like wheatgrass and kale. At least now I know who my real friends are, Kaysee." There's something more to what he's saying, something lingering under the surface. A warning? Doug and his "real friends" slink away and pile into a shiny black SUV. They peel out of the parking lot blaring death metal music.

"Kaysee, what's going on?" Jason whispers. He's standing right behind me close enough for me to feel his breath on my neck.

"Just don't—you can't—you wouldn't," I stutter. Words are elusive. What am I supposed to say? Lie and say everything's okay? Tell him the truth?

"Kaysee," Baihe runs up to me and pulls me into a hug. And it's too much. Tears explode, and I'm ugly crying, heaving, unable to take a breath.

"Where were you?" I ask Baihe. "Doug was here with some friends."

"I know," she shakes her head. "I saw him leave."

"They were going to have—" my eyes dart to Jason. "They were going to have a rave."

"*Ai ya*," Baihe whispers the Mandarin phrase. She's never told me the meaning, but I've always guessed it meant something was seriously messed up.

"A rave? What rave?" Jason asks as Zel and Toby step next to him.

"Wait. Is a rave what you...?" Zel trails off.

"Yes!" I cry out. "A rave is exactly what I told you it was." Zel gasps and grabs Toby's arm.

"What am I missing here?" Jason asks holding up his hand. "What rave?"

My eyes meet his and I wipe at the tears streaking down my cheeks. "He needs to know," I say, all my energy evaporating. I've held up this lie long enough. It's time to be who I really am, flawed and confused and a dumpster fire. But that's me. I can't deny it.

"Jason, I'm the Inman vampire. Baihe's a vampire. Doug is too, and I just stopped him from killing everyone in the museum," my words come out emotionless. Just facts. He stares at me, his eyes squinting in concentration. He must be playing through every interaction we've had. Every moment. Every touch.

"But, no," he says. "What about Zel?"

I shake my head, "No, she's not."

"But you are?" He asks. "You are a vampire? For real? Like, that's actually a real thing?"

Snarling at him, I reveal the splendor of my vampire teeth. "For real," I say.

"Big yikes," Toby whispers aghast.

"But you can't tell anyone. None of you can. They'll come after us if you do," I say. I don't know what kind of reaction I expected from them. Disbelief is reasonable. But now that I've told them, I'm instantly regretting it. Oscar is going to lose his mind when I fill him in on my spontaneous confession. I might have just ruined everything. "Seriously, you can't tell anyone," I plead.

"Can't tell anyone what?" The question comes from behind me, the voice syrupy and fake.

"Brittney Frickin' Bell," I snarl as I turn.

With her hair and makeup perfect, Brittney Bell stands next to her cameraman. The camera on his shoulder is pointed in our direction.

"Nothing!" I yell. "We were just leaving."

"Zel?" Brittney Bell asks as though she's seeing an old friend. "I still haven't gotten that comment from you." Zel shrinks behind Toby.

"It's time for you to go," Baihe steps between me and Brittney Bell, whose eyes have suddenly glossed over. "You and your associate will leave now and forget that you saw us. And you'll leave Zel alone."

Blinking a few times, Brittney Bell gazes at each of us before saying, "Hank, grab the camera. We need to get back to the studio." They saunter away.

"Did anyone else hear?" I panic looking around the well-lit patio and parking lot.

"No one else is here," Baihe says, her voice smooth and calm. She's probably trying to persuade me so I'll stop losing my shit, but even she can't break through this epic disaster.

Dropping to sit on the stairs, I pull my braid out and run my hands through my hair. "Oh my god. Oh my god. Oh my god." I can't stop saying it. My mind is short-circuiting. I'm hyperventilating and sobbing. "Everything's falling apart."

Baihe sits next to me and wraps me in her arms. She turns to Zel. "We need to get her home."

"I just don't understand what's going on here," Jason says, his arms crossed tight over his chest.

"I'm with you," Toby agrees biting his thumbnail.

"Jason, you're giving me and Toby a ride home. We'll talk on the way," Baihe takes charge. "Zel, you're taking Kaysee home. Text her mom to fill her in, just avoid the part where Doug wanted to eat everyone at the museum, okay?"

Even though the night is warm, I pull the snuggie around me after I buckle myself into Zel's car. I need the comfort of the warmth surrounding me as I cry the whole drive home. "Everything is falling apart," I whisper to the passing cars.

27
WE'RE COMING FOR YOU

The only thing I say to anyone for the next two days is, "Leave me alone." Often, it's yelled through my bedroom door. Oscar tries to convince me to open the door by sitting outside and singing show tunes very off-pitch. He lasts over an hour before he gives up.

The sun rises and sets. My phone blows up with text messages. But I stay in my bed with the covers over my head. I'm just not ready to face the world and don't know when I'll ever be ready again.

"Kaysee, you need to come out," Oscar says through my door again.

"Leave me alone," I reply.

"Yes, love, I've done that for a few days now."

"So?"

"So, you need to pull yourself up and come out of your room." Oscar turns the doorknob. It clicks with the effort, but the lock holds strong. "I'm sorry it's come to this."

The scraping sound of metal on metal fills my room. I pull the blanket off my head and sit up.

"Oscar, what are you doing?" I ask as the door shudders.

"Stand back," he orders. There's a crash against the door and the snap of hinges breaking as Oscar tumbles into my room. He catches himself on my desk chair, rights himself, and straightens his shirt.

"You're coming with me," he says seriousness filling his expression. "I can persuade you or you can come of your own volition, but either way, you're following me."

"Where are we going?" I ask not ready to face the world or anything else outside my bedroom for that matter.

"I was going to take you to the kitchen, but now we're going outside. Staying in bed for two days hasn't helped your aroma, love. You smell like Doug."

I take a quick pit sniff, and he's right. I smell like Cheetos and leftover pepperoni pizza. Disgusting! Groaning I stand and follow Oscar who's waiting for me at the top of the stairs. He leads me outside to the patio and gestures for me to sit in the swing.

Pulling up a patio chair, he sits across from me. The sun is dipping below the horizon allowing darkness to overtake the world. "Look, I'm sorry for revealing myself," I say running my hands up the rough ropes of the swing.

"That's been taken care of," Oscar says. "Baihe made a wise decision that it was acceptable for Jason and Toby to know our little secret, so she only persuaded them to not tell another soul."

"They must have been freaking out," I worry.

"Actually, no," Oscar chuckles. "They handled the news surprisingly well. Not much surprises people anymore."

I scoff. "So, can I go back to my room now?"

"No, you cannot. We need to talk." Oscar sits back in his chair, resting his hands in his lap. "What you're feeling isn't uncommon for a young vampire like yourself."

"Oscar, I'm not in the mood for another 'your vampire body is changing' talk."

"Too bad, it's what you need," he smiles devilishly. "We all went through depression like this after being changed. It's part of the grief cycle of becoming a vampire."

"But I have a right to be depressed," I argue. "I outed myself and was overheard by Brittney Bell. I could have ruined everything for all of us."

"But you didn't."

"But I *could* have." I stand. "It's losing the art contest. I was so angry. And this whole Instagram picture thing, and I was stupid to start the Twitter account. I'm totally deleting that today. Now Toby and Jason know about us too. I've brought too many people in, too many people who could tell the world. And I'm not just talking about angry villagers with shotguns, I'm talking about the dangerous vampire world too. Did you know that I had to chase Doug and his friends away from raving at the museum?"

"I did know that," Oscar sighs. "He hasn't been seen since then."

"See? I ruined that too. Now Doug is running wild through southwest Missouri leaving a path of death and destruction. It's my fault. I should have shoved him in the car and locked him in the basement."

"That actually doesn't work so well with Doug," Oscar says. "We tried it once in Montana. He did surprisingly well alone in a basement with nothing but a computer and bags of Fritos."

"Stop trying to make me laugh," I tell Oscar as my lips turn up slightly.

"Kaysee, we've all been through this, more than once actually," Oscar stands and rests his hands on my shoulders. "Vampire life isn't easy. And being a vampire in high school is particularly hard. Always has been. Always will be. But you're going to be around for a very long time. You can't spend the next decade hating yourself. Trust me, I tried that."

"Really?" I raise my eyebrows. "What happened?"

"I will spare you the details but let me say that there is a town in Denmark that lost many of its citizens in 1905... and a rather large cow as I recall."

Now, I do laugh.

"There she is," Oscar smiles. "Trust me. You don't want to live a life regretting that you hated yourself for so long. Now, for the love of god, check your phone. Zel and Jason won't leave me alone. They've even shown up on the doorstep multiple times. What a bother."

"Thank you, Oscar," I say pulling him into a hug. "I couldn't do this vampire life without you."

"You're welcome." He pushes me away. "Forget what I said about the phone, love. Get thee to the toiletries. I think the smell is somehow worse outdoors."

Smiling, I head inside. What Oscar said makes sense. It doesn't completely clear away all the garbage in my heart but it gives me an ounce of hope. A long, hot shower and washing my hair three times helps more. I put on my comfiest workout clothes and grab my phone. The battery died sometime early Sunday morning, but

I plugged it in before my shower and now it's flashing with notifications like an over-decorated Christmas tree.

There are literally 107 texts from Zel. She gave up after the first 30 or so and just repeatedly texted "Call me ASAP" for the final 77. Messages from Jason grow in their concern and sadness. His last text tears at my heart.

I guess you need space. I'm here when you're ready.

My heart aches to see him, but I need to do something first.

I pull out a blank canvas and the picture I'd printed of him from when we went hiking. It's the one of him standing against the sky where he looks like he's flying. I set it on my desk and take out my paints.

I painted late into the night to finish the project. After a few texts with Zel, we made plans to hang out between track practice and school. My feet are itching to move. When Oscar drives us to track practice, I leap from the car. Mrs. Kelsey is taking us on what she calls a long run today. It's only four miles. I finish ahead of the others far enough that I have time to run a mile and a half on the track before school starts.

Cruising through my first classes I don't need one sip of vamp juice. When I step into chem class and see Jason, my heart skips a few beats. The paint wasn't dry on my project when I left for track practice, but it will be tonight. Butterflies fill my stomach as I approach our lab table. Sitting hunched over his notes, Jason has his back to me. The last time I saw him I was a flaming hot mess. He must think I'm insane and unhinged.

"Hey, Jason," I say meekly.

He turns to me and it's like a slow-motion cheesy Hallmark movie. His hair shifts with the movement and he has to brush it out of his eyes. His eyes crease with a deep smile and I melt like butter on a hot pan.

"Kaysee," he says my name tentatively.

"We have some things to talk about—if you want to talk, that is," I say.

"Yeah," he chuckles. "We have a few things to talk about. But not here. You know Mr. Garcia hears everything in this classroom."

"Did someone say my name?" Mr. Garcia asks from across the room making us laugh.

"Come by after school?"

I nod. "Yeah."

"You two look like you're sharing sultry secrets," Zel teases as she walks over holding Toby's hand. When he meets my eyes, Toby is overcome with sheepishness. It's cute but doesn't compare to the smoke and heat coming from Jason.

"I told him not to worry," Zel whispers conspiratorially leaning close. "You won't eat him."

How weird is this? My friends and my big secret. They know I'm a vampire, and they're not running for the hills. It makes me wonder if I should have told them sooner.

We have a big test coming up next week, so Mr. Garcia gives us the class time to work on the study guide. As we look up answers in our notebooks, Jason and I steal glances and grin like goofballs. I guess I've gotten used to the idea that I do really like Jason.

As I'm following him out of class, I take a peek at my Twitter feed. There's a DM notification. I don't recognize the sender but open it anyway.

I will find where you live. We're coming for you. And you can't run away from us.

I have to clutch my phone to keep it from falling from my hands. Jason stops and looks back at me questioningly.

The message is signed *Vanhelsing510.*

28

VANHELSING510

It's a joke. Just a joke. Some internet troll messing with me. Just a joke, right?

No, it's not. It's the mob with pitchforks and shotguns. Damn it. I'm screwed. Again.

"It's someone messing with you," Zel says at lunch. We're crammed on a bench with Oscar and Baihe far away from anyone else. Jason stands behind us. His schedule changed after Christmas, so he doesn't have lunch this period, but he skipped French class when he saw me turn white as a ghost.

"We can't be sure," Oscar says. "What's the person's name?"

"The profile just says Vanhelsing510. There's not much else but a picture and some weird tweets."

"We can reverse search the picture, but first you should be safe and turn off your location," Jason says. "Then we should set you up with a VPN."

I turn to him, smashing my thigh against Zel's. "You speak computer?"

"Yeah," he shrugs. "My oldest brother used to mess around on them, and when he went to college to study cybersecurity. He showed me a thing or two."

Thrusting my phone in his hands, I command, "You do it. See what you can find."

After a few minutes of quick tapping, Jason has installed a VPN to vary my IP address and given me an extra layer of anonymity. He's also turned off my location and searched the handful of pictures on Vanhelsing510's page.

"It's all just internet junk pics, nothing that would lead us back to him." Jason passes my phone back to me. "Sorry."

The bell rings, and we all grab our backpacks and uneaten lunches. "Kaysee, wait up," Jason jogs to my side.

"Thanks for all that tech stuff," I say taking a swig of vamp juice.

"No problem, that was easy," he replies with a dismissive shrug. "But, hey, how about I come to your house tonight? Maybe you shouldn't be out on your own after dark."

I laugh. "You forget that I am a blood-thirsty human drinker, right? I think I can handle myself."

"Still, I'd feel better knowing you were safe at home and not having to use your vampire skills to murder someone to keep them from murdering you."

"I guess, if you put it that way," I cringe. "Come by after school. We can talk, and I have something for you."

"Oh, you do?" Jason wiggles his eyebrows suggestively. I punch him in the shoulder but smile when I walk away.

♥

Two more threatening messages pop up in my Twitter inbox before the end of school. I keep telling myself to stay calm, but each one makes me more nervous. All through art class, I take pictures with my phone. If I can't run, at least I can look at the world through the filter of a camera lens, and pretend everything is shiny and pretty.

"You look like a tea kettle about to whistle," Baihe says after buckling her seat belt. Oscar pulls Mom's car into the after-school traffic jam. "When we get home, I want to show you some defensive techniques."

What she means by this is taking me in the front yard and showing me multiple ways to hit or kick a guy in their junk. It's only after I point out that some vampires or angry mob people are girls, that she laughs and shows me some different moves.

I'm relieved when I spot Jason walking down the sidewalk to my house. Pausing from the lesson on how to use my elbow to cause significant damage, I jog over to meet him.

"You're still alive, that's good," Jason says.

"I'm not dead yet," I reply. "Of course, it is really hard to kill me now."

"Yeah, I've been meaning to ask about that. Remember when we went hiking?"

I grimace. "And I broke my leg." He follows me to my front porch.

"I knew it! I heard it crack, and knew it broke," he says as though he's answered the final question on a game show and won a million dollars.

"Yeah but, it was healing very quickly, and I didn't want you to think I was weak."

Jason closes the distance between us and lowers his voice. "Weak is never a word I'd use to describe you. You took all the bullying from me and never backed down. I've always known you were strong."

My breath hitches as sparks shoot through the air between us. "You were really mean. I actually cried many nights at Zel's house."

"I was angry after my mom died. You were one of the many people I took out my anger on." He takes my hand. And oh, holy expletives, his hand is so strong and rough from years of using free weights. It sends a shockwave up my arm.

"I forgive you," I practically drool. I'm a puddle, my are knees weak. There is a flash in his eyes, and I think he's going to try to kiss me again. I can feel his desire echoing through his pulse.

I lick my lips and lean forward. What the hell? I'm stopped short when a sharp rock pelts me on the side of the head.

"First lesson, Kaysee," Baihe says holding a few decorative garden stones. "Never let your guard down. You have to remember that! Oh, hi, Jason." She waves at him oblivious to what was going on between us. I love Baihe, but right now, I'd like to practice using my elbows on her sensitive body parts a few more times.

Wiping the trickle of blood from my temple, I nod toward the house. "Let's go through to the backyard. I need to get that thing for you."

"Are you okay?" Jason stares at the blood smeared on the side of my face.

"I'm fine, totally fine. Vampire healing," I shrug and lead him through to the back patio.

Before I grab my newest art project, I slip into the bathroom and clean the blood off my face. It's not really that bad. A bruise is dancing under my skin with colors changing from deep purple to cobalt blue to canary yellow.

"Okay," I begin sitting across from Jason and holding the painting so he can't see it yet. "I did this one fast, so it's not my best. But I wanted to do this for you as a thank you and an apology. Yes, you've been a total asshole in the past, but this year you've been really cool."

Jason laughs and leans forward. "If it's a picture of an actual ass hole, I don't want it."

I groan and roll my eyes. "Here, take it," I say and thrust the painting at him. I watch his eyes move across the canvas. It's monochromatic blue with dynamic variants in the hues. In the center is his picture, but I've blended it into the canvas. Below the picture are treetops in deep azure shadows. The blue of the sky wraps around him and is filled with wispy clouds and the silhouette of a flock of birds flying toward the sun. It was rushed. I'd love to go through and sharpen some places, but overall, I'm proud of this painting. I've always enjoyed painting on photos and blending them into a larger work. With this piece, it all flows in such harmony that it's hard to tell where the photo ends and the painting begins.

"This is really good," Jason says still studying it.

"It's nothing, really," I say. The same feeling I have every time I share my art is creeping over me. I'm exposed like someone is seeing me naked.

"Yes, it's freaking awesome. It looks like an album cover," he looks at me and smiles. "It's amazing. So—so, I don't even know how to say this. It's just...will you go to prom with me?"

His sudden shift knocks me off-kilter. Did he just go from "Your art is nice" to "Will you go to prom with me?"

Misreading my confusion he says, "You don't have to. It's fine. I wasn't sure if I was gonna go anyway."

Starting somewhere deep in my gut, joy blossoms over my entire body, revealing itself with a wide grin clearly displaying my vampire teeth. "You're okay going to prom with a vampire?" I ask.

"I'm okay going to prom with you, *Kaysee*."

Someone, get a towel! I'm a puddle melted on the floor again. There's no hope of me taking solid form again anytime soon.

I manage to compose myself for a brief moment to say, "Yes. I'd love to go to prom with you."

29

A Short Presentation on Slaying Vampires

In the three weeks between Jason asking me to prom and the day before prom, life is nutballs crazy. Track practice and my first two meets take my mind off the DMs that continue to roll in from Vanhelsing510. Greg, the shot putter from the track team, now eats lunch with us every day. He and Oscar have spent many hours cuddled up on the couch binge-watching Netflix.

Zel, Baihe, and I find the perfect dresses for prom. Zel's dress tapers through the legs and is tight enough that when she walks her steps are so short that she looks like she has to pee really bad. Baihe picks one with long slits up both sides of the skirt. She said it's so she still has the flexibility to kick ass. Mine is simple, the way I like it. Emerald green, not too tight, not too long, and not too cleavage-y.

The only weird thing is that Doug hasn't shown up anywhere. No one has heard from him. Oscar keeps saying that he'll return like a stray cat after it's been fed. I've literally considered leaving a package of Cheetos or Oreos outside at night to lure him back. Not knowing where he is worries me more than I let on. If he's really with those evil vampires, what could he be up to?

I keep tweeting as the Real Inman Vampire and have amassed a decent following. I have over 59,000 followers and get lots of interaction with my posts even if they are vague.

"See you at my house tonight?" I ask Jason as we walk out of the chem lab holding hands. We haven't done much more than hug or hold hands yet. I don't know why he's waiting to kiss. I'd love to flex my feminist power and pin him to a locker one day. But he hasn't initiated, and I'm too chicken. Maybe it's my teeth? Maybe it's because Jason knows that I could easily kill him or turn him into a vampire. That would really interfere with his plans for college and med school.

"Yeah, should I bring anything?" He asks giving my hand a squeeze.

"I don't think so. Oscar said we just needed to be there," I smile at him, something I'm having trouble stopping is smiling at Jason.

He deposits me in the commons for lunch and pulls me into a hug before going on to French class. My arms tingle from where they were wrapped around his muscled torso. Sure, I studied anatomy in biology last year, but for real, I never knew someone could have so many muscles. I bite my lip smiling like the village idiot watching Jason walk down the hallway and wondering how in the world I ended up with a guy like him.

♥

The whole team's here in my living room. Mom made snacks and Dad's passing around vamp juice and Cokes. I take one of both to drink with my apple slices. It feels like a birthday party when I was in first grade, but it's not. It's a far cry from that.

"The best way to kill a vampire, as we all know, is a stake to the heart," Oscar says standing in front of a whiteboard on an easel. He's drawn a crude outline of a person with a red X on the heart.

We all nod in agreement. Jason snatches one of my apple slices. Greg sits on the other side of him, a notebook and pen poised to take notes. Oscar shared our little secret with Greg saying that if my boyfriend knew about our vampire lifestyle, his deserved to as well. Across from us, Zel has her fingers intertwined with Toby's. He's trying his best to hide how freaky this all is to him, but he's failing.

"But chopping off their head is also just as effective," Baihe says drawing her own red X on the whiteboard man's head. "Remember that vampires can heal fast, but if you cause enough damage, we don't have time to heal before we bleed out. So, you can go for an artery too." Baihe is way too perky talking about killing.

"That's a good point," Oscar nods. Greg scribbles furiously.

"Oh," Baihe jumps with excitement, "and don't forget that if a body part is cut off, it can't grow back. That goes for ears, eyes, fingers, testicles—"

"Where's the bathroom?" Toby's face has gone green. "I need to, um..." He holds his hand tight over his mouth.

"This way, sweetie," Mom grabs his arm and drags him to the hall bathroom. I shoot Zel a questioning look. She cringes and shrugs. Toby may not be up to vampire slaying after all.

Jason raises his hand, "I don't see why we're doing this now. Do you really think there'll be vampires attacking the prom? It seems a little trite."

"While it might be trite, it's also efficient," Oscar explains. "It's fairly common for vampires to attack large crowds but ones that are not too large. A rock concert is fun in a seedy bar, but in a full stadium, things get out of control. Proms are perfect. There's a lot of blood to choose from, including some that will be laced with alcohol or more commonly the pure blood of a virgin."

"That's a thing? Virgin blood?" I ask bewildered. "You've never said anything about that before, just diabetic blood."

"It's a thing," Baihe says with an apologetic shrug. "Some vampires get off on it. But not all of us!" She holds up her hands defensively. Every time I think I understand how to be a vampire, new crap like this pops up.

I take a swig of vamp juice as Oscar turns his attention to the outline of the school gym drawn on the other side of the whiteboard. He's marked the bleachers and all the exits. "In each of your kits, there will be extra strong bike chains. I found them on the Amazon and was assured by the advertisement that they're impervious to being cut. During prom, all the exits will be open except the emergency exit leading outdoors."

"And you know this how?" I ask.

"I had a special conversation with Principal Cole," Oscar winks. "She was very helpful."

"Okay, so there's seven of us, but only five exits," Zel points at the board. "So, I volunteer to *not* be carrying one of those unbreakable large chains. They won't go with my dress."

"Actually, there will only be five of you at the prom. Greg and I have decided to stay in for the night," Oscar says.

"You won't be there? What do we do if the evil vampires do show up for a rave?" I ask.

"No worries, love. We'll be on standby at Greg's house. He's a mere two blocks from the school. If anything happens, you can text me, and we'll hop on over ready for the melee." Oscar smiles reassuringly, but I'm still not happy with this whole thing.

"Couldn't we all just stay home?" Toby asks returning to his seat next to Zel.

"And miss prom?" Zel screeches. "I'm not going to let Damn It Doug and his sus vampire idiots keep me from going to prom."

Oscar points to himself, Baihe, and me. "Whether we're there or not, it's likely Doug will show up with his friends. Damn It Doug has always had a flair for the dramatic."

"And he holds a grudge like no one I know," Baihe adds.

"After locking the doors, what do we do next?" Greg asks, pen ready. His enthusiasm makes me wonder whose idea it was to keep him on standby. I think he'd be much more useful than Toby.

"First, let me say the last door to be locked is the emergency exit. Leave someone standing by to let me and Greg in should you need us," Oscar says. "The best plan is to keep Doug and his blokes outside. Gather everyone together in the gym and stay safe. But, should any of the other vampires breakthrough, be ready to fight."

"We put some things in your kits for that too," Baihe says pointing to the bulky backpacks lying on the floor next to her. "We'll each need to bring our kits and have them ready."

"How do we know if Doug is attacking?" I ask. "It'll be dark, loud, lots of people."

"We need a signal," Jason nods at me. "I have an idea for that. Anyone know who the DJ is for prom?"

30
LEVITATING

The mirror isn't big enough for me, Zel, and Baihe to get ready at the same time. We still cram in the bathroom together anyway. Being an only child, I've never had the joy of sharing life with anyone like this. Mom and Dad have been so absent for so long. Growing up I thought I could walk out the door, and if I kept walking, they probably wouldn't know I was gone until I was somewhere near Denver. Having my parents hovering to take endless pictures now is weird. We had to shut them out of the bathroom because they were way too overstimulating.

Baihe and I let Zel do our makeup and touch up our hair. She's a wizard with eyeliner and makes us both look freaking amazing. Baihe's lips are deep red, and her hair is twisted into two buns high on her head with two chopsticks sticking through each bun. Following my very clear directions, Zel gives me a look that's natural with a hint of glitter on my eyelids. She did this awesome thing where she uses her flat iron to give my hair layers of waves. When she's done with herself, she looks like a young Jennifer Lopez on her best day. Her lips, her hair, the fit of her dress over her hips. She's killing it. I snap a great picture of Zel and Baihe laughing as Zel brushes her hair. It's priceless.

Before we go downstairs to meet the guys, I check my Twitter feed again. There's another DM from Vanhelsing510.

You can't hide forever. I'm going to find you soon.

I've kept the messages to myself, but Jason followed me on Twitter and has been checking out the comments. Vanhelsing510 is all over there too, mostly trying to rile people up. He blends in with the other Twitter trolls. It's the DMs that make my skin itch.

Starting the Twitter account was supposed to take the attention away from Zel's picture, make it look like the whole thing was fake. Things aren't happening the way I expected. But I'm going to put this whole thing aside for tonight and just enjoy prom...as long as Doug and Jeff don't show up and ruin it by eating everyone.

As we walk down the stairs to Toby and Jason waiting in the living room, I snap a few pictures of the two of them standing together. They're both hot in their own way. Toby is rockin' geek chic with a patterned tuxedo that would look ridiculous on anyone else. Jason is in a traditional black tux that fits him perfectly and makes him look like a young James Bond.

Mom and Dad make us pose for pictures. We're standing on the stairs. We're sitting on the couch. We're fake laughing on the front porch. I make Mom take a few special pictures of me, and Zel with the swing in the backyard. We take turns sitting while the other stands behind spinning the swing. Everything is perfect. A light wind flutters new leaves on the trees and lifts my hair carrying the warmth of late spring to add to our joy. The laughter we share isn't fake one bit. Prom hasn't started, but I'm already having the time of my life with my best friends.

Zel's parents let us use the family minivan to go to prom. Her mom convinced her dad saying that we'd ruin our dresses if we had to push Zel's car through town when it breaks down again. Jason and I slide into the far back seat, and he immediately reaches for my hand.

Leaning over to whisper in my ear, his breath tickling me, he says, "You look amazing."

I giggle and stop myself from biting my lips. I don't want to mess up my lip gloss this early in the night. "You look pretty too," I say smiling my new smile. It's where I lift my lower lip higher than usual so that it covers the tips of my vamp teeth. I've been practicing it for the past week.

"It's prom time, bitches!" Zel yells as she pulls out of her drive-way. We whoop and holler. She hits the gas and all the colors of blooming spring flowers fly past us, their vibrance candy for my eyes.

It's been a shitty school year, but we're going out with a bang. The principal even said we didn't have to wear masks for prom. We're ready to let loose and have some fun. But at the back of my mind, I remember that I also need to keep my eyes and ears open for Damn It Doug and Evil Jeff.

"Shit!" Zel spits as she pulls the minivan into the school parking lot. "Shit! Shit! Shitty shit!"

Leaning to look out the windshield I see the source of Zel's "shits." The Channel 10 news van is parked outside the gym. Standing behind it is Brittney Bell checking her reflection on her phone.

"It's not so bad," I say. "She hasn't bothered us in a while. Maybe she's just here to cover prom." As I say the words fingers of doubt clench my heart.

"Actually," Zel begins but trails off. She pulls into a parking space and turns off the minivan. "She's been messaging me, like a lot. But I ignored them. I thought she'd drop it."

"Look," Jason says, "screw her. Let's go in and enjoy prom. Forget Brittney Bell."

"Yeah, forget her," Baihe adds with a mischievous smile. "I'm ready to dance."

We shuffle out of the car and grab our kits from the trunk. The chains make them awkward to carry. As we walk, I try to forget everything that's in them even as their bulk slaps against my thigh with every step. Oscar might have gone a little overboard in preparing us to fend off Doug and Jeff.

Seeing Zel, Brittney Bell runs over, her high heels tapping the sidewalk like a tinny drum. "Zel, you're here." She smiles like they're old friends again. It makes me want to gag. "Any comment on the Inman vampire?"

"It's just a joke, a hoax," Zel says with an eye roll and keeps walking.

Brittney Bell tsks. "But where did the photo come from? My people did some research and determined that the original source was your post on Instagram."

Toby steps between them. "No comment," he says with authority and tugs Zel by the hand toward the school. As she passes through the glass doors into the commons, Zel waves her middle finger at Brittney Bell. I guess she did have a comment after all.

When we pass our tickets to Mrs. Cole, she gives our bags a questioning glance. Baihe is on it in an instant. After a few words whispered amidst intense eye contact, Mrs. Cole looks past us and yells, "Next."

Stepping into the gym we're assaulted with flashing lights and the thumping beat of Billie Eilish. There's decorations of crepe paper and a tree artistically made of discarded masks. Seems appropriate considering the theme of prom this year is "Unmasked." It's culturally insensitive, but the principal let it slide since virus cases have dropped to nearly nothing.

Jason takes my hand and leads me to the bleachers. We stash our bags in the openings at the ends. Baihe, Zel, and Toby stash theirs under the bleachers across the gym. The DJ, a friend of Zel's brother, switches the song to Dua Lipa's "Levitating," and it captures exactly how I feel. So light I'm levitating. The pressure of the art contest is gone. It didn't turn out the way I'd wanted, but it's over. And the person I thought I didn't want pulls me to the dance floor.

I let myself be free, and I dance. In the past, I only went to dances because Zel dragged me along. I'd shuffle to the music for a few songs, then settle on the bleachers with a few cookies and watch everyone else having fun. I felt safe in the shadows, watching life happen around me.

Not tonight. Tonight, I'm dancing. I'm living it up. I'm not staying in the shadows. I'm finally being so bold I'm levitating.

My feet surprisingly aren't killing me. We've been dancing nearly nonstop for two hours. Zel bowed out a few songs ago and is now sitting in the bleachers with her feet on Toby's lap. He's rubbing her arches and smiling at her like someone totally in love. It's the way I've been smiling at Jason tonight too. But I'm too scared to say or do anything about it. So, we just keep dancing, and my vampire healing abilities take care of my feet all night long.

"You want a break?" Jason asks between songs, sweat trickling down the side of his face. He tossed his suit jacket and bow tie a while ago. His shirt is unbuttoned a few buttons with his sleeves rolled up showing off the defined muscles of his forearms.

I nod, still smiling. He takes my hand and leads me to the hallway outside the gym. It's quiet here, the music muffled. We can see out the glass doors where the Channel 10 news van is still parked. I quickly forget about Channel 10 News when Jason leads me to a bank of lockers a little way down the hall.

He sighs and waves his hand through his hair. "This is a lot more fun than I thought it would be," he says with a wide smile.

"I think so too," I reply and dip my gaze. "It helps to have someone fun to share it with."

"That's exactly what I was thinking," Jason says stepping closer. I straighten, my back flat against a cold metal locker. Jason grazes his knuckle under my chin and tips it up so that I'm looking him straight in the eyes.

Heat builds between us and my heart catches.

"Kaysee, I've been into you for a long time," Jason says. He trails his fingers down my arm leaving me trembling from the joyous shock they produce.

Jason scoffs. "Everything's been crazy. Never in a million years did I think that I'd be friends with vampires or I'd ever tell you how I felt."

"I guess you won me over by showing me how human you actually are, and I lured you in by being non-human." My gaze is drawn to his lips which are inching closer.

"Human. Vampire. You're just Kaysee to me. Kaysee with green eyes that capture art through the lens of a camera. Kaysee who doesn't take my shit. Kaysee who sees me as the bastard I am but still hasn't run away."

"Running away is an option?" I ask easily slipping into our usual banter. And mentally I'm kicking myself. He's being hella sexy and I'm making jokes. Argh!

"No," Jason rests his hands on my arms. "Because if you run away now, you'll never know what it's like to kiss Jason Hancock. I have been dying to do this for months."

He leans toward me, and my hands find their way up his back. Everything is in slow motion. He's not rushing this, but inches closer and closer, his breath mixing with mine. My eyes are drifting shut ready to let my other senses languish and celebrate the sensation of his lips on mine.

"What the hell?" Jason jumps. Both our heads whip toward a blazingly bright light shining into the hallway from the commons' doors. Jason looks back at me. "Doug?"

"We'd better check it out," I say pulling him with me. Vampire rage brews in my gut. If it is Doug, I'll kill him just for ruining this moment. At the corner, we squint at the doorway, shielding our eyes with our hands. And I shake my head in frustration. "Brittney Freakin' Bell."

The light is set up to shine on her in front of the doorway to the school. She stands next to someone and it looks like she's recording an interview. I squint trying to make out the interviewee through the glass doors. Seeing the silhouette, hair stands up on my arms. The interviewee has a scrawny stature I'd recognize anywhere.

"Damn it, Doug," I whisper in frustration. "Stay here," I order Jason and round the corner hugging the wall. It's hard to see much because of the bright light pouring in. I don't want to get too close. It could just be Doug being Doug and here to mess things up like he always does. But it could also be so much worse.

I'm too close now, the sharp light spilling on my feet. Through the window, I capture a swift movement of someone stepping forward. When the light hits the side of his face, I cringe. Evil Jeff. This is not good. All the curse words flash through my mind. But I don't have long to revel in my wrath because when Brittney Bell laughs at something Doug says, she angles her head back just right, and Doug lunges.

A splatter of blood sprays the glass door as Doug latches on. Evil Jeff goes for the cameraman as I scream, "No!"

In shock, I step fully into the light. Doug and Jeff lift their heads from their victims and meet my eyes. Recognition fills their faces with sinister smiles. Jeff turns to the side and whistles. And four more vampires appear, hungry and ready to kill.

"Kaysee?" Jason steps into the hall.

I turn and race for him. "Coldplay!" I scream. "Coldplay!"

31
OPERATION COLDPLAY

Tossing two chairs at the doorway to block the vampire's path, I race for the gym. A few people linger in the hallway, probably trying to steal kisses like Jason and me. But, damn it, Jason didn't even kiss me.

I am totally going to kill Doug for so many reasons, I think as my blood boils.

"Get in the gym!" I command shocking the lovebirds with my insistence so much they immediately obey. The first beats of "Something Just Like This" pound from the gym. Coldplay's haunting opening notes ripple over me heightening my senses and sending a shitload of fear up my spine.

I reach for my phone strapped to my thigh. Abuelita for the win again. When Zel told her we needed places to keep our phones during prom, she created a thigh phone holster for me and a wrist one for Baihe. Zel just hid hers in her cleavage, always a safe place.

My fingers stumble over my screen to tap in my passcode. Once the phone wakes up, I hit send on the pre-written message I had waiting to send to Oscar. And behind me, a sickening laugh echoes through the commons.

At the bleachers, I crash into Jason. He catches me and hands me my kit. I kick off my heels and pull the bike lock out of the bag. "I'll get this door, you get the other side," I say squeezing his arm. Fear flickers in his eyes. "Go!" I order and turn to the door closest to me.

I steal a glance across the gym and see Zel wrapping her bike lock around the boys' locker room door. We've been through the plan. We all have a part. Mine is to lock the door closest to the commons. And I'm heading there when I see Doug jump out into the doorway, a few steps from entering the gym. I squeal in surprise and stumble to a stop. Doug laughs at me. It's a game for him.

"Doug, you can stop this. Just turn around and leave," I say stepping closer to the door with the bike lock dangling from my hands.

"Pshaw!" Doug cackles. "This is not going to be like the last time. You can't scare me away. Oscar is nothing. Baihe is an idiot. And you are just a baby vampire who knows nothing!"

"I know enough to know that you can't kill all these people." I wave at everyone dancing behind me.

"You are a moron," Doug spits. "You've never tasted warm blood, straight from the veins. You only know what Oscar's told you about being a vampire, which is really nothing. There's a whole world out there, Kaysee."

"He's right," Jeff says stepping next to Doug. "Don't fight us. Join us and see what it's like to really be a vampire. To have the power of eternal life or death in your hands."

"Kaysee!" Baihe runs up behind me. I barely hear her calling my name over the music. "Don't listen to them!" She tugs on my arm, but I shake her off.

Walking toward them, I keep my eyes on Jeff. He peers at me as though he's already devouring my flesh. Adrenaline floods my body making my hands shake, but I fight to keep steady, focused.

Doug's friends arrive behind him and Jeff, licking their lips and baring their teeth. There's a stocky, white guy with a thick mullet. Next to him is a huge African American guy who looks like he could play for the NFL. On the sides are two girls, wearing slutty dresses. One has a black bob and oddly looks like Miley Cyrus. The other girl from the art show, Bianca, has long, stringy hair and looks like Angela from *The Office* on her worst day. They all share a deep hunger filling their eyes.

I take a slow breath and whip my gaze back to Evil Jeff. "Kiss my ass," I say stepping back and lunging for the doors. I grab one side, and Baihe yanks the other. We slam them shut and press our weight into the doors. On the other side, the evil vampires are pushing against the doors trying to dislodge us and begin their rave.

"Where's Oscar?" I scream at Baihe as a strong jolt hits the door.

"I don't know," Baihe says shifting against the assault.

"Jason!" I scream hoping that he can hear me over Chris Martin. "Jason!"

A group of people near the door are watching us confused. Toby bursts between them. "Give me the chain," he holds his hand out.

I pass him the chain as Jason arrives and adds his weight to the doors. Toby shimmies between us to thread the chain through the door handles and clicks the lock closed. We all jump from the door that still throbs from the vampires' efforts to break through.

"How many?" Baihe asks.

"Only the six," I say stretching my shoulder. I'm pretty sure something just got torn, but I can feel it already healing. "There might be more. Get to the door to let Oscar and Greg in." I turn to Jason. "We've got to get this under control."

Glancing around the gym, I see some people still dancing, others mingling by the snack table. Zel rushes our way, her legs encumbered by her tight dress. She passes Indigo, Maeve, and Maddy huddled by the bleachers. They've seen what's going on and are looking at me searching for answers with their quizzical gazes. The gym is full of students, teachers, parent chaperones. Doug wants to kill them all. But I won't let that happen.

"The hinges aren't going to hold," I say as the doors rattle against the bike chain.

Zel reaches me clutching her kit. "Get to the top of the bleachers," I order her before turning to Toby who's shaking like a leaf in a tornado. "Toby!" He snaps his gaze to me. "Get your shit together, then get your kit, and go to the top of the other bleachers. Go!"

A look passes between Toby and Zel like they're caressing each other with their eyes. "Go!" I yell again clapping my hands to break their spell. They turn and scamper for the bleachers.

"Jason, get behind us and move people to the center of the dancefloor. And find Oscar," I'm desperately ordering him as something metal crashes against the gym doors. The chain rattles and a few bolts pop from the hinges. When I look behind me, Jason has disappeared into the crowd that's still bumping, grinding, and twerking unaware of their potential demise.

"You ready for this?" Baihe asks pulling two chopsticks from her hair.

I scoff. "I'm a pacifist, vegetarian vampire. There is no way I'll ever be ready for this," I say my heart pounding against my chest in tune with Coldplay's beat. From the kit, I pull out a knife and a sharpened stake then sling the bag over my back. The weapons feel wrong in my hands. But I'm going to have to fight to save my friends and to save the prom. Setting my feet into the sturdy stance Baihe taught me, I lift my weapons. Ready or not, here they come.

After a few moments of the door resting still, I get my hopes up that Doug and his gang have given up. But the explosion of bolts being ripped from the cement block walls tells me otherwise. The doors crash forward and land on the floor twisted in a cloud of dust. Light from the hallway backlights the evil vamps. They stand ominously eying the room.

A clank rings through the gym when the NFL vampire drops a fire extinguisher on the floor. Jeff steps into the gym, a disco light dancing across his face. He laughs and says, "Dinner time, lovies!" With a snap of his fingers, the vampires rush toward us.

Baihe sends her chopsticks sailing lodging one in NFL vamp's neck. He falls to his knees screaming in pain. The other chopstick sticks into the Miley vamp girl's stomach. With the chopstick protruding from her hot pink dress, she looks like a demented popsicle.

Bianca, the Angela-wreck-of-a-vampire, lunges for me with Doug on her heels. She reaches out, but I swipe with my knife and catch her arm making her squeal and stumble back. I steal a glance at Baihe who is facing off with Evil Jeff. He sneers at her, enjoying taunting his kill. Baihe attacks him with a flurry of badass kicks to his face, his gut, then his face again.

I realize I shouldn't have taken my eyes off of Doug when he crashes into me dragging us both to the floor. He lands on top of me, smiling. "Isn't this just like the first time we met?" He jeers. I respond by driving my knee into his groin with epic force, and it feels so good to watch him turn green as he falls to the floor next to me.

When I'm on my feet again, I'm blinded by a splatter of red. The scent of hot sauce and imitation orange flavor assaults my nose. Red sprays over my outstretched arms. And it douses Bianca making her scream in pain. Looking over my shoulder, I smile at Zel. She beams back at me and lifts another water balloon.

This was another of Oscar's ideas. It's a distraction and a defense. The vamp bombs are a mix of Sunny Delight, cayenne pepper, and Tabasco sauce that will knock anyone off guard. Actually, all that acidity burns the skin too, I realize as sprinkles of fire ignite over my arms. Wiping my arms over my prom dress, I watch Bianca dance in pain trying to wipe away the spicy concoction. She's covered in it like that old horror movie *Carrie*.

Baihe is fending off Jeff and the NFL vamp with kung-fu kicks and punches. I whip my head around looking for mullet vamp and Miley vamp.

"No!" I yell, running for a cluster of oblivious seniors dancing in a circle. Mullet vamp and Miley vamp are sneaking up on them, their eyes gleaming. They're across the gym, closer to where Toby waits with vamp bombs in the stands. Red splatters next to the seniors, but misses the vamps by a long shot. Maybe we should've put Jason on vamp bomb launch duty. As if reading my mind, Jason bursts back through the crowd and yells at the senior circle to get out of the way. They stare at him confused, their eyes glazed over by alcohol. The group shifts after Jason shoves one of the basketball players. They move toward the center of the gym but not fast enough.

Mullet vamp jumps on a tall girl from the volleyball team, knocking her to the ground. Before he can bite her, I lift my stake and drive it into his back. The Coldplay song ends. In that moment of silence before the next track, I hear the stake squish into the soft flesh near mullet vamp's kidney. It makes me retch. A vamp bomb explodes on the floor behind me at Miley vamp's feet. She slips in the sticky liquid, grabbing at me to keep from crashing to the floor.

BTS's *Butter* blares across the gym to cheers. Jason steps past me and cold cocks the Miley vamp. She crumples landing in the vamp bomb juice like she's going to make a snow angel in it.

"Jason," I yell, grabbing his arm, "go help Toby. And text Oscar again."

He hesitates, his hands holding my arms. I can feel his speeding pulse beat against my skin. Giving me a once over, he turns and bounds up the bleachers for Toby.

Baihe shrieks behind me making me spin and lift my knife. Jeff has caught her kick and holds her foot, twisting it with vengeance. A vamp bomb explodes against his back, ineffective against his leather jacket. Bianca vamp lies motionless on the floor with two chopsticks impaled into her heart. Jeff glances her way, then twists Baihe's foot again.

I move toward Baihe but NFL vamp steps between us. His eyes gleam with murder when he looks from me to Indigo, Maeve, and Maddy who are huddled behind me. They stand frozen, like a picture. Terror is etched across each of their faces. Swiping my knife at NFL vamp, I catch his stomach. He doesn't even flinch, just turns toward my art friends. Maeve screams, her voice towering over BTS and drawing looks from people on the dance floor. More people are taking note of the battle happening right behind them. Football meathead Tagg steps up to NFL vamp.

"What are you doin', man?" Tagg slaps his chest and peacocks.

NFL vamp sniffs as though he's trying to smell Tagg's scent. With a dismissive chuckle, he lifts Tagg and tosses him into the bleachers as though Tagg was a rag doll. Tagg's scream and the sound of his crash draws attention from the whole room. Everyone stops dancing and turns our direction. A few teachers step toward the action with confusion and concern filling their faces.

"Get back!" I yell waving my knife. Light glints off the blade. The benefit of years of active shooter drills is evident when everyone on the dancefloor pushes toward the back wall of the gym and cowers behind the snack tables.

"Duck!" I hear Jason yell, and I drop to the floor in a flash. An explosion of red hits NFL vamp in the face and rains down on me. Another vamp bomb from Zel hits him on the back of his head. NFL vamp screams in pain as the acid and spice from the vamp bombs cover his skin. I stand and drive my knife into his gut. He drops to the floor in a pool of red, a mixture of his own blood and the vamp bomb juice.

My hands shake with the attack. Squeals erupt from the dancefloor. The music comes to an abrupt halt. I'm turning to help

Baihe when I feel like I've been hit by a car, lifted, and slammed to the floor. Stars explode across my vision, and all air is vacuumed from my lungs. I flail to get to my knees finding the mullet vamp standing over me. I'd never seen him coming, but he obviously had it out for me after I'd stabbed him in the back.

"I recommend staying down now," mullet vamp hisses.

"Leave," I gasp having trouble making my lungs breathe again. The thumping bass opening of Lizzo's *About Damn Time* echoes against the gym walls as I swing my bag off my shoulder and pull out two more stakes. Getting my feet under me, I swipe at mullet vamp. I'm too unsteady and miss, to which he laughs and jumps on a shivering girl in a shiny black dress.

Another vamp bomb explodes against his back just before Jason careens into him. They roll across the gym floor coming to a stop with mullet vamp pinning Jason to the floor. He snarls opening his mouth wide to clamp down on Jason's neck when something smashes into his head. A heavy ball leaves a noticeable dent in his head and dazes him long enough for a javelin to sail straight through his heart.

Before mullet vamp hits the floor dead, I whip my head to the emergency exit and find Oscar and Greg racing in. Greg picks up his track shotput from where it'd landed next to the mullet vamp, and Oscar yanks his javelin out of the dead vampire.

Baihe is splayed on the ground to my left holding her ankle, but I can see that she's still alive. To my right, Jason cradles his bad knee, his face oozing pain. Toby is huddled in the bleachers above Jason while Zel has descended toward me. I wave at her, motioning her back to safety.

"Well, look who's come to join the fun," Evil Jeff says stepping toward Oscar. In response, Oscar moves in front of Greg protectively.

"If it isn't the Middle Ages Euro-trash here to ruin the fun," Oscar jabs holding his ground.

Jeff laughs. "Nice, I see you haven't lost your sense of humor, poppit." He steps over the Miley vamp's crumpled body, looking at her with remorse. "You know, I really liked her. She was always up for a good time."

"It's time to leave, Jeffrey," Oscar says. "This time for good. No more Cleveland, no more Kelmis, no more mass destruction." He lifts his javelin pointed at Jeff's heart.

Jeff flinches. Grabbing Jason by the back of the shirt, he lifts him off the floor and holds Jason like a shield against his chest. The movement makes Jason groan in pain. "I'm not done with the fun yet, old friend. You know, you can still join me. Go back to our good old days of clearing out villages and keeping the loveliest ladies for ourselves," Jeff winks. "Forget Kelmis, remember Todesfelde?"

"Jeff, let him go," I say standing. The look on Jason's face breaks my heart. He's trying to smile, but he can't hide his fear and pain.

"Oh, baby vampire girl wants me to let him go?" Jeff mocks me fluttering his eyelashes.

"You should eat him," Doug says limping to stand at Jeff's side.

"Shut up, Doug!" Jeff, Oscar, and I say in unison, shocking us all. I've heard that hostage negotiations hinge on being able to relate to the attacker. Maybe our mutual hatred of Damn It Doug can work in our favor.

Behind Jeff, I catch a glimpse of Baihe sitting up and stretching her foot. She's moving with stealth, and I wonder what she has planned.

"Let's be reasonable," Oscar says stepping forward. "You want to eat your way through this gym. We want to protect everyone. Obviously, we can't all have what we want. How about you let the bloke go, and we take this outside like gentlemen?"

Jeff lunges forward, dragging Jason with him. Everyone in the room recoils in shock. A mutual cry of horror fills the gym. "You think I'm a gentleman? Far from it, old friend," Jeff hisses, baring his razor-sharp teeth. He jerks Jason's head back, exposing his neck.

"No!" I shriek, my vocal cords shredding. So many thoughts crash into each other in my head as I race for Jeff, not one of them is warning me that it's a bad idea to take on this murderous, asshole vampire alone. So, nothing stops me from throwing my arm between Jason's neck and Jeff's teeth as I career into the pair. We tumble toward the snack tables. Jeff's teeth clamp down on my arm as he flails to right himself and crashes into the table. Screams peel through the gym when the punch bowl and cookies fly. They land on the people clustered behind the table. Everyone's covered in red punch that drips like blood. A girl with punch splattered across her pink 80s-style dress faints, landing on the bleachers at an awkward angle.

All I can think is that I have to get Jason away from Jeff. Crashing my fist into Jeff's jaw, he releases his bite on my arm. I shove Jason with my feet. He uses the momentum to roll a few yards away to where Oscar helps him to his feet. Jeff grabs for me, but I elbow him in the gut and push myself up to get a few steps away. Baihe is limping in my direction and yells my name. When I turn, she tosses me a broken mop handle, one from her pack. It falls a few feet short of me. I scramble for it, lifting the jagged tip and pointing it at Jeff. At his heart. And I send it sailing.

The wooden stake floats through the air in slow motion. Lizzo's rhythm thumps against my body. I stop breathing. My heart stops beating. For the two seconds of the stake's flight, I'm literally dead.

"Fotze!" Jeff screams in German when the mop handle impales his shoulder. He stumbles back, struggling to remove it. A vamp bomb explodes against him, covering his side in red as Toby races past me for closer range. He unleashes, throwing more vamp bombs at Jeff, each one making Jeff scream and curse more.

"Hey!" Doug yells, tackling Toby. They tumble to the floor as Zel's squeal reverberates from the top row of the bleachers. She's instantly scrambling down to help Toby, but Baihe gets there faster. Even though she's limping heavily, she gets to Toby before Doug can do much real damage. She punches Doug with the intensity of splitting a stack of bricks. There's a strange cracking sound and Doug crumples to the floor in a heap. Zel pulls Toby up and wraps him in her arms.

Seeing Zel and Toby fawn over each other, I swivel my gaze to Jason. He's standing with Greg's help. There's still fire in his eyes for the fight, but Greg is pulling him away from the fray.

Stepping to my side, Oscar lifts his javelin and says, "Do you want me to end this?"

"Will it ever end?" I ask. Junior year was supposed to be the year I got the guy, got the art scholarship, and got out of the shadows. I'm definitely out of the shadows now. I look around the room at all the frightened eyes glaring at me waiting for my next move. What a disaster.

"It never does end, love, just another verse of the same song in a new key," Oscar says sounding deflated.

"Can you make them all forget?" I nod at the people cowering in their prom dresses and tuxes. Jeff still struggles to remove the mop handle, jerking awkwardly, the only one who appears to still be dancing. Ed Sheeran's *Perfect* not matching Jeff's spastic rhythm.

"I can make them all believe whatever you wish," Oscar says. He's got my back. He always has.

"Then get rid of him, but don't kill him," I say. "I can't live with that."

"As you wish," Oscar drops his javelin and approaches Jeff. I watch in awe as Oscar grabs the mop handle and twists it until Jeff looks him in the eyes. I can't hear what Oscar says when he persuades Jeff. It takes longer than usual, but soon Jeff is glassy-eyed and nodding.

Oscar drags Jeff out of the gym by pulling the mop handle like Jeff is a toy. When the emergency exit door closes behind them, I drop my bag to the floor feeling like the world has crashed against me. I'm speckled with vamp bomb juice that stings my arms. There are splinters in my fingers from the stakes, but my vampire healing is already pushing them out of my skin.

"Kaysee," Jason limps to me and pulls me to his chest. I wrap my arms around him holding tight and never wanting to let go. His hands trace up my back and into my hair as if he's making sure I still have all my parts. Ed Sheeran continues over the gym, but I'm unaware of anything else except Jason and where our bodies touch.

"Jason," I whisper, leaning back to trace my fingers across his face. Blood trails down the side of his cheek. His hair is a wild mess, and his dress shirt is torn on the shoulder. He's never looked more attractive.

His eyes meet mine, and I can feel his desire. And I need him too. Our lips crash together, sending a shockwave through my body. Running my hands through his hair, I pull him closer. His kiss is hungry, like he's been starving. I know the feeling.

When he pulls back to catch his breath, we're both smiling like maniacs. I don't even try to hide my vamp teeth. This is just who I am. I may not have won the art contest like I'd wanted, but I got that kiss. And, damn it, I saved the prom.

"And cut!" A voice echoes off the gym walls as *Perfect* comes to an end. Everyone turns to the busted-out gym doors to find a blood-covered Brittney Bell.

Damn it. I thought she was dead.

32
SIZZLE

The story we created is that a few seniors decided to pull a prank and destroyed the prom. That's what everyone thought after Oscar persuaded every single person at prom and made them wipe any pictures from their phones or social media. Baihe cleared away the dead vamp bodies. Don't ask. I have no idea what she did with them. There was one body missing though, Doug's. Damn it.

"He's like a cockroach," Oscar sighed standing in the middle of the gym with people lined up in front of him. "Impossible to kill and keeps coming back." He shook his head and went back to persuading people. His excuse worked wonders and explained why people were covered in red punch and spicy Sunny D.

The hard part of covering our tracks was convincing Brittney Bell and her cameraman to wipe their footage. It turns out that they'd been filming most of the time we were fighting Jeff and his crew. In the end, she agreed to copy it onto a flash drive that I'd keep safe in case we need it someday. I'm glad Jason knows about tech stuff because he discovered another copy she'd already stored on the hard drive of her laptop when he was wiping everything.

What really bites about all this is that Brittney Bell is now a vampire too. Damn It Doug struck again. Because I screamed and distracted Doug and Jeff from finishing feeding, they didn't kill Brittney Bell and the camera guy, just like when my family pulled Doug off me the day before school started. Bitten but not killed, now a nearly-immortal vampire like me.

We're stuck with her and Hank, the middle-aged camera guy. He's surprisingly cool about being a vampire, but Brittney Bell will not stop with the questions. Oscar moved into her apartment and is sleeping on her couch for a few weeks to help her transition. Based on the last few texts I've gotten from him, it's not going great. But we have no other choice. The world is not ready for a vampire Brittney Bell yet.

While Oscar has been away, he missed Mom and Dad's big announcement. The vamp juice is done. It's completed and even has a few different flavors. Baihe and I tried each of them and gave many thumbs up to them all. I also noticed that the perfected formula energized me more and held me over longer between meals than the early version.

Now, Baihe is working with Mom and Dad on marketing. The first order of business is a name for the vamp juice and the three flavors. They've gone back and forth, Mom insisting that sticking with "vamp juice" would be okay while Baihe shakes her head vehemently and proceeds to tell another horror story of vampires being massacred because they were discovered. Last I heard, Baihe was lamenting that there was already a Monster drink because that would actually be perfect. And Mom was reading from her phone synonyms for "bloodsucker." Keeping my head low, I slip out the front door.

Today, I'm not thinking about any of that. I'm not letting thoughts and concerns drift through my mind about being a vampire or about not getting the art scholarship. I'm not worried about Zel's Instagram pic of my teeth or my Real Inman Vampire Twitter account. Vanhelsing510 disappeared after the prom anyway, so I haven't even looked at Twitter all week. Should I be worried that he's so quiet after trolling me for weeks? Probably. His sudden silence makes me wonder when he'll pop up again. But I absolutely refuse to worry today.

Instead, I'm running. It's a longer trail at Buseik State Park. I didn't love it at first because the terrain is so rough. But having to avoid tripping on jutting rocks or falling down the side of a hill helps clear my mind, helps me focus on just the next step. And with the overcast skies overhead, I'm free to run through the trees without being scorched.

When my phone pings four times in quick succession, I slow and pull it from the pocket of my running pants. All the messages and the four that came through five minutes ago are not surprisingly from Zel. She's spending the weekend with Toby and his family at their lake house. Her parents almost didn't let her go. But then Abuelita met Nai Nai. They formed an instantaneous bond. There's something about Chinese grandmothers and Latin grandmothers. They're very much alike. Zel's messages are all about the funny things Nai Nai does that horribly embarrass Toby, much like Abuelita often does to Zel.

I'm happy for Zel. Hey, I'm happy for Toby too. If I couldn't catch the hot nerd, I'm glad Zel did. I scroll through the messages, ending with a tirade of emojis interspersed with a description of watching *The Avengers.* Zel complains they have to stop the movie every ten seconds when Nai Nai starts challenging the implausibility of the Marvel Universe.

As I round the corner of the trail and catch sight of Jason's camp chair near the parking lot, I smile. And I also trip on a root. I hope he didn't see that. Brushing dirt off my knee, I jog up to Jason who stands to meet me. He's not who I'd hoped for. Instead, he's oh, so much better.

"One more?" he asks smirking. I love the way his lips look when he smiles like this. I used to hate that smirk when he made fun of me in middle school. But discovering who he is, learning he has a caring and loyal heart, I'm falling in love with the smirk now.

"I think five laps is good for today," I smile back draping my arms around his waist.

"Good, because there's something I really need to do right now," he says brushing loose hair off my forehead.

When his lips meet mine, I tingle from the top of my head to the tips of my toes. It's like this every time we kiss, which we've done a lot of in the two weeks since prom. His lips move against mine with familiarity, tugging at my lower lip in a way that always makes me laugh. I'm still sizzling when he breaks away.

He smiles down at me, his lips reddened. "I got another text while you were running."

"What? The one you were waiting for from Elon Musk? You've been asked to join the team going to Mars?" I tease. "Because I might too. There could be some real benefits to having vampires on Mars."

Jason laughs and shakes his head. "Seriously," he says, his voice dropping.

"Jason Hancock being serious," I give him a peck on the lips.

"Your mom texted," he sighs, pulling me tighter against him. "It's almost curfew. She said that with Doug and Jeff on the loose, she doesn't want you out after dark."

"Oh, come on, we can push it a little, right?" I wiggle my eyebrows in a manner I hope portrays seduction.

Jason laughs, not the response I was hoping for. "Wax Lips, after reading online about the supposed gas leak at a frat house in Nebraska that killed 10 guys, I'm not risking anything. If I don't get you home, you know that Baihe will kick my ass anyway. And my knee still isn't great after prom." He nods at the thick brace hugging his leg. I smile to hide how I really feel, which is worried to near-death that Doug and Jeff are raving across the Midwest.

"You're only worried about Baihe? You do realize that I still have the power to drink all your blood, right?" I joke trying to force down my anxiety and hold on to this moment a little longer. Just another snuggle, another kiss before I have to return to the real world.

"But if you drink all my blood, I won't be able to do this," he says nibbling at my ear. I quiver and giggle. "Or this," he captures me in a movie-worthy kiss. For real. He pulls me close and dips me back, the wind blowing my ponytail as sparks fly so much I'm worried we'll start a forest fire.

So, junior year didn't turn out exactly how I'd planned. I'd never planned to become a vampire, but it turns out that it's been one of the better things to happen to me. It made me bold. It made me brave. It made me do things I'd never imagined. Like, really, I was hit by a bloodmobile, battled a vampire horde, and lived to tell about it.

Oh, yeah. And I got the guy. The blazing hot guy who's still kissing me, making my skin sizzle and my heart swell as the sun lazily drops below the horizon.

ACKNOWLEDGEMENTS

When working on any big project, especially writing a book, no one does it alone. I am grateful to have been surrounded by a wonderful group of friends and family who helped make this book possible.

Amy Brewer, thanks for your insight into the story and for your endless encouragement.

My book club ladies; Elizabeth, Jessi, Sarah, Amy, and Jennifer; I am a better person having you all in my life. thanks for your continued support and all the beta reading!

To the Good Selling Authors group, you are my favorite group of writer friends. I love seeing you all succeed and am grateful for your kind words as I fill pages.

To my children, Simon & Junia, I know it's hard to have Mom step away to work on writing. Thanks for your grace and for being good for Dad when I ran off to write at the library. Please never tell me how many treats he bribed you with for that good behavior. That can be your own little secret.

To Brian, I know you don't fully understand how I come up with stories and how I am bursting to get them on the page. But you support me anyway. I love laughing with you and am beyond grateful for all the ways you've supported my work. Wo ai ni and ya he kafei.

JUNIOR YEAR BITES 317

grateful for all the ways you've supported my work. Wo ai ni and ya he kafei.

About the Author

A native of the Missouri Ozarks, Annie Lisenby is a mom, a theatre teacher, and an author. She's lived abroad and across the country but is happily settled in rural Missouri with her husband and two kids now.

As an actor, Annie performed on stage and onscreen. She was an extra for film and television for three years. If you look quick enough, you'll see her in "The Office," "House," and a really great Dirty Vegas music video. She also worked as a stunt performer in her younger years and enjoyed being set on fire, but not performing high falls.

Annie's debut novel *A Three-Letter Name* was chosen as best novel by an indie author from Missouri by the Indie Author Project.

Learn more about Annie at www.annielisenby.com.

Want more of Kaysee and her vampire friends?

Senior Year Sucks

Coming 2025